Praise for *The Alienation of*

"Brady ......minds a way to ...... together a fast-paced young adult novel feel with a substantive agenda. Stefani's storytelling skills and elegantly simple language immediately get you involved in an emotional, suspenseful, off-balance reading experience that is equal parts drama and science fiction."

—**Ian Kahl**, author of *Anxiety is a Rambling Dagger,* and *That Faraway Place*

"Beyond our everyday world there lies the alternative reality of childhood, a universe populated by strange beings and powered by our collective imaginations. *The Alienation of Courtney Hoffman* is a doorway for readers of all ages that returns us to that world from which so many have become disconnected. Brady G. Stefani's ability to connect us to that larger, weirder reality is a gift from an ever-changing, ultimately unknowable cosmos."

—**John E. L. Tenney**,
Paranormal Researcher

"Stefani's *The Alienation of Courtney Hoffman* is a thought-provoking and emotional journey through a young girl's mind as she struggles to understand who she is, where she came from, and who she is supposed to be—all while deciphering between reality and the tricks our minds can sometimes play on us. Stefani beautifully demonstrates how difficult life can be for anyone who thinks or acts a little differently, and reminds us that, more often than not, the things that terrify us the most are the things trying to save us."

—**Jessica Stevens**, author of *Within Reach*

"As the father of two teenage girls, I can tell you that Brady Stefani must have some sort of supernatural helmet that helps him think and write in their language. But *The Alienation of Courtney Hoffman* is much more than a novel for teens. This fast-paced adventure kept my attention, blazing back-and-forth from reality to an alter-world so close by that it's creepy. Here's a page-turner that captures a lot about childhood struggles through an imaginative story filled with surprises."

—Jim Schaefer,
Pulitzer Prize-winning journalist
and writer for the *Detroit Free Press*

"Brady Stefani has written a wonderful coming-of-age tale of an adolescent girl who is struggling to grasp what is real and what is not real. While conveying the actual inner experience of an adolescent is a difficult task, because of the unconscious and incomprehensible facets of the mind, Stefani uses a scientific metaphor to accurately convey the demands, perils, and triumphs of adolescence that must be traversed to become an adult. With *The Alienation of Courtney Hoffman*, Stefani has achieved an important literary form that will be of interest to adolescent and adult readers alike."

—Melvin Bornstein, M.D., Clinical Professor of Psychiatry
at Wayne State University, Training and Supervising Analyst
at Michigan Psychoanalytical Institute,
and editor of *Psychoanalytic Inquiry*

the
ALIENATION of
COURTNEY
HOFFMAN

the
ALIENATiON of
COuRTNEY
HOFfMAN

a Novel

Brady G. Stefani

Published by SparkPress, a BookSparks imprint,
A division of SparkPoint Studio, LLC
Tempe, Arizona, USA, 85281
www.gosparkpress.com

Published 2016
Printed in the United States of America
ISBN: 978-1-940716-34-3 (pbk)
ISBN: 978-1-940716-35-0 (e-bk)

Library of Congress Control Number: 2015960213

Cover design © Julie Metz, Ltd./metzdesign.com
Cover photo © Michaela M. Frunek
Formatting by Kiran Spees

For Beckett, Blaze, and Heather Stefani.

Also, for the chosen many who experience the alienation of mental suffering. Know you are not alone, find your pathway out.

Once in a while you get shown the light
In the strangest of places if you look at it right.

—*Robert Hunter/ Jerry Garcia*

ONE

Lightning ripped across the northern California sky, then splintered down through the rain and disappeared behind our neighbor's house. Letting the door slam shut behind me, I ran away from the warmth of our porch light into the darkness of our backyard. My mom would've killed me if she'd caught me outside that late at night. Especially in a thunderstorm, and on the night before my fifteenth birthday, with the big party she had planned for tomorrow. But I had to get out of the house before I fell asleep and they came for me. And they were coming!

A gust of wind blew my hair against my face. I swiped it out of my eyes just in time to see a plastic lawn chair tumbling through the air. I covered my head with both arms, but a leg of the chair smashed against my elbow. *Ouch!*

I dropped onto the wet grass, pulled my knees into my chest, and rocked nervously back and forth. Water soaked up through my nightgown and my underwear, making me shiver.

None of these things mattered, though. Because something far worse was happening inside my head. A memory of me as a little girl, on the night my grandpa Dahlen disappeared from his cottage, was trying to claw its way into my consciousness. And I didn't want to think about that night. Ever.

Still, I couldn't stop it, which didn't make sense. I was awake, and outside, where I was supposed to be safe, yet the aliens from my dreams were somehow messing with

1

my thoughts, rearranging things, trying to make me think about that night! But how?

And why? It happened eight years ago, and my grandpa was dead now.

Although, before he disappeared, he'd—

No! Stop, Courtney! I yelled at myself.

I bit my fingernail and took a deep breath, hoping to calm down.

No luck. I was remembering the musty old-books smell from my grandpa's bookcase. Butterflies rushed into my stomach and I sprang to my feet.

"All right. Is that what you want me to do?" I shouted into the rainy darkness. "Remember my grandpa? What happened that night? If I do that, then will you leave me alone?"

I wiped the rain from my eyes, and suddenly it was like I was right there, in the cottage. His notebook sat on the plaid couch, opened to a map he'd drawn of the ancient wormholes linking the alien world to our own.

I stumbled backward over a tree root and my butt hit the ground; my head clunked against an even bigger root. *Oww!* I started to sit up. But suddenly the memory I'd been running from took over the screen in my mind. I fell back into the wet grass and watched the scene unfold as if I were seven years old again, right there in the cottage.

It was raining outside, and the air smelled like old, musty books and burnt hamburgers. I glanced over at my grandpa Dahlen. He was busy in the kitchen, forking ears of corn out of a pot of boiling water. Standing tiptoe on the comfy reading chair, I reached up to the bookcase and ran my fingers along the dials of what he called his ham-radio/alien-transport machine.

"Courtney!" Grandpa stared at me over his steamed-up glasses.

2

"Fine." I plopped down on the reading chair and crossed my arms over my chest. Then I lowered my eyes. Blood was seeping through my shirt again from earlier in the day, when my grandpa's nun friend had stopped by with a guy with a tattoo gun. They'd come to give me a tattoo. I hadn't wanted a tattoo! But my grandpa had told me it was important, and the way he'd said it, I'd believed him. So now I had a blue mark on my rib cage that looked like four dead bugs arranged in a square.

"So tell me this, Grandpa," I said. "If these aliens who visit you are really your friends, then why do they make you keep everything secret?"

He turned away from the steaming pot and eyed me with suspicion. "Because people are frightened of what they don't understand. And frightened people can be dangerous, Courtney," he said. "Now come sit down for dinner."

I slipped into a wobbly kitchen chair, rested my elbows on the wooden table, and stared down at my burnt hamburger. "Mom doesn't believe in aliens, so does that make her dangerous?" I asked.

Grandpa chuckled. "Your mother is only interested in facts and evidence. Even when she was a child, she had no tolerance for intangibles. Or even comic books, for that matter. Can you imagine?" He set a plate of corn on the cob in the center of the table, then sat down across from me. "But dangerous? No. I think we're safe from her." He flashed me a wink.

I winked back. People always told me that I shared his silvery-blue eyes. Hearing someone say it would make my mom cringe, though, because she thought Grandpa was crazy. And the last thing she wanted was for me to turn out like him. But she and my dad were spending the weekend with their old law school friends on Lake Tahoe, so they'd dropped me off with Grandpa on their way.

"Well, if these alien things are real living creatures, then did God make them?" I asked. "Or are they just imaginary?"

"Good question."

I smiled proudly. I was about to finally get the truth from him.

"How's your burger?" he asked.

"But you didn't answer—" I started to protest, when a bang on the front door made me jump.

My grandpa ran over and covered his ham-radio/alien-transport machine with an afghan.

More quick pounding! Grandpa shoved his notebook under the couch.

I tried to read his expression, to see if he was frightened or just cleaning up, but he wouldn't look at me. He rushed to the door and glanced through the peephole, and I held my breath.

When he unlocked the door, three men barged into the cottage.

I immediately recognized them as professor friends of my grandpa's from when he'd taught at Berkeley. But what were they doing out here at night? I mean, hadn't they heard of cell phones?

They stared over at me. "Hello, Courtney," said one, a tall man with a thick beard and black suit coat.

I shot my grandpa a pleading look, like *Make them go away.* But he quickly shook his head. I stomped into the guest bedroom and slammed the door.

"They're coming," one of the men whispered, loud enough for me to hear. He sounded worried. Which made me worry. About what, though, I wasn't quite sure.

I bit my thumbnail, and it tasted like wormy dirt from the woodpile. *Gross!* I wiped my mouth with the bottom of my shirt.

"She's not safe," another man said.

Not safe? I froze. *"She"? As in me?* My heart started racing, and suddenly I couldn't get enough air into my lungs.

I grabbed the black metal latch of the window next to me and opened it. The *chirr-chirr* of crickets filled the bedroom, and I breathed in the smell of wet leaves. Pressing my face against the screen, I glanced up at my grandpa's ham radio tower, standing tall along the side of the house. The siren on top of it glistened with rain under the silvery moon. It would sound off if any bad guys snuck into the backyard and tried to mess with my grandpa's things. Or that's what he'd told me, anyway.

Suddenly a familiar shiver trickled down my neck. *Oh wow!*

I turned away from the window and locked eyes with Astra. "Nice of you to show up," I said.

She was a few years older than me. Like eleven, maybe. She was sitting cross-legged on the floor next to the closet; her eyes shone bright green against her pale skin and black hair. She bit into her plump bottom lip, which meant she was worried about me. "You think I'm going to climb out the window and run away?" I asked her.

She didn't answer. For an imaginary friend, she wasn't very talkative. But she seemed to show up whenever I was in trouble. And there was no getting rid of her; our minds were connected. My grandpa said she was probably a real person somewhere, and that we shared consciousness because we came from the same bloodline. As crazy as the idea seemed, I liked to think that there might be someone real out there who would understand me if we ever crossed paths. Most people just thought I was weird like my grandpa.

"I'm glad you're here," I told Astra.

Outside my door, I could hear the men pacing around on the creaky wooden floorboards.

"When?" my grandpa asked.

"We don't know," another man said.

I didn't like the sound of that. My stomach tightened with nerves. I sat down on my bed and rocked back and forth, staring at Astra.

"You're crying," she said. Or I could hear her voice in my head, anyway.

"No I'm not." I swiped my cheek. Then I looked down at the spot of blood on my shirt. "I got a tattoo," I said, trying to change the subject.

A siren wailed outside. *The alarm!* I jumped up, turned toward the window. But the bedroom door burst open behind me. I spun back around, and my grandpa stood in the doorway.

"Grandpa! What's happening?" I started toward him. He quickly shook his head and then pressed his finger to his lips: *Stay quiet.*

I nodded.

Grandpa looked scared. And he was never scared. My heart pounded against my rib cage. Astra was gone. This was bad.

Bright light lit up my grandpa's face. It was coming through the window behind me. *Oh no!* I whipped around to see who was there, and someone grabbed me from inside the room.

I started to scream, but a hand covered my mouth. My feet lifted off the floor. Frantically I twisted my head around to see who it was, but I was being dragged backward, down the hall, into the bathroom. Kicking at the bathroom wall, I bit into the hand covering my mouth, and for a second my head was free. I whirled around to see my grandpa, his finger gushing blood from where my teeth had cut into his skin.

"Grandpa? What are you doing?"

He whispered something in my ear. Then he lifted me up, ignoring my flailing legs.

The next thing I knew, I was underwater. Screaming!

TWO

"**It's** party time. It's party time." My nine-year-old sister, Kaelyn, banged on my door, then skipped down the hall and clomped downstairs.

I stared at myself in my bedroom mirror and tugged on the neckline of the red dress my mom had bought for me for my big fifteenth birthday party, which was starting in ten minutes. As hip as the dress supposedly was, it looked stupid on me, curving in and out in places my body didn't. I was like a stick figure drowning in red. A pale stick figure with a black bruise on my left elbow from where the flying lawn chair had hit me last night.

I pulled the dress over my head and tossed it on the floor, then climbed into bed.

I'd told my mom a month ago I didn't want a dumb party. Just the thought of sitting around with a bunch of people and pretending to be happy—when horrible things were happening inside my head—made me want to throw up.

A car door slammed outside, and I heard voices. I crawled to the end of my bed and glanced out the window. Lauren, my best friend, and Christie, my second-best friend, were here for the party. *Great!* Lauren's mom was coming in too. *Even better.* Then a red SUV pulled in behind them, followed by a small blue car, which parked on the street in front. More cars, more party guests. What was I going to say to these people?

I grabbed the clothes I'd worn earlier out of the laundry

hamper. As I pulled on my shirt, a shiver of electricity trickled down my neck. *No way!* It had been forever since I'd felt that shiver, but I knew exactly what it meant.

"Astra?" I spun around.

She wasn't there. I could feel her presence, though. *Weird.* I quickly wiggled into my pants. Another shiver. *Huh?*

I glanced around again, but no sign of her. "Not a good time for tricks, Astra! I'm having a birthday party." I hadn't seen her in almost two years, but with the craziness last night, and all the dreams I'd had the last few weeks about alien visitors, I wasn't completely surprised that she was trying to make an appearance.

"Astra?" I threw open the door to my closet where she sometimes showed up. No Astra.

"Astra! This isn't funny. You're worried about the aliens in my dreams. I get it," I said, scanning the room for signs of life. "They were trying to get me to think about my grandpa's cottage. But I took care of—"

"Courtney?" My mom charged into my room.

Oh no, what did she hear?

She was wearing the same dress she'd bought me. Only hers fit perfectly.

I met her stare. Her eyes were icy gray; her expression was calm. Biting my fingernail, I glanced down at the lime colored NOT ALL BEANS ARE GREEN T-shirt and tight pink-and-black plaid pants I was wearing. It was hard to believe I was her daughter.

"Is there a problem?" my mom asked.

"Not really." I tried to smile. "I'm just about to get dressed." I picked my dress up off the floor.

"Because it sounded like you were talking to someone," she said.

"Just myself." Again I tried to smile.

Mom's eyes narrowed, which meant she was in

cold-blooded attorney mode now. "I thought we were finished with the make-believe friends."

"I am, Mom!"

"Mental health is a slippery slope, Courtney. So unless you want to end up crazy like your grandfather did, you better forget about him *and* your imaginary friends."

"I will, I swear." I tried to look sincere, so she'd know I was telling the truth. I really did want to forget about all that.

"You've been talking about him in your sleep the last few nights, yelling so loudly that your sister can hear you through the wall," she said. "And it frightens her."

"No I haven't," I said. I flipped the dress around in my hand and pretended to study the label.

"The past is the past, Courtney. It's time to put a lid on that imagination of yours and grow up. You understand me?"

I nodded.

"Good. Because I've been through this Martian visitor nonsense with my father, and I'm not going through it with my daughter. Get it together, young lady, or you'll find yourself in the adolescent psych ward at St. Ignatius. Understand?"

"I get it already, Mom. Grandpa who. Jeez."

"Well, I certainly hope so. For God's sake, he gave you that tattoo, then tried to drown you in the tub. Who in their right mind would do such a thing to a child?"

I dropped my head in shame.

"Now put your dress on. Your real-world friends are downstairs waiting for you."

"I get it, Mom." But she turned and strolled out.

I swallowed hard to keep from crying, and I tried not to think about my grandpa. Only it didn't work. My chest felt warm, and fuzzy, and hollow, all at the same time. I missed my grandpa.

He couldn't have been as crazy as my mom made him out to be. Her relationship with him had always been strained, so I'd spent far more time with him during his last few years than she had. Sure, he'd had his weird ideas about alien visitors and bad people out to steal his plans, but the way he'd explained things, everything had made sense. And he was the kindest person I'd ever met. He wasn't *crazy* crazy. He was just weird smart in a scientist kind of way, and I was his favorite person in the world, so he told me things. And there was no harm in that.

Or was there?

The red dress fell from my hand and landed on the floor again. No, my mom was right—having dreams about alien visitors was one thing, but he'd tattooed me and tried to drown me. Not to mention that he'd drowned himself two weeks later in a bathtub in Switzerland, six thousand miles from where we lived in northern California. Only a crazy person would do those things. A dangerous crazy person.

As soon as I heard my mom's heels reach the bottom of the stairs, I plopped down inside my closet and pulled the doors shut. I could still feel Astra in my head, but she was far away now. *Fine by me!* I was finished with all of it. I was fifteen years old; it was time to grow up. No more thoughts about my grandpa! Or aliens! Or Astra!

Then I saw her, Astra, in my mind. My stomach tingled with excitement. She was sitting in a diner, at a booth, by herself. A cup of coffee in one hand, a red colored pencil in the other. "Astra!" I said. But she didn't seem to hear me, and she didn't respond in any way as if she had.

She was older than the last time I'd seen her. Which made sense. Nineteen, maybe. But it was definitely her— same intense green eyes and straight black hair.

There was a sketch pad on the table in front of her, opened to a drawing of something on fire. Or more like beams of red light jetting up from the ground and down from the sky. It was kinda creepy, but beautiful.

I stood up in my closet to see if I could move closer to Astra. Though Astra had visited me a hundred times, I'd never visited her before. And here I was, watching her frantically scratching in her sketchbook with her blood-red colored pencil. "Astra?" I tried again, louder.

Suddenly she looked up from her drawing and turned to her left. Like she was staring at me. I gasped! Then I bumped my bruised elbow against the back of my closet, and I yelled in pain.

Astra was gone from my mind.

Staring at the back of my closet doors, I rubbed my elbow. Then I grabbed my hair in my fists and pulled. *I need this weirdness to stop!*

"Knock, knock. Earth to Courtney . . . anyone home?"

Shit! It was Lauren, right outside the closet doors.

I unclenched my hair just as she yanked the doors open. She had a short blue dress on, and her blond hair was pulled up in a bun. "Hello, Miss Hoffman," she said. "It's your birthday. Are you coming to your party?"

"Hey, Lauren." I half-waved, and then hugged her, before pushing past her into the room. "Help me with my dress."

THREE

By the time I'd locked my bike up and slipped in the side door by the ceramics room, the tardy bell was ringing. *Great.* In the three weeks since my birthday, I'd missed more school than I had in my whole life before that. I was just so exhausted all the time. But at least today was Friday.

I dragged my feet all the way to my locker, pulled it open, and grabbed my Earth science book.

"No way. Look at the circles under your eyes." Nicola Meyers glared over from the next locker. "Sleep-starved or what, Courtney?"

I tried to focus my drowsy eyes on Nicola, her smug little nose and perfect teeth. I bit my lip. As much as I despised her shallow ways, I was too exhausted to come up with a witty comeback. Plus, I did look like crap. I hadn't slept more than a few hours all week. And when I did sleep, I had nightmares about aliens creeping into my bedroom.

Without looking away from Nicola, I let my eyelids droop shut.

"Oh, you did *not* just close your eyes," she said. "You are so weird, Courtney. Wait till I tell Josh." Meaning Josh Sale, my sort of boyfriend, whom I hadn't spoken to in three days. Well, by boyfriend, I meant we kissed a couple times. And he'd told he me he liked me. And he was definitely crushable.

Nicola's locker slammed shut, and her zebra stripper

clogs clapped away. I was alone in the hallway. Already late for class. Maybe I had time for a quick nap, standing up?

"Hey. You okay?"

Ugh. I recognized the voice. I opened my eyes. The emo snowboarder pixie chick from my art class was coming over. Dirty-blond pigtails stuck out the bottom of her scratchy-looking ski hat, which had two wool Viking horns flopping around on top.

"You okay, Courtney?" she repeated.

"Yeah, thanks, Haven." I shut my locker. "I'm just really out of it."

"It's Haley," she said.

"Oh, jeez, sorry, Haley. I'm just . . . I gotta go." I turned and walked in the wrong direction.

FOUR

I rested my ear flat against the wall above my headboard. I could hear Kaelyn in the next room, breathing in her sleep.

Lucky her. I couldn't sleep. For all the wrong reasons, too. Craziness, mostly.

Trying to ignore the sinking feeling in my gut, I dug my flashlight out of my dresser. *Fifteen years old and still afraid of the dark. Sorry, Kaelyn. So much for me being your brave big sister.*

I leaned back against my headboard and shined the light at my pink dresser. Then up at my soccer trophies, my blue ribbon from the science fair, my homecoming corsage, a spelling bee runner-up award, and my photo collage of Lauren and me on the ski lift making goofy faces.

Sliding down to my pillow, I pulled up my comforter. The clock on my nightstand read 3:13 a.m. It was Saturday night—or Sunday morning, actually. Which meant I had to be at soccer practice in less than six hours. Or was it five? My mind was too tired to hold a thought.

I clicked off my flashlight and let it fall from my fingers.

What felt like minutes later, a strange buzzing woke me out of a harmless dream about fishing with my grandpa. My eyes opened to the darkness. My breathing was heavy and my skin felt prickly and damp with sweat, which didn't match up with the fishing dream. Something was wrong.

The floor creaked, and my soccer trophies clinked against each other. *Oh no!*

A scraping noise. Something was in my bedroom! The buzzing in my ears grew louder.

The trophies on my dresser rattled again. Butterflies rushed through my stomach.

I tried to sit up, but my body was still asleep; it wouldn't move.

A shadow stretched across the ceiling above me. *What's happening?*

I managed to raise my head off my pillow. And standing there at the foot of my bed were three lanky creatures with huge black eyes. Alien creatures. I recognized them from my dreams. Two of them were males with thick chests. And the third one, the least ugly one who always seemed to be in charge, in my dreams anyway, she was female, and less aggressive in her mannerisms. But this was no dream, I was awake!

"Hello, Courtney," the female said.

"AHHHHH!" I screamed.

By the time my mom rushed in, the aliens were gone.

"I'm sorry, Mom." I jumped out of bed and tried to hug her, but she backed away. "It was just a bad dream about soccer. I swear! I didn't mean to yell."

She shook her head and stormed out without a word.

I turned on my lights, gathered myself up into a ball, and started sobbing. What was happening to me?

By the time I got to practice the next morning, everyone was standing on the goal line, one foot on a soccer ball, listening to Coach Davies. I had totally missed warm-ups. The last Sunday practice of the season, of the school year, and I was loser-late.

I ran across the field and squeezed in between Christie and Lauren. "Hi. What'd I miss?" I said, trying to sound funny.

Lauren shot me a quick look. "Courtney, you look horrible," she whispered.

I lowered my head in shame.

"Seriously, man," Lauren said. "Like crazy-grocery-store-lady-with-dark-circles-under-her-eyes horrible."

"Yeah, thanks," I said. I could feel my lower lip trembling. *Please don't cry, not now.* Tears streaked down my cheeks, and I closed my eyes in defeat.

Bad move. Waiting for me behind my eyelids were the three alien visitors from last night!

My heart jumped, and my eyes sprang open. But they were still there in my mind, staring at me with their giant, black, insect-like eyes.

Coach Davies blew his whistle. "Let's go, girls. Partner up. Short passes."

I shook my head, somehow managing to dislodge the image of the aliens from my mind.

"Courtney?"

Lauren was talking to me, but I didn't look at her. I stared blankly at the soccer field. A dark shadow was creeping across the sky, toward me. This was the beginning of the end. My end! I could feel it.

"Courtney?" Lauren yanked me over to the sideline, put her hands on my shoulders, and tried get me to look up at her. "Hey, I was just kidding. Oh, man. Court . . . are you okay?"

I shook my head. I wasn't okay. Not even a little bit okay.

"Courtney! You're scaring me."

"I gotta go, Lauren. I'm sick." I pulled away.

But she grabbed me by the arm, and I didn't want to make any more of a scene than I already had, so I let my body go limp.

"Sick how?" she asked.

I didn't answer her.

"Is it more nightmares?" she asked.

A couple weeks back Lauren had found me crying in the locker room, and I'd told her about my nightmares—dreams about aliens coming into my room while I was asleep. But last night was different! I was awake, and they were there!

My lower lip trembled again, and more tears flowed.

"Oh, Courtney. You have to talk to someone," Lauren said.

"No!" I focused my teary eyes on Lauren's. "I can't tell anyone anything. My mom's already pissed at me. Lauren, you have to swear not to mention this to anyone! Promise, right now!"

"All right, all right. I promise. But only if you tell me what's going on."

I could feel my secret boiling up inside me. It wanted out. I was sick with worry about going crazy, and exhausted from telling myself the aliens weren't real. Lauren was my best friend; I could trust her.

"You swear on your life not to tell anyone?" I asked.

"Cross my heart, hope to die," she said.

"They're not nightmares, Lauren. My grandpa was right about the aliens. They're real, and they visited me in my bedroom last night. I think they're trying to drive me crazy, like they did to my grandpa. Either that, or none of it's real, and I'm already crazy."

The color drained from Lauren's face. "Oh God, Courtney. You need serious help."

I ran to my bike and unlocked it without looking back.

FIVE

Sunday nights were the worst for falling asleep. I clicked on my flashlight and shined it at the ceiling above my bed.

Tomorrow at school, kids on the soccer team would be telling people how I'd bolted from practice. I'd called Lauren earlier tonight, and she'd sworn she hadn't told anyone about our conversation. But that wouldn't erase what Coach Davies or the other kids at practice had seen.

Hearing my mom's footsteps, I doused my flashlight and buried it under my comforter just as she pushed open the door. The big light came on, and she marched in and handed me a glass of warm milk.

I sniffed it, thinking she might have put something in it to help me sleep. Ever since she started dating Dr. Anderson—seriously, that's what Mom made me call him, Dr. Anderson, not Mr. Anderson or Roger, but Doctor, like he was so important I had to acknowledge his title. *Whatever.* Since she'd started dating him, she'd been watching me like a hawk, obsessed with my sleep-related well-being.

"It's just warm milk, sweetie," she said. "But it should help with your nightmares."

I didn't want to argue with her, but warm milk? *Seriously, Mom?* I could drink straight from the udder of the sacred cow and it wouldn't help my crazies. My mind was drowning in unholy groundwater where no cow dared tread.

I took a test sip anyway, then guzzled it down. "Thanks." I handed the glass back to her.

As soon as she left, I crept over to my closet and grabbed the duct tape and box of aluminum foil I'd stashed behind my shoe rack. Back on my bed, I twisted up a strand of tape, and then I wrapped it around the window lock until the latch was totally immovable. Then I pulled out a sheet of foil and taped it across the top of the window, shiny side out.

The reflective surface would prevent the aliens from beaming in, or so I'd read on the Internet. I taped up two more sheets of foil so the whole window was covered. It looked good—secure. Five school days left until summer vacation. I could do this! Keep sane. I hoped.

"Courtney?"

Shit! My door flew open and my mom stared in, at the tinfoil on my window.

"It's not what you think it is, Mom." I jumped out of bed. "It's a science project."

Narrowing her cold eyes, she took a deep, loud breath. "I've had all I can take of this alien nonsense, Courtney! You have the whole house on edge. And your friends are worried about your safety."

Friends? She must've talked to Lauren. *Oh, perfect!*

"Mom, you don't understand. I was just joking with Lauren about aliens."

"No, young lady, I do understand! There's no such thing as aliens! Not on Earth, not in outer space, and certainly not in your bedroom! You want to pollute your mind with that gibberish, fine. But *not* under this roof!"

"Okay, sorry, Mom. I'll take the tinfoil down right now."

She slammed my door and stomped downstairs.

Ten minutes later I heard a car pull up in the driveway. I peeled back a piece of tinfoil and peeked out the window. My mom's boyfriend, Dr. Anderson, was standing outside his car, staring up at my window, shaking his head.

I plunked back down in bed.

The hallway light shone through the crack under my door. I could hear my mom and Dr. Anderson whispering.

"Courtney?" Dr. Anderson pushed my door open. He was wearing green hospital scrubs and a beige cardigan sweater.

I glanced at my alarm clock—10:20 p.m.—then back at Dr. Anderson. *What a joke!* He always dressed like he was fresh out of surgery or something. But the truth was, he worked in an office as a pediatrician two days a week, and he probably hadn't set foot inside a hospital since medical school. Plus, for a pediatrician, he certainly knew nothing about kids—or the way they think, anyway. But that didn't stop him from trying to look important, and from constantly giving me advice about making responsible decisions when it came to sex and alcohol.

Ugh! Why my mom liked him, I had no idea. Except that he liked fancy restaurants and put up with her holier-than-thou crap.

"What do you want?" I asked him, annoyed.

He sat down on the end of my bed.

Ew, creepy!

"How you doing?" he whispered, pretending like he didn't want my mom, who was standing right outside the open door, to hear our private conversation.

"Fine until you showed up," I said, loud enough for my mom to hear.

Dr. Anderson got up and strolled over to the door. He whispered something to my mom. Then he shut the door and sat down in my desk chair.

"Your mother's upset," he said, turning to face me. "She thinks you're experiencing mental problems."

"Yeah, and that's your business how?" I asked.

"You want to know what I think, Courtney?" he whispered.

"No. I have school tomorrow. What I want is to go to sleep!"

"I think you're making things up," he said. "Trying to trick your mother into thinking you're something that you're not."

"Something I'm not?" He made me so mad, my chest felt like it was on fire. "You have no idea what you're talking about!" I yelled.

"Oh, is that so?" he said, creepily calm. "Well, I have colleagues who are interested in people like you. So if you want to play crazy, that's fine with me; let's play crazy."

"Mom!" I yelled. "Get this sicko out of my room!"

My mom barged in. "Let's go. Downstairs, Courtney."

"Me? But—"

"Right now, young lady!"

"Fine." I followed her down the stairs.

She walked past the laundry room and opened the door to the garage. "Wait for me in the car," she said.

"What? Why? I'm in my pajamas."

SIX

A lady in a white lab coat walked into the room and stood at the foot of my bed. Her ID badge read DR. KIMBERLY WU. She looked young for a doctor, maybe in her twenties, but smart.

"Hi, Courtney. I'm Dr. Wu. Do you know where you are?"

I nodded. She tilted her head like she wasn't convinced.

"In St. Ignatius Hospital," I said, less than enthusiastically. "Up by Napa. On the psychiatric floor."

"That's right." Dr. Wu smiled. "Can you tell me why you're here?"

I pulled at the plastic hospital band cutting into my wrist. "Because my mom thinks I'm crazy, and her stupid boyfriend helped her bring me here. He claims to be a doctor, but I doubt he's a good one."

"Oh." She glanced at the clipboard in her hand, then at me. "Let's forget about your mom's assessment for a minute. Tell me what you think is going on with you."

"What I think?" Whatever my mom and Dr. Anderson had told the hospital when they'd admitted me was probably on the clipboard, so lying wouldn't work. "I'm having bad dreams," I said. "About alien visitors. But the dreams are so real, it's like it's really happening." I bit my thumbnail and waited for her to laugh, or shake her head in disapproval.

But she didn't. The look in her eyes was sincere, like she really wanted to understand.

"So just nightmares?" she asked, as if it was okay if it was more than that.

"Kinda," I said. I pressed the up button on my bed control so I was practically leaning forward. "Except, well, when I woke up last night, the aliens were still there, and I couldn't move my body. So maybe they're real?" I felt tears welling up in my eyes. "Or I'm going crazy." I wiped my cheek.

"Hey." Dr. Wu sat down next me on my bed and placed her hand over mine. "There are no aliens after you."

"How do you know?"

"I do. Trust me. Sometimes parts of our mind wake up while other parts are still asleep. If we get stuck in this hypnagogic stage between dreaming and wakefulness, we can dream with our eyes open, and it can seem very real. I believe that's what's happening to you," she said.

"Okay. So I'm going crazy?" I asked. Then it dawned on me that the term *crazy* might no longer be politically correct. "I mean, like, mentally ill? Like my grandpa did?"

"No, Courtney."

"Huh? You sure?" I swiped a tear from my cheek, then glared at Dr. Wu so she would know I wouldn't settle for anything less than the truth!

"It may feel like you're going crazy when that happens, but you're not."

She sounded truthful.

"Okay. I guess that could be it." I took a deep breath. "So can you fix it so that other stuff doesn't happen?"

"We certainly can try," Dr. Wu said. "I'll start you on some medication. After a few nights of sound sleep, you should start feeling normal again."

"Really?" *Normal again!* A wide smile broke across my face. "And so you'll tell my mom and Dr. Anderson that I'm not crazy?"

"I sure will."

"And I can go home now?"

Dr. Wu frowned. "We're going to have to keep for you a few nights."

I felt the blood drain from my face. "But I have school tomorrow. It's our last week. And everyone will know I'm not there. They'll find out about this place, and I'll be the joke of the school."

"I'm sorry, Courtney."

Great!

On my way back from the bathroom, I rounded the corner and saw a girl crouched down in the hallway outside my room. My heart stopped, then my feet.

Astra?

But where was the tingly feeling I always got when she showed up?

Whoever this chick was, she definitely wasn't a patient, because she was wearing a tight red corset and a black skirt that was torn and frayed at the bottom.

I slowly started toward her again in my hospital scrubs. She was too busy typing on her phone to notice me. But when I got within a few feet, her head jerked up, and blazing green eyes locked onto mine.

It *was* Astra!

"Hi!" I said aloud.

She stood up, and the metal studs on the back of her corset made a scraping noise against the painted cinderblock wall. *That's weird.* Imaginary Astra never made any noise, other than talking. And I could smell incense coming off of her clothes.

"How's it going?" she asked, shoving her phone in her pocket.

Her voice was different, coming from her lips and not from inside my head.

"Okay," I said. I bit my thumbnail. There was no getting around the question, as ludicrous as it might sound. I had to ask. "Are you real?"

She moved closer to me, closing the gap to less than a foot. I held my breath, hoping no one was behind me in the hallway watching me talk to a possibly imaginary friend, but I was too entranced to turn my head and look. Astra held up a black fingernail and poked me above my collarbone.

"Ouch," I breathed, glancing down at the red mark on my chest.

"I'm real," she said. Then she smiled. "Jeez, dude! What kind of drugs are they giving you in here?"

Ignoring her question, I stared at her. "I can't believe we're actually meeting," I said. I felt myself smile. "I have so much to tell you."

"Shh! You'll get in trouble." She motioned behind me, and I looked over my shoulder at the two orderlies, both eyeing me.

I turned back to Astra—but she was walking away.

"Hey," I called after her.

She waved back at me over her shoulder and kept walking, around the corner and out of sight.

My heart pounding wildly, I looked down for the mark where Astra's fingernail had pressed into my skin, but it was gone.

I hurried into my room and shut the door. How was I going to explain what had just happened to me to Dr. Wu? *No.* I couldn't tell her. That might change my diagnosis to crazy.

Oh no! Either my imaginary friend had just turned out to be a real person who came to visit me in the hospital, or else I had hallucinated the entire thing. And I was wide awake when it happened, not in some hypno-whatever stage between dreaming and waking up. This was bad. Dr. Wu was wrong about me.

I climbed into bed. Closing my eyes, I took a deep breath. I could feel the medicine the nurse had given me right before I went to the bathroom slowing my thoughts down and making me drowsy. So maybe that was it? The medicine was playing tricks on my brain?

SEVEN

Monday, I slept for almost the entire day. The only parts I remembered being awake for were when the nurses came in to administer my medication.

Then Tuesday morning, Dr. Wu stopped in my room and told me I was cleared to join the general population in the activities room for family visiting hour. I jumped out of bed, fixed my hair, then hurried down the hall. It seemed like a week since I'd talked to anybody normal.

Apparently visitation wasn't mandatory, because no one from my family showed up. I thought at least my dad and his girlfriend, Rachel, would come. Knowing my mom, though, she probably hadn't even told them I was in here. After a half hour of standing by the door, waiting, I wandered over to the far window and gazed out at the parking deck, trying not to cry.

"Hey, you," came from behind me.

I whipped around. It was Astra. A burgundy dress and torn black stockings clung to her pale body. "We meet again," she said.

I glanced over at the orderlies, but neither was watching. Then I turned back to Astra. I could smell the perfume coming off her skin, see tiny, dark freckles on her pale cheeks. She looked real.

I poked her arm with my finger. Definitely real! I gave her a huge hug; then, suddenly embarrassed, I backed away.

"Oh, all right." She straightened out her dress. "You're happy to see me."

"So, we know each other," I said. "You recognize me, right?"

"Dude?" She glanced around like she thought someone was watching, then back at me. "We met last night, outside your room."

"No, I know. But before that . . . Your name *is* Astra, right?"

"Astra?" She laughed. "Never been called that."

So she didn't use the name Astra.

And wait. Was she saying that she didn't recognize me from all her visits? How could this be?

Pretending to scratch my eyebrow, I covered my mouth with my hand in case anyone tried to read my lips. "We were imaginary friends," I whispered. "But my grandpa said you might be real."

"Dude, what?" She shook her head. "You messing with me?"

"No. I'm serious," I said. "You visited me like a hundred times, going back to when I was like five years old."

She narrowed her eyes into an inquisitive gaze. Then she nodded, like she almost understood what I was talking about.

"So . . ." Covering my mouth again, I leaned closer. "You here to break me out?" I asked.

Astra laughed again, loudly. "Slow down, *Twelve Monkeys*," she said. "I'm here to pick my brother up. He's being discharged. But I wanted to catch you before I left."

I felt my face heat up and turn red.

"You okay?" she asked.

I shook my head. "I don't know why I just said that stuff about knowing you. I'm crazy. Just forget what I said."

"You're not crazy," she said.

"Oh yeah? And how do you know that?" I asked, suddenly

suspicious that she was lying about not recognizing me. "You've seen me before, haven't you? Like in your head?" I had to try one more time.

"Dude!" Astra smirked. "Not sure about that one. But I know you're not crazy, because my brother's just like you."

"Like me how?"

She leaned her head in so her mouth was inches from my ear. "He's visited by aliens," she whispered.

"What?" Only Astra would know about the aliens. "Wait. So if you're name's not Astra, then what is it?" I demanded.

"I'm Agatha Kirlich." She held out her hand for me to shake it.

Agatha Kirlich? Sounded like a made-up name if I'd ever heard one. I kept my hands at my sides, and eventually she gave up on the handshake.

"So, Agatha Kirlich, if that's really your name . . ." I narrowed my eyes. "How did you even know I was visited by imaginary aliens?" I asked.

She grinned. "I overheard the nurses talking when you we're being admitted. Not a lot of alien-abductee patients around here. So I popped down and read your chart."

"Oh really?" I guess it was possible.

"Yeah, really. And I can help you with your problem. But you have to get out of this place first," she said. "You don't belong here."

I glanced down at my hospital scrubs and my patient wristband, then up at Agatha Kirlich. She was nineteen, maybe, and super pretty, just like Astra. Same green eyes and straight black hair. Even the same long pale legs.

"Dr. Wu said I could go home in a few days," I said. "But . . ." My eyes welled up and tears streaked down my cheeks.

"But what?" Agatha asked.

"My mom's horrible. I need to call my dad to pick me up,

except they took my cell phone away when they admitted me."

"You can use the phone at the nurses' station during visiting hours," Agatha said.

"I can?"

"Yeah, for sure," Agatha said. "But listen to me, dude. You have to call me soon as you get out of here. I'd give you my number now, but they might search you. I'll find you on Facebook and shoot you my info. Okay?"

"Okay. I'm Courtney Hoffman."

"I know. I saw your chart, remember?"

"Oh yeah." I smiled.

"I gotta bolt, Courtney." She held out her hand for me to shake it.

This time I did. Her hand felt warm and strong. "You're definitely real," I said, smiling.

"Yup," she said. She leaned into me again. "And so are the aliens, Courtney. Don't let anyone tell you different!"

"What?" I asked. But she turned and sauntered out the door.

EIGHT

My dad was sitting at the kitchen table, working on his laptop, when I came downstairs. He glanced up. "I'm sorry, but you just missed breakfast."

Oh. Nobody had told me anything about a schedule. "Sorry."

"He's just kidding, Courtney." Rachel set a plate full of blueberry waffles on the table. "We made you your favorite. Sit down and relax."

My dad smiled at me.

"Thanks." I smiled back. Blueberry waffles used to be my favorite, when I was like six years old. But it was the thought that counted. Plus, anything was better than the hospital food I'd been forced to eat for the past five days. And these weren't just frozen toaster waffles; they were real ones from a waffle maker. I poured syrup until it filled every last waffle hole; then I hoisted a forkful to my mouth.

"Oh gosh, these are delicious," I said, my voice muffled by the wad of waffle still in my mouth. I was so glad that my mom was letting me stay at my dad's house for the entire summer. She was a total control freak, after all. And even though Dad was supposed to get Kaelyn and me every other weekend, and two weeks during the summer, the most my mom ever actually let us visit was for an occasional weekend, or a few days during holiday breaks. But she was sick of my shenanigans, and Dad agreed to take me for the summer. Of course part of the agreement was that my sister would stay with Mom for the whole summer, because she had soccer almost every day. And of course, I'd miss Kaelyn. But I'd only been at Dad's for like ten hours, and I already knew I liked it better than home. And it was still June. So that meant two-plus months without having to deal with my mom.

"Thought for the day, ladies. Ready?" My dad turned his laptop so we could see it. Then he read aloud, "'Life is strange; then you die.'"

"Boo. That's morbid. Ignore him, Courtney," Rachel said.

I laughed, covered my mouth.

"After breakfast I'll take you to the club and we can get you sized up for golf clubs and a tennis racquet," Rachel said. "Sound fun?"

I wiped the syrup from my face. "Yeah, totally!"

That night, I swallowed my medication, then sat down on my queen-size bed with the old laptop my dad was loaning me and logged into Facebook. My first real contact with the outside world since I was carted off to the hospital six days ago. Thirty-three unread messages. *Yikes!*

The first seven were drama-laden apologies from Lauren, begging my forgiveness for having told my mom about our conversation at soccer practice. The next twenty were "get well soon" messages from everyone else at school. Five more from Lauren, updating me on who'd hooked up with whom at senior graduation parties and reassuring me that everyone, including Josh Sale, missed me. Apparently Josh didn't miss enough to call or email me, but whatever. Not like we were really boyfriend and girlfriend.

The last message was from Agatha Kirlich. She'd found me! Suddenly my face flushed with embarrassment for all the crazy things I'd said to her that day in the hospital. I'd been in a total state of confusion. She may have looked shockingly similar to Astra, but that was just a coincidence or a projection of my mind. And besides, Astra was never real!

Ignoring the butterflies in my stomach, I clicked on Agatha's message. She wanted to meet for coffee at the Holy Donut, which was a diner a few miles from my house in West Bridge. I'd never been inside it, but I'd definitely seen it before. I messaged her back that I was forty miles away, at my dad's house, and would be there for the summer.

Her reply popped right up. *Let me call you now. Cell number?*

Shit! I pulled at my hair. Not that I didn't want to talk to her. I did. Even if she wasn't Astra, I felt a strange bond with her. I wanted to tell her I was okay, and find out more about her brother and his alien-visitor problems. But *no.* There was something dangerous about her. I couldn't put my finger on it, but I felt it in my gut.

No cell! I messaged back, which was basically true. Even though I had my phone I didn't want to use it, because my mom controlled the account and had a way of monitoring my activities.

I slammed the laptop shut. Leaned back against my headboard.

After a full minute, I opened the laptop again and went to Agatha's Facebook page. Blazing green eyes stared back at me from the picture on the screen, and I held my breath. *Oh wow!* She totally looked like Astra. I scanned through her info. She was definitely a real person, though, with real friends, and pictures, and posts. She lived in West Bridge! *Talk about weirdness.*

I bit my fingernail and kept scrolling. She'd graduated from West Bridge High, my high school! She was four years older than me, though, so we never would've met there.

Maybe I saw her when I was a kid at some point, and her face just got stuck in my head in an imaginary-friend kind of way? Weirder things had happened, especially to me.

She had a blog, so I opened the page. *Have You Been Visited by Aliens?* jumped out on my screen. I clicked the blog, but it was written in another language. I scrolled through it anyway. At the bottom of the blog was a picture of an old wooden church. *Ancient alien wormhole, Trondheim, Norway.*

Wormhole? A drawing of my grandpa's flashed in my head.

I clicked off her page, back to mine.

A new message from Agatha popped up. *This doctor I work for, Dr. Straka, can help you with your alien problem. He understands these things. Give me your dad's address. I'll pick you up and take you there. Your parents will never have to know.*

Oh gosh. I hadn't had any extraterrestrial nightmares or nocturnal visitors in the past six days, not since I'd started on the medication at the hospital. *I'm sorry, Agatha, I know you're trying to help. But I can't get into this right now.* I deleted her message.

Another message from Agatha popped up. The link to Dr. Straka's website. *This chick is definitely persistent.* I clicked on it, expecting more craziness. But Dr. Straka looked pretty normal. I scanned through his home page. He specialized in sleep disorders and hypnotherapy. And treating patients without the use of medication. I liked the sound of that. As much as my medication was working, it made me feel spacey and tired all the time. I clicked on Dr. Straka's bio page and read through the list of all the awards he'd gotten for helping people and volunteering his services. He seemed totally legit. And smart.

I sent Agatha a quick message. *Appreciate the info. I'll get back to you.*

Then I shoved the laptop under my bed, flopped back onto my pillow, and closed my eyes.

Tomorrow I'd have my first tennis lesson at the club. Normal life stuff. I tried to think about it. What I'd wear. My mind wasn't cooperating, though, which frightened me.

I rolled onto my side, covered my face with my other pillow.

You're fine, Courtney. I was fine. I just couldn't get the image of Agatha's blazing green eyes out of my head.

NINE

Most days, Dad and Rachel worked at home in their respective offices until about two or three p.m., and then we'd all go to the club. Tuesdays, though, they both worked at their real offices, so one of them would drop me off at the club on their way into work.

But today was Tuesday, July 3. And in preparation for the big Fourth of July party tomorrow, the club was closed. Which meant I was home alone.

Yikes! Alone and I did not do well together.

I pulled out my laptop and checked my messages. No new ones from Agatha. She'd sent me like six messages over the past ten days, trying to convince me to call her, or to let her pick me up and take me to lunch, or to see Dr. Straka. I hadn't responded to any of them.

I felt horrible for mostly ignoring her, but only a crazy person thought aliens were real. And she definitely did. And I had no room for craziness. Anyway, a few days ago, she moved to Norway to become a model or something. So obviously all offers to meet up with her were off the table for now.

I shut my laptop and slid it under my bed.

Still in my pajamas, I strolled into my bathroom and stared at myself in the mirror. A loud clap of thunder shook the bathroom window, and I flinched. Grabbing my prescription bottle off the counter, I shook out a pill, popped it in my mouth, and chased it down with tap water. Eleven days had passed since they'd let me out of the hospital, and not one nightmare. Eleven days of normal sleep. No waking up still dreaming, no imaginary visitors. No butterflies in my tummy, no scary thoughts. I was myself again. Only tired, and foggy from the medication.

I leaned my head down toward the sink and splashed cold water on my face. Grabbing a towel to dry my face, I felt a shiver of electricity trickle down my neck. *Whoa.*

I froze! The little hairs on my arms stood up.

You can handle this, Courtney.

I turned around slowly, expecting to see Astra standing behind me. But she wasn't.

A smell of incense or burning candles filled my head, though. *Huh?*

I decided to ignore it. I turned back around and grabbed my toothbrush out of its cup, glanced at myself in the mirror. Then I saw Astra.

Not behind me, but in my head.

She was standing in an old, empty church, wearing a gothic black dress and big boots over torn stockings. Her face was corpse white, covered with powdery makeup. Even weirder, it was like I was standing on the bumpy stone floor of the church, ten feet from her.

"Astra?" My voice crackled. But she didn't seem to hear me. And if she could see me, it definitely didn't show on her face.

I glanced around the church. Big photography lights hung from the metal posts next to the altar, and there were drums and a guitar, and a video camera. Candles and incense sticks burned in old metal lanterns hanging from the walls.

Astra tossed her backpack over her shoulder and walked right past me. She grabbed the handle of a fifteen-foot wooden door that seemed to lead outside, and yanked on it. But it didn't budge.

She whipped around and stared toward the church altar. "Unlock the door, Jorg. You're not funny."

A guy with flaking corpse makeup on his face and black circles around his bright blue eyes got up from one of the pews. Tall and lanky, he clomped over toward Astra in big black boots. Half a dozen baby-bird skulls dangled from a wire around his fake-blood covered throat.

Gross! He looked dangerous, too!

Astra bit her lip.

My breathing grew faster.

"Why are you here?" the scary Jorg guy asked Astra in a cool, Scandinavian-sounding accent.

"Well, I'm not here for church service, am I?" Astra said.

I smiled to myself, reveling in her familiar sarcastic confidence.

"The video shoot is over, Jorg," Astra said, peering up at him. He was actually pretty cute, despite his death makeup: gorgeous blue eyes, square jaw, and totally kissable full lips.

"Everyone's gone," Astra said. "Let me out."

"You're American," he said towering over her. "Why are you in Norway, Agatha?"

"Agatha?" I blurted out. "Norway? What the hell?"

Agatha turned quickly to her left and stared in my direction. My heart stopped. "It's me, Courtney," I said. "Can you see me?"

She stared past me for a long few seconds, then returned her attention to Jorg.

"I already told you. I came here with my older brother," she said. "He's having some mental health problems, so we thought visiting our aunt Ketti's farm might help him clear his head. Now open the door before I slit your throat for real."

Jorg snatched Agatha's backpack and held it up out of her reach. "Not until you tell me why you're *really* here."

Twisting the leather choker around her neck, Agatha glanced down at the stone floor, then back up at Jorg.

"Okay," Agatha said. "My aunt died a couple years ago, but she used to talk about a place where people like my brother could go to learn about the visitors in their dreams. We thought maybe my aunt left some instructions, or a note. But she didn't. Just pictures of this church. Can I go now?"

He unzipped Agatha's backpack and pulled out a sketch pad. The same sketch pad I'd seen Astra drawing on in the diner, back on my birthday! So they *were* totally the same person, and this proved it. *I knew it!*

"Now you're going to critique my artwork again?" Agatha asked sarcastically.

"Eight hundred years ago, this church was built over a gateway to the alien world," Jorg said. "But a hundred years ago, Magi priests from America tore open the floor and dug up the ancient texts and a sacred alien helmet. They stole our portal to the alien world and severed our communications with our alien ancestors. That's why people like your brother are so messed up. They've lost their link to their other half."

"People like my brother? You mean you know others?" Agatha asked with nervous excitement.

Jorg locked his eyes on Agatha. Her chest rose and fell with her breath.

He opened her sketch pad. "This drawing of yours." He held up a color pencil drawing of a crumbling parking lot with bolts of red lightning jetting up through the cracks and down from the sky. "Is it the apocalypse?"

"I think so," Agatha said. "I see it in my dreams sometimes, like a vision."

He turned the sketch pad around and started reading to himself.

"Who's the girl in your poems who talks to the aliens?"

Agatha shook her head. "She's in my dreams. Imaginary person, I guess. I never really see her face. But—"

Jorg slammed the notebook shut and stomped closer to Agatha. "Well, in your imagination, does she save the worlds?" he asked through clenched teeth. "Or does she cause the apocalypse?"

Agatha shook her head. "I don't know, I swear."

Jorg tossed the sketch pad to her and she caught it against her chest. Then he stepped around her, reached up, and flipped open the metal door lock. "Go back to California. I'll be in touch."

Agatha pulled open the huge wooden door, and suddenly she and the church were gone from my mind.

Gazing vacantly at my reheated pizza lunch, I heard the doorbell. I crept across the foyer, to the huge double doors, and peeked out the peephole. Lauren, my supposed best friend, was standing there. Totally unexpected, unannounced.

I thought about running upstairs and jumping into bed. But—

"I see you, Hoffman." She tapped the outside of the peephole with her finger.

Crap! A hollow feeling moved into my stomach. I opened the door and stared blankly at her. I had no idea what to say.

Luckily, awkward moments didn't bother Lauren. "Hey, Court, I really gotta pee," she said, hugging me. "Oh man, you grew. Like, how tall are you?" She released me from her hug and stepped back to look at me.

"Seriously, Courtney, you look great," she said. "Hey, do

you like my hair? I know—I hate it. Wait, I'll be right back. I gotta pee." She pushed past me into the house.

I stood there, motionless, still in shock. I guess I wasn't quite sure how I felt about Lauren after she'd spilled my secret to my mom. The same secret she'd sworn on her life, on the sideline of the soccer field, not to tell anyone!

When she returned from the bathroom, she made me take my shoes off and stand back-to-back with her to make sure she was still taller. "Phew," she said. Then she felt my chest. "Okay, that's all you. How do you like my bra?" She arched her back and stuck out her chest. "You can barely see it, right?"

"Yeah. Looks great," I said. "I mean, it looks like nothing. Like it's not there. But you, or, you know, your shirt, and everything underneath it look great."

"Thanks." She smiled.

I glanced out the front door, which I still hadn't closed. Lauren's mom's white SUV was parked crooked on the driveway, the left front tire on the lawn. The windows were down, and the radio was blasting.

"So, you got your driver's license?" I asked, even though I knew she wouldn't turn sixteen until next December.

"No, but I got my learner's permit. My mom's getting her hair done, so I kind of dropped her off for an hour and a half, so I could practice parking." Lauren checked her phone. "Took me like forty mins to get here, but I got lost. So I'm cool to stay for like ten minutes. Then I gotta fly."

Ten minutes? I felt like I should invite her into kitchen to sit down. But I didn't really want to.

"So, how are you, Courtney? Are you better and everything?"

"Yeah, all better," I said.

Lauren's phone rang, and her eyes grew wide. "Oh no! It's my mom!" She stared at the phone until it stopped ringing. A half minute later it beeped. She lifted it to her ear and listened to the voice message.

"I'm totally busted," she said. "I gotta motor."

We quickly hugged good-bye. Then Lauren ran out to her mom's car and jumped in. After backing up, cranking the wheel, and going forward again, three times, she managed to turn around on the lawn and shoot down the driveway and onto the street.

TEN

Today was the last Friday of summer vacation, and the club was packed. Dad and Rachel were off playing golf, so I sat by the pool wearing my scratchy fringe cover-up over the blue-and-white bikini Rachel had bought me, trying to enjoy my last few hours before moving back to my mom's house for the school year.

"Hey, Courtney."

Lexi Martin and two other girls I sometimes played tennis with plopped down a few lounge chairs away. I half waved at Lexi. "Hey back," I said.

"Sunny enough or what?" Lexi said. She glanced up at the sky, annoyed, then flipped onto her stomach.

I leaned back in my chair and closed my eyes. The screen in my mind went orange with sunshine. Then I watched the orange slowly turn black, like maybe a cloud had covered up the sun. Suddenly an image of me as a little girl, floating in a bathtub, dead, jumped into my head.

I shot up out of my chair and pulled at my hair. Then the picture of me drowning was gone from my head.

Sitting down, I glanced at Lexi and the other girls to see if they'd noticed my freak-out. Luckily, they were dead to the world. *Okay, that was totally weird. But you're fine*, I told myself. I wrapped my arms around my knees and rocked back and forth, trying to forget about what I had just seen in my head. Obviously, it wasn't a memory. But I had seen it before, in a nightmare. *You're fine.*

I glanced at the pool. Slivers of sunlight jetted down into the deep blue water. I took a slow breath and tried to think how beautiful the sun and the water looked.

But I couldn't concentrate. A strange buzzing sound was rising up in my ears. And my brain felt weird, like a giant magnet was pulling my thoughts out of my skull. *What is happening to me?*

I scooted my body to the edge of my chair. Sweat dripped off my forehead, and I wiped my face against my forearm. My skin smelled like sunscreen and chlorine. But there was another smell coming from me too: the musty-book smell from my grandpa's cottage. *Oh God! No way am I going through this again.* I needed that smell the hell off me!

I rushed over to the edge of the pool, and I was about to jump when I shot a quick glance down into the water. Only I couldn't see the water, or the bottom of the pool, or anything real. Just a picture in my head of a drawing my grandpa had made in his notebook: a giant gate made of twisted metal antlers. And behind the gate was a spiraling tunnel of light. A wormhole to the alien world, my grandpa had explained to me. I stood there, staring, my mouth open in disbelief.

"It's only water."

"What?" I whipped around. Trevor, the lifeguard, was smiling at me.

"You're staring at that pool like you expect a monster to burst out of it," he said. "What's happening?"

"Nothing." I brushed past him and sat down on my lounge chair. *What is happening to me?* I wondered, bouncing my knees. Except for that one day when I had a vision or whatever of Agatha in Norway, I'd been normal all summer. And now, on the day I was supposed to move back to my mom's house, I was losing it.

I leaned back against my towel and tried to slow my

thoughts down, but the buzzing sound and the magnet feeling in my skull were back. I jumped to my feet.

My eyes darted around the pool—to the kids lined up for the diving board, Trevor and his buddies by the lifeguard platform—then up at the clear sky. The buzzing grew stronger. There was something up there: a cloud. Not one of vaporized water and frozen crystal that meteorologists would recognize. This was an invisible cloud of magnetic alien energy. The buzzing had been my warning. I could feel them watching me now, messing with my thoughts. A surge of electricity rushed into my head.

No! I stood up and pulled at my hair, hoping the pain might jar me back to sanity. Then I paced along the edge of the deep end. *There's no cloud, Courtney. No such thing as aliens.*

"Courtney!" someone called.

It was my dad.

I whipped around. He and Rachel were over by my chair, waiting for me. It was time to go. Time to move back to my mom's house.

Shit. I walked over and stood in front of them, my body electric with nervous energy.

"You okay, sweetie?" my dad asked.

"What? Yeah." I tried to smile. *Don't look up at the sky. Act normal.* I swung my bag over my shoulder and ignored the musty-cottage smell and the magnetic tickle inside my skull. "Summer's over. Let's go," I said.

ELEVEN

Dad and I spent the forty-minute drive back to Mom's house listening to soft jazz. Definitely not my favorite. But I was so exhausted, the music barely even registered.

When we pulled into the driveway, I sprang to attention. My mom's house looked different than I remembered it. I quickly unbuckled my seat belt and leaned toward the windshield to get a better look at my bedroom windows. *Oh, wow.* New yellow curtains. The tinfoil and duct tape were gone.

I took a deep breath and climbed out.

"It's four thirty. Your mother and sister aren't here, huh?" My dad gazed at the garage where he used to spend Saturday afternoons hanging out, tinkering with whatever as he watched college football games on his giant TV.

"Yeah, they're shopping for school clothes," I said. I checked my phone for any text updates from Mom, but nothing. "I think Kaelyn has a soccer game tonight, so they'll probably be home soon."

Dad carried my suitcase onto the front porch, and I grabbed my backpack and followed him. I tilted back the cement frog statue and slid out the spare house key, then started to unlock the door.

"I'm gonna miss you, Court."

I looked at my dad. "You're not coming in? You're not gonna wait for Kaelyn?"

My dad tried to smile. "Your mother and I . . . it's better if I'm not here when she gets home."

"But . . . you're gonna leave me here alone?"

My dad chuckled. "You'll be just fine, kiddo." He hugged me awkwardly.

"I know, I'm just kidding," I said. But I wasn't.

After my dad left, I plopped down on the couch in our family room. I wanted to feel happy to be home. *I get to see my sister, and hang out with Lauren and everyone,* I reminded myself as I stood up, then made my way back into the foyer. I grabbed my suitcase and dragged it up the steps, thump by thump, and then down the hallway to my bedroom. *I mean, why wouldn't I be happy to be home?*

I felt something streaking down my cheeks. I stopped and wiped my eyes. They filled up again. My lower lip trembled. I couldn't keep it inside me anymore.

I slithered down the wall and onto the floor and started bawling. I was sick with guilt about what had happened at the pool. I'd promised myself after the hospital that I'd never think about aliens or my grandpa again, and I hadn't all summer. But—

My phone vibrated. It was Lauren. I raised my phone to my ear while I wiped my eyes. "Hello?"

"Don't freak out, Hoffman," Lauren said.

"Why? What's going on?" I climbed to my feet.

"There's a vicious rumor going around that you're no longer at your dad's house, but you're locked up in a mental hospital again and never coming back to West Bridge."

My heart jumped. "Are you serious?"

Lauren laughed. "Well, it's only a small rumor. Actually, Josh started it like two seconds ago. Hold on, he's right here."

"Lauren, I can't talk right—"

"Courtney? Courtney Hoffman? Where are you?" It was Josh Sale, the guy I'd sort of liked before my problems started.

"Hey, Josh," I said. It sounded like they were in the car; the background noise was super loud.

"Stay strong, Chezwick!" Josh yelled. "We're coming to break you out!"

"Give me the phone!" Lauren yelled. She got back on the line. "He's so dumb. So where are you?"

"Right now?" I looked down at my suitcase. If they knew I was home, they'd be over in ten seconds. Not that it wouldn't be cool to see them, but . . . The truth was, I wasn't quite in the mood for Lauren. And I definitely couldn't let Josh see me with my eyes all puffy like this.

"I'm still at my dad's house," I lied. "On the golf course. Golfing."

"Hoffman, seriously? But you'll be home tomorrow for Chip's birthday party, right?" Lauren asked. "Everyone's going to be there."

"Yeah, probably." What the hell was she doing in the car with Josh anyway?

"Probably?" she asked. "Earth to Courtney: unless you wanna eat lunch at the loser table all year, you gotta show up at Chip's and show everyone how you're . . . you know, all normal again."

"Yeah. I know," I said. "Okay, my shot. Gotta golf." I hung up.

Even in the daytime the upstairs of our house was creepy, because every little creak came up through the floor vents and sounded like wild animals hissing. Humming loudly to myself, I unpacked my clothes and then went down to the kitchen. I was starving, but I didn't want to eat and spoil my appetite. It was almost six o'clock; Mom and Kaelyn would be home soon, and I had a feeling they'd pick up Thai food for dinner on their way out of the mall like we always did.

Wishful thinking. At eight o'clock, Mom texted me that Kaelyn's soccer game was just finishing up and that they were going out with the team for pizza afterward. I heated mac and cheese up in the microwave and plopped down in front of the TV to watch a movie. But at nine o'clock the channel changed—my mom's shows had started recording—and I couldn't get my movie back on.

I dragged myself up to bed.

Apparently, my mom had confiscated my night-lights while I was at my dad's house, so now my bedroom was so dark that I could barely see the foot of my bed. *Seriously, Mom?*

I pulled open the drawer of my nightstand and felt around inside until I found my flashlight. Leaning back against my headboard, I swept the beam of light across the foot of my bed and over to my new curtains.

Outside my window, my mom's car door slammed; I hid my flashlight under my comforter. Feet clomped up the stairs and down the hallway. I clicked my flashlight off. The toilet flushed, and my sister's door banged shut. I could feel my mom, more than hear her, fidgeting outside my bedroom. Finally she knocked.

I pulled my sheets up and pretended to be asleep. But through my covers, I saw the big ceiling light turn on and my mom stroll in. She sat down next to me on my bed and smoothed a wrinkle from her chic business skirt.

"You still awake?" She uncovered my head.

"Pretty much." I glanced up through one eye.

"Well?" she asked. "What do you think?" She raised her manicured eyebrows like it should be obvious to me what she meant.

What do I think? I shoved my hair out of my eyes. Then I looked at my mom again for a clue, but I had no idea what she was asking. We hadn't spoken more than ten words to each other all summer. So we weren't exactly finishing each other's sentences. We weren't even on the same planet, for that matter. But I wanted to be, starting now. I wanted a new beginning.

"Think about what?" I asked politely.

"The curtains, Courtney."

"Oh!" I sat up and pretended to admire the bright yellow sheets of fabric. "Yeah, I like 'em, Mom. Much nicer than the tinfoil."

"That's not funny."

"It's not?" My heart sank, and I slumped back down.

"Since you brought up the tinfoil incident, this might be a good time for us to talk about rules."

The tinfoil incident? Was that what she was calling it now?

"I don't know what your father puts up with at his house, but I'm expecting you to behave responsibly."

"Of course. I will, Mom."

"Your sister's not a little kid anymore. She's impressionable and she looks up to you. I'm not going to stand by and let you poison her mind with nonsense."

"Mom, I won't. I'm all better. I promise."

"I know you won't." Mom stood up and gazed admiringly at the curtains, then stared down at me. We locked eyes.

Ten o'clock at night and she looked flawless, like a movie star ready to play the role of a beautiful, no-nonsense attorney. I looked like a hurricane victim, fresh out of a sea-soaked ditch.

"I'll not be intimidated by your stare," Mom said.

"What? No. I wasn't staring like that, Mom. I swear. Please, sit back down."

She grabbed the socks I'd been wearing earlier from the floor and folded them. "Zero tolerance, Courtney. That means first sign of any Martian nightmare shenanigans, or one word about your grandfather, and Dr. Anderson and I will march you straight down to the hospital again. But this time your father's not gonna bail you out. This time you're going to stay in there until I'm convinced you've got your imagination under control. You understand me, young lady?"

Beautiful, no-nonsense attorney moms may be great for cross-examining witnesses or organizing school fund-raisers or looking amazing at soccer games. But mine sucked at the things that really counted. Like giving hugs and saying all-important mom things like "I'm your mother, and no matter what happens you can always talk to me about it" or "I love you, and there's nothing we can't get through if we put our minds together."

"Do you understand me?"

Looking into her icy gray eyes, I felt a shiver. Grandpa's warm, silvery-blue eyes had definitely skipped over her generation.

I love you too, Mom.

"Courtney! Do you understand me?"

"I understand," I said.

"Good." She kissed me on top of my head. "Lights on or off?"

"Off, please," I said. She flipped the switch, and my room was swallowed in darkness.

"Door open or closed?"

"Closed, please."

Cree-aak, thump. Solitary confinement.

TWELVE

A buzzing noise woke me out of a dream about eighth-grade soccer camp. I lifted my head off my pillow and the noise stopped. Probably just the air conditioner or something, I hoped. Flopping back down, I pulled my extra pillow over my head and tried to will myself back to soccer dreamland.

I was almost there, too, when I heard my soccer trophies rattle against one another. The hairs on the back of my neck stood up. *Not good.*

The floor creaked. My eyes sprang open. *Please, not this again!* I yanked my pillow down and stared around me into darkness.

The floor creaked again, louder. I gasped. Then I heard the crackle of electricity. My bed started to vibrate. It was shaking!

Oh God! I wanted to scream, except I couldn't. Mom would wake up and run in and turn on the light, and if there was nothing there, she'd go ballistic.

The air-conditioning clicked off, and I let out my breath. Maybe I'd imagined it?

I could hear my heartbeat, strong and steady. But no buzzing noise. *Phew.*

Then I heard footsteps by the foot of my bed. *Ahh!* I kicked off my comforter and sprang up. But light burst in between the crack in the curtains, striking me in the face.

I dropped back down to my mattress and squeezed my eyes closed.

This is bad! I could feel the warmth from the light against my eyelids. *Really bad!* I had to roll off the bed and get to the light switch. *One, two, three, GO!* I twisted my body. But it didn't twist. I tried again, but nothing. I couldn't budge. I was paralyzed.

Slowly I cracked my eyes open. Silhouetted in the light were three alien creatures. Their long, lanky bodies shuffled awkwardly toward my bed. *This isn't supposed to be happening!*

What would Dr. Wu tell me? *Stay calm. It's just a dream. Try to wake up.*

But I was awake! And they were standing over me now, staring down through their monstrous, oval-shaped eyes— bigger than my fists. My eyes darted from one creature to the next. Their skin glistened grayish blue in the light coming through the window. My heart pounded, and it was getting impossible to breathe in enough air.

The alien on my left, the female, must have heard my heartbeat, because she leaned in to listen to my chest. I bit my lip to stop it from trembling.

She raised her head and moved it up my body until her eyes were inches from my own. I could feel her breath on my face. Her nostrils twitched open and closed like two slimy snails being electrocuted. I tried to move away, to sink deeper into my mattress, but I could only stare up.

Please leave me alone! I tried to beg her, but my voice didn't work.

She heard me, though, because she turned toward the other two and made a screeching sound. Then she jerked her head back around and her eyes locked onto mine. My brain tingled. I could feel my thoughts being read—could feel that she was reading them.

Please! I yelled at her with my thoughts. *You have to go back to my dreams or wherever it is you came from.*

Don't fight it, Courtney, a strange, crackly voice said. It came from inside my own head, but I knew it was her speaking. *We're connected now.*

I tried to shake my head. *I don't want to be connected,* I thought at her. *I have friends and a family and a life, and you're gonna screw everything up again. I'm an A student and the junior captain on the varsity soccer team. My sister looks up to me. I'm a good person. You'll make me crazy, and my mom is not cool with that.*

She tilted her head and studied me, her eyes gleaming in the dusty light, her snail-nostrils twitching. *We need you, Courtney.*

No, you don't need me, I swear, I protested. *I'm not like my grandpa. You need someone who's not afraid of you. You should find a Goth girl who listens to creepy music and likes zombies and witches and stuff. There're tons of them out there, and they'd be happy to help you.*

No. It's you we're after.

Well, don't be after me. Please. I'm begging you. Just leave!

Not without you.

What? What does that mean?

There was a silvery thing in her hand now. Metal and twisted. A tattoo gun? She raised it over my head, and a needle poked out of the end.

What are you doing?

She pointed it right at my right eye, and I tried to squirm out of the way, but I couldn't move. I felt the needle plunge straight down into my eyeball.

AHHH! My body lifted up off the bed, and white light flooded my mind. I was leaving my bedroom. I could smell the musty books in Grandpa's cottage; I heard yelling. I was being pulled through the cottage. I felt warmth against my legs. The aliens were dragging me into the bathroom. *Oh my God! They're going to drown me in the bathtub!*

Stop! I thrust my body with all my strength—and I knocked my flashlight against my bedroom wall. I could move! I kicked off my comforter, scrambled to the door, flipped on the ceiling light, and looked back. The aliens were gone.

I hurried over and checked my right eye in the mirror. No blood or needle marks. My teeth were chattering, but I didn't care. I rubbed my hands over my body to see if anything was broken.

"You okay, Courtney?"

"Ah!" I spun around. It was Kaelyn, standing in the doorway, her gray eyes beaming out from behind her mess of blond hair.

"You scared me," I said, feeling my heartbeat. I hadn't seen her all summer, since the tinfoil incident. I had to act normal.

"I like your pajamas, Kaelyn." My voice was shaking. I tried to smile. "How are you?"

"Were the aliens here?"

My mouth dropped open. I couldn't help it. I grabbed my sister and pulled her into my room. "Don't say that," I said. She was only nine. She shouldn't be thinking those dangerous thoughts. "There's no such thing as aliens. So don't talk like that. Ever, okay?"

"Your pajamas are wet."

"What?" I backed away and looked down at my pajama pants. They were wet. Fifteen years old and I'd wet my bed. As if I wasn't already humiliated enough.

"Did the aliens make you pee in your bed?"

"I told you not to talk like that." I covered my wet pajamas with a book from my desk. "Now please, just go back to your room."

"But I want to meet them. I want to be like you and Grandpa."

"Kaelyn, that's not funny. You're gonna get us in trouble with Mom. Go back to bed."

"Not fair!" she said. And she stormed out.

I shut my door and tore off my wet pajamas.

Staring at myself in the mirror, I dug my fingernails into the ribs below my left armpit. *I hate you, Grandpa. This is all your fault!* I pressed harder, and the pain rose until I couldn't stand it. I pulled my hand away and watched the bluish indentations from where my fingernails had dug in my skin slowly return to normal color. Hardly normal, though. My grandpa's mark was still there. A blurry tattoo of four dead insects. His last gift to me.

I grabbed my phone off the floor and crawled into my closet. My hands were shaking as I pulled up Dr. Straka's website. Agatha had told me that I could call Dr. Straka anytime, day or night, and that if he didn't answer I should leave a message. That he'd call me right back. I scrolled down to his phone number. Took a deep breath. Then I pressed CALL.

THIRTEEN

I **steered** my bike through the shaded patch of side-walk in front of the Holy Donut diner and the temperature instantly dropped ten degrees. Five seconds later I was back in the sunlight, pedaling hard again. Sweat poured off me.

According to Dr. Straka, his office was in a medical plaza somewhere between Solomon Grace Hospital and the old abandoned mental-hospital building. Even though I must have driven by Solomon Grace—and the boarded-up old mental hospital, for that matter—a hundred times with my mom on our way to indoor soccer, I couldn't picture a medical plaza.

I grabbed the bottom of my yellow FOSTER THE PEOPLE shirt, pulled it up, and blotted my face—but my shirt was already soaked with sweat, and now my blue sports bra showed through. *So much for my cool, not-crazy outfit.*

I rode by the emergency entrance for Solomon Grace Hospital, then continued alongside a brick fence and past a field of tall weeds. Then, seeing the sign I was looking for—MEDICAL PLAZA—I swerved around two orange construction cones and into a bombed-out-looking parking lot. The front tire of my bike plonked into a chunk of asphalt, and I bounced and skidded to halt.

Oh wow! A six-inch-wide crack snaked its way across the whole parking lot, starting way over by the abandoned mental hospital. My front tire was wedged in one of the snakey branches of the giant crack. I stared across the parking lot at the abandoned psychiatric building. Supposedly it had once been part of Solomon Grace, but it had been run-down and empty for as long as I could remember, and now it looked like it was leaning to one side.

I glanced at the opposite end of the parking lot, at a row of medical offices that probably hadn't been painted since before I was born. *This is Dr. Straka's medical plaza?* Two cars were parked out front. I jerked my bike tire free, pushed my sweaty hair out of my eyes, and started pedaling toward the offices.

A tattered couch took up most of the waiting room. Instantly recognizing the chick sitting on it, I felt my stomach go viral with butterflies. Agatha Kirlich, her freckled cheekbones perfectly framed in thick black hair.

"The doctor will be with you shortly," she said matter-of-factly, flipping through the stack of medical files on her lap without glancing up. *So much for her modeling career in Norway.*

I parked myself on the other end of the couch. The slit in Agatha's skirt was open, and I tried not to notice, but I could see all the way up the side of her leg to her red underwear. I wiped sweat from my forehead and sank back into the lumpy couch.

Agatha stared over at me with her electric green eyes. "We need to talk!"

"Yeah?" My voice crackled. I could feel my heartbeat picking up speed.

She uncrossed her legs, clunking her big black Viking boots against the floor, and then sat up on the arm of the couch so she was facing me. "So how goes the battle?" she asked.

"The battle?" My throat tightened. "I'm all better now. I'm actually just here because I had a nightmare last night, but I'm cool now. Like, all better, and cool and stuff." I was talking so quickly my words were practically blurring together.

Agatha squinted her eyes just enough to let me know that she knew I was full of it. My eyes retreated to my lap. *Please hurry, Dr. Straka.*

"We really need to talk, Courtney," she said, less antagonistic. "Let's step outside."

"No thanks," I said, my knees bouncing up and down.

"Hey. You're shaking."

"Am I?" I couldn't look at her. I shoved my hands under my knees to stop them from knocking against each other. But my whole body was shaking with adrenaline.

"What's wrong, Courtney?"

"I know you think they're real, Agatha," I said. "And maybe your brother is visited by real aliens. But my visitors are imaginary—they have to be. And the more I think about it, the worse it will get. So I just need Dr. Straka to hypnotize me like you said he could, and make them go away."

I wiped my eyes before any tears could escape.

I was sweating again. Standing up, I pulled my shirt up and blotted my face.

"Whoa!" Agatha's hand clamped around my elbow. "Let me see that tattoo."

"No." I pulled my shirt down, suddenly self-conscious.

"I'm not kidding." Agatha stood up. "Show me."

"No way."

She pouted her bottom lip. "Please. Just a lookie."

"Fine." I pulled my shirt up and showed her the horrible tattoo on the ribs below my armpit.

"Dude. What is that?"

"I don't know." I yanked my shirt down and slumped back down on the couch.

"You have a medieval symbol of four birds tattooed on your rib cage, and you're telling me you don't know what it is?"

"They're insects," I said. "And I was seven years old when my grandpa and his nun friend let some guy carve me with his tattoo gun. Then my grandpa died. So no, I don't exactly know what they're supposed to mean."

She stood up and grabbed my hand. "Now we *really* need to talk. Outside. Let's go!"

I pulled my hand back. "No, I'm here to see Dr. Straka."

"He can't help you, Courtney."

"What?" I stared at her. "You're the one who told me he could. His website says he's an expert on sleep disorders, and that he fixes things with hypnosis instead of medication."

"Things have changed around here," Agatha said quietly. "I can help you, though. My brother can help you."

Lowering my eyes, I shook my head.

Agatha sat down right next to me on the couch and rested her head awkwardly on my shoulder. "Have the aliens made you draw the insects from your tattoo yet?"

"Draw them?" I scooted away. "What are you talking about?"

She raised her head and stared at me. "My brother drew the same symbol as your tattoo all over the wall of his dorm room. That's why he was in the hospital with you back in June."

"Seriously?" Part of me definitely wanted to know what she was talking about, but I needed to stay focused on my appointment. "Never mind." I covered my ears. "Don't tell me!"

"The aliens were giving him a message, Courtney. They were trying to tell him—"

The door across from us swung open, and I jumped up.

Dr. Straka stepped out into the waiting room. His hair was shaggy and longer than it had been in his website picture, and he looked more like an old surfer than a doctor. But as long as he could fix me, what did I care?

He handed Agatha a stack of medical files. "Beautiful day out there, girls. You can go home, Agatha. I'll see you in a few weeks, when I get back from Vermont," he said. Then he winked at me. "Ready when you are, Courtney." He turned and walked back into his office.

I glanced at Agatha, and our eyes locked.

"Tell him you have to reschedule," she said.

I shook my head. "I don't want your help."

"Well, you need it." She grabbed my hand and wrote a phone number on my palm. "Call me when you're finished."

"I can't."

I stepped around her, but she blocked me and pushed her mouth against my ear. "You can. And whatever you do, do not let Straka take you over to Solomon Grace to meet his friend Dr. Delmar. Something bad is going on over there."

I bit my lip and pushed past her.

Dr. Straka was busy flipping through a file when I walked into his office. I gently shut the door behind me and started toward the black couch.

Glancing up, Dr. Straka pointed to the yellow chair in the center of the room.

"But shouldn't I lie down on the couch so you can hypnotize me?" I asked.

He looked up again. This time he smiled warmly, like we were old friends, then he leaned back in his recliner. "Let's start with you in the chair."

Shit. The chair looked like it was for talking, and I wasn't in the mood for talking. I just wanted to get to the hypnosis part, get fixed, and get home. Annoyed, I took a seat in the scratchy yellow chair.

"Now tell me what's going on, Courtney."

"I'm not sure." I tucked my hands under my legs and glanced over at the hypnosis couch, then around the office. Two Beach Boys record covers and a Grateful Dead concert poster hung in frames on the wall. *Hmm?* Suddenly I wasn't feeling so confident anymore.

"Looking at your file, it seems like you spent a few days in the psych ward in St. Ignatius this past June?" he asked.

My eyes darted back to Dr. Straka. *How does he have a file on me?* Trying not to look frightened, I fake-smiled and readjusted myself in the chair.

"If you want my help, you need to tell me how you ended up in St. Ignatius," he said. And the way he looked at me, I suddenly got a strange feeling that I'd made the right choice. That he was the one who could help me.

"Okay." *Here goes nothing.* I took a deep breath, then exhaled. "My mom and her boyfriend locked me up in there because I was having dreams about aliens. But Dr. Wu gave me some medicine, and it fixed everything. Well, until yesterday . . . at the pool I started feeling weird things, like I was being watched . . . and then last night I had the dream-thing I told you about on the phone, and that's everything." I decided to leave out the part about my vision of Agatha in Norway. Imaginary friend turned real was a whole other can of worms, and I wasn't ready to open that one yet.

"Oh, and I can't go back to Dr. Wu," I said, "because my mom will find out and have me locked me up again!"

I leaned forward in my chair. "That's why I need you to hypnotize me! I need to make them go away before school starts on Tuesday!"

I bounced my knee while Dr. Straka wrote in my file. He looked up at me and I stopped, sank back into my chair.

"Anyone else in your family experience visitations from extraterrestrial beings?"

"Do we have to talk about this?" I asked. I squirmed uncomfortably in my chair, then bit my thumbnail. "Can't you just hypnotize me and make 'em go away?"

"You need to talk about it, Courtney. Now what about other family members? A grandfather, maybe?"

Grandfather?

"I don't know," I said dismissively. My skin felt itchy. I scratched my neck and then straightened out my skirt.

Gazing at me, Dr. Straka tapped his pen against his lips. "On the phone last night, you told me that the aliens came back again, but that this time it was different. Tell me what you meant by that," he said.

I nodded my head and felt my lip start to quiver. "Different like way worse."

Dr. Straka lowered his glasses. "Worse how?"

I leaned forward in my chair again. "Last night the female alien who's in charge had this gun with a long pointy needle, and she shoved it into my eyeball, and I lifted right up out of my bed. Then next thing I knew I was in my grandpa's old cottage—I don't know how they did it, but they took me there! And it was because they wanted to—"

My words caught in my throat. I could hear myself saying "kill me" in my head, but something was stopping my mouth from saying it out loud. A buzzing sound filled my ears. *Oh no! They're coming for me!*

"They wanted to what?" Dr. Straka asked. "Courtney? Tell me about your grandfather's cottage. What did the aliens want to do there?"

I could hear his words, but his voice was far away. I was leaving my body, I could feel it. The musty-book smell was back too. The aliens were taking me to the cottage!

"No!" I jumped up. "Something's happening, Dr. Straka. Right now. They're trying to take me away. You have to help me!"

"Okay. I'm here. Let's take a deep breath."

I tried, but I was breathing so fast I couldn't get enough air. Music blasted from over by Dr. Straka's desk, startling me, and I crashed back down into the yellow chair. Dr. Straka grabbed his cell phone out of the drawer and the music stopped. The musty-book smell and buzzing faded. The aliens were gone.

"Sorry about that, Courtney. But I have to take this call. Make yourself comfortable."

"Seriously?"

He swung open his door and walked out.

How can he just leave me like this? Taking deep breaths, I made my way over to the couch to lie down.

After what seemed like forever, Dr. Straka strolled back in. "Please sit up, Courtney."

"I can't," I said. "Not until you hypnotize me."

"I'm not going to put you under hypnosis today."

"What?" I sat up too quickly, and my head swirled with dizziness. "Why not?" I asked, balancing myself against the couch.

Dr. Straka picked a fuzzy sport coat up off the desk chair and put it on, wrinkles and all. Then he clipped a hospital ID badge to it.

"My colleague runs a sleep clinic," he said. "I spoke with him this morning about you, and that was him again just now. I'd like for us to have a consultation with him before we proceed with any treatment."

"But—"

"There are no buts in mental health, Courtney," he said. "You'll be much safer over at Solomon Grace."

"Solomon Grace?" I stood up. *This is exactly what Agatha warned me about!* I shook my head. "No way you're gonna lock me up in Solomon Grace."

He smiled like we were old friends again. "Nobody's locking you up. We're not even going into the main hospital."

"We're not? Then where would we be going?"

"To an office in the building across the parking lot. You'll see." He tucked my file under his arm and held open the door for me. "Come on. Let's walk over there."

"All right, I guess." I walked out into the waiting room, and Dr. Straka followed me.

"You'll like Dr. Delmar," he said. "You'll see."

Dr. Delmar? I stopped in my tracks. He was the doctor Agatha had told me not to go see. And I wasn't gonna ignore her advice on this one.

"I'm actually feeling better now, Dr. Straka. And um, I think I need to get home. Maybe I'll just come back tomorrow." I tugged at the door to the outside, but it was locked.

"Courtney, I'm leaving for Vermont tomorrow morning, for two weeks. I have another office there, in Woodstock, and I have some patients there I need to see." He unlocked the door and swung it open for me. "I don't think you want to wait that long."

"Two weeks? Oh right, you said that to Agatha. Wow." I definitely couldn't wait that long.

Right! So maybe . . . Well, even if Agatha *was* trying to help me, it wasn't like she knew everything. I mean, it was easy for her to tell me not to go see Dr. Delmar, but then she wasn't the one with aliens trying to drown her!

"So this Dr. Delmar can help me?" I asked.

Dr. Straka smiled. "He's an expert on the kind of things that are happening to you."

"You're not lying, are you?" I asked, narrowing my eyes.

"No, Courtney." He smirked. "I wouldn't lie to you."

"Okay, fine. But it better work." I stepped outside.

Whistling cheerfully, Dr. Straka locked up his office. Then he started across the bombed-out parking lot, in the opposite direction of Solomon Grace, waving at me to follow him. And so, reluctantly, I did.

FOURTEEN

Lauren's older brothers used to tell us stories about sneaking into the abandoned psychiatric hospital, about the creepy things they'd find in the old padded rooms and underground tunnels. Well, apparently it was no longer abandoned. Because that was exactly where Dr. Straka was taking me.

"Are you serious?" I stopped right on the edge of the giant crack in the asphalt and squinted up at Dr. Straka. "You wanna take me in *there*?"

Dr. Straka chuckled. "It's not a very pretty building. But extraordinary circumstances sometimes require us to visit extraordinary places. Think of this as an adventure."

"It's a dump, Dr. Straka. And it looks abandoned. So, extraordinary or not, no way am I going in there." I pulled my phone out of my pocket.

"It's not a dump, Courtney. It's under renovation. Two months from now it will be a state-of-the-art sleep laboratory."

"Yeah?" Now that he mentioned it, I could see a couple of construction trucks parked along the side of the building. "But still. Isn't there somewhere else you can take me to be fixed? Like, a normal place that's already renovated?"

He tapped his finger against his lips. "You're being visited in your bedroom by extraterrestrial beings?"

"Imaginary ones," I said.

"Imaginary or not, you've been having conversations

in your head with these aliens. You can't just march into any old doctor's office or hospital with a story like that, can you?"

"I guess not." I stared down at the crack. It looked super deep.

"No, you can't. People will take it the wrong way."

"But Dr. Delmar won't?"

"No, he'll take it the right way."

"Fine."

We made our way across the rest of the bombed-out parking lot to the old building. The front doors and windows were boarded up, and a huge trash dumpster the size of a freight truck sat off to one side. Other than that, there was just broken asphalt and garbage.

Dr. Straka took me around to the side of the building, past the construction trucks and an old rusted-out school bus with all its wheels missing, to a service entrance.

He tapped his ring against the heavy steel service door. And while we waited for someone to answer, I made a print of my shoe in the dirt and scratched my initials next to it with my toe. If I disappeared, at least there'd be a clue.

The door creaked open, and a security guard poked his head out. "We're taking a backstage tour," Dr. Straka said, smiling. He held up his laminated ID, and the security guard stepped aside. Trying not to think about Lauren's brothers' stories, or about anything Agatha had warned me about, I kicked a stone against the school bus and followed Dr. Straka through the door.

The place was filthy. My feet stuck to the floor as we made our way down a long corridor. Then we slipped under a strand of yellow caution tape and continued along the back of an old gymnasium with broken chunks of ceiling scattered across the floor. Someone had painted *Helter Skelter* in big red letters on the wall.

"Are you sure we're supposed to be in here?" I asked.

Dr. Straka laughed. "Positive, Courtney." We stepped into a rickety elevator and creaked up to the fifth floor. When we got off the elevator, two construction workers were busy pulling down the old ceiling tiles with crowbars. They looked surprised to see us, but then quickly went back to work.

The soles of my shoes squeaked against the smooth tile floor of the long hallway. Tiny rooms with old metal bed frames and thick steel doors with deadbolt locks lined both sides of the hall. *Yikes.*

Dr. Straka stopped in front of a large wooden door with a faded sign above it that read FACILITY LIBRARY. Taped to the door was a new piece of paper with DR. VINCENT DELMAR, MD typed across it.

Raising his fist, Dr. Straka tapped his ring against the door.

He waited, then tapped again.

When there was still no answer, he pushed the door open himself, and we walked in.

Whoever this Dr. Delmar was, his office was cold and dusty, with books stacked everywhere and stuffed animal heads on the walls. I sat down on a wooden stool and glanced up to see a dead elk staring down at me. Its glass eyes were glossy and sad, and its twisted antlers were covered in cobwebs.

Dr. Straka sat on the desk across from me. Then he quickly stood up. "Ah, Dr. Delmar."

An older man—he was like sixty, I guessed—came into the room and sat down directly behind me.

"Your mother and Dr. Anderson had you committed when you told them you saw aliens in your bedroom," he said. His accent reminded me of our old cleaning lady from Poland. But friendlier. "Do you know why that is, Courtney?"

Startled by his directness, I turned around on my stool and faced him. "Because they thought I was imagining things," I said. His hair was disheveled and his glasses were like a hundred years out of date. I cleared my throat. "And I guess because they thought what I was saying made me dangerous to myself?"

"Yes, but why did your mother think it was dangerous that you were imagining these aliens?" His teeth shone yellowy-gray as he moved closer to the lamp.

"Because aliens aren't real," I said. "And you'd have to be crazy to think they are. And I guess crazy people are dangerous."

"Yet you receive visits from aliens in your bedroom," Dr. Delmar said.

"Sometimes." I looked down in shame. "Not real aliens, though—imaginary ones. I know aliens aren't real. I'm not crazy or dangerous, if that's what you think."

Suddenly nervous about Dr. Delmar's intentions, I turned back toward Dr. Straka. "Tell him I'm not dangerous!"

"It's all right, Courtney," Dr. Straka said. "Dr. Delmar's one of the good guys."

"Let me be frank with you, Courtney," Dr. Delmar said, and I twisted around so I was facing him again. He picked up the petrified-insect paperweight on the bookshelf next to him. "Dr. Straka and I see many patients who have dreams and night terrors involving alien monsters and flying saucers. But they're just dreams. Your case, however, is much different."

"It is?"

He put the paperweight down and looked up at me. "The visits from your alien friends are not dream experiences. You're wide awake when it happens."

"I know." I gazed down at a dark crack in the wood floor. He was right. They weren't just half dreams like Dr. Wu thought. This was much worse than that. *Oh god! Do I have something serious, like schizophrenia?* I could feel him staring at me, but I couldn't look up. "So what's wrong with me then?" The words barely made it past my lips, and I almost wished they hadn't.

"There's nothing wrong with you."

"What?" My eyes shot up to meet his.

"Your emotional reaction to strange visitors in your bedroom is quite normal," he said.

"Normal?" Nobody ever accused me of being normal.

"You can thank your remarkable brain for what's happening to you," Dr. Delmar said. "It has a feature that most human brains don't—one that allows you to enter into a parallel world, or an alternate dimension, where you can see and communicate with entities that normal people cannot. It's an extraordinary gift, really."

"Well, I don't want a gift," I said, fidgeting on my stool. "I want you to make them go away!"

"These aren't childhood monsters, Courtney," Dr. Delmar said. "We can't just shove them back into your subconscious or shine a flashlight on them and make them disappear."

"Then what are they?" I asked. *Please don't say real live aliens.*

"They're extraterrestrial beings of advanced intelligence."

I felt a lump in my throat. "You mean the aliens in my bedroom are real?" I swallowed hard. Deep down, somewhere, I'd known it all along.

"That's right, Courtney," Dr. Straka said.

"Alien beings of advanced intelligence have been selectively visiting people on Earth for thousands of years," Dr. Delmar said. "People like you who were born with specially developed brains—a genetic variance inherited from your ancestors. You're part of a chosen bloodline. You should feel quite lucky."

I grabbed my head with both hands and squeezed it, hard. "You're telling me that I have a special brain that allows aliens to creep into my room at night and torment me? And that I should feel happy about this?"

"Not in so many words, but yes." Dr. Delmar smiled.

"But that's impossible, isn't it?" I asked. "I mean if they're real aliens, they'd have a spaceship, and my neighbors or the police or someone would totally have noticed if there was a huge flying saucer parked over our house! This has to be a mistake. Or wait . . . This is a test, isn't it—to see if I'm crazy, right?" My eyes darted from doctor to doctor.

Dr. Delmar dragged his stool forward so he was right in front of me.

He closed his eyes. "People are always looking up at the night sky for suspicious lights." His eyes opened, and I quickly looked down. "I understand why—it's quite exciting, in a silly way—but the truth is, the visitors we're dealing with don't have to travel by flying saucer. They punched their holes through the time-space continuum long ago. They're intergalactic travelers, but they live closer than you would ever imagine, Courtney. Their universe is right outside our window—closer than the moon. We just can't see it."

"I think I want to go home," I said.

"No you don't," Dr. Delmar said. "I'm just getting to the part where you come in. There are a small number of humans, like you, who can sense the aliens' presence. Your brain acts as a portal and allows these visitors to slip between their universe and ours. You're a genetic anomaly, young lady. Your alien visitors are as real as you and me. And chances are they want something from you."

My face went numb. "That sounds like something my

grandpa told me, about a portal between worlds," I said. "But he was crazy."

Dr. Delmar shook his head. "No, he wasn't."

"You knew my grandpa?" I asked. I scooted my stool back from Dr. Delmar. "My grandpa Dahlen?" This was too much.

"Samuel Dahlen, yes. He and I crossed paths many years ago at Berkeley." Dr. Delmar glanced at Dr. Straka. "He was a brilliant man. In fact, he was one of the few humans in recent history with an alien brain center that was so highly developed that it allowed him to openly communicate with alien visitors in our universe. With any luck, you could develop—"

Oh God! I felt sick!

"I wanna go home. Right now, Dr. Straka!" I stood up, and the room swayed. "I'm gonna throw up."

I leaned over and grabbed my knees for balance. My stomach flip-flopped, and I lowered myself down to my hands and knees. *Ugh!* I rested my elbows on the wooden floor and laid my head against my arms like I was praying.

"She has a flair for dramatics," Dr. Straka whispered.

"Everything okay, Courtney?" Dr. Delmar asked.

"No," I mumbled into my arm. My stomach heaved, but it was empty. Just thick spit and stomach bile came up into my mouth.

"Would you like to hear the good news now?" Dr. Straka asked.

"No, thank you." *This is how my grandpa went crazy. Believing in aliens.* But shit—it kind of seemed like I was going to go crazy either way. Or else end up drowned in a stupid bathtub. So . . .

"What is it?" I asked without looking up.

"The fact that the aliens are real doesn't mean Dr. Delmar can't help you make them go away," Dr. Straka said.

"Oh yeah?" Still hunched over, I glanced up.

"Courtney, I run a special program that helps people like you," Dr. Delmar said. "If you'd like, I can run a couple of tests on you to determine if you're a good candidate."

"And if I'm a candidate, you can make them go away?" I asked.

"I believe so. It's a simple matter of deactivating the alien part of your brain."

"How long would it take to do that?"

"It's a process. But the tests should tell us if you've inherited your grandfather's brain anomaly."

"And how long do the tests take?"

"A few hours," Dr. Delmar said. "We have to administer anesthesia to induce sleep. Then we monitor your brain activity and see if we can activate the alien center that seems to be causing your visitations."

"All right, I'll do the test." I sat up on my knees, then grabbed the stool I'd been sitting on and pulled myself up. "But I'm going to a birthday party tonight, so I have to be out of here by seven o'clock."

We got off the elevator on the second floor. Dr. Straka flipped a light switch, and the hall lit up. The old sign on the wall read ADOLESCENT WARD.

"Let's go right in here," Dr. Delmar said.

I followed him into the room. It was tiny, with bars on the windows and no bed or chairs to sit on. More like a prison cell than any hospital room I had ever seen. Maybe it was a prison cell?

This was a huge mistake.

I turned to run out the door. But a nurse with white hair rolled a bed into the room, forcing me to back up against the wall. Then another nurse, a man with tattoos all over his forearms, rolled in a crazy-looking machine.

Mistake or not, it was too late to escape.

The white-haired nurse handed me a blue hospital gown.

"You want me to take off my clothes?" I asked. "With everyone watching?"

"Honey, we've seen it before," the nurse said. "Now everything off but your underwear and bra. Let's go!"

I dropped my clothes and quickly covered up with the gown, making sure to keep my tattoo hidden under my arm.

"Now on the bed," the nurse said.

I sat down on the mattress and she poked a needle in my arm.

"Ouch! What are you doing?" I asked.

She taped a plastic tube to my wrist and hooked the other end up to an IV bag. "This will relax you," she said. Then she used gooey gel to attach little wires to my scalp.

Dr. Delmar sat down across from me and adjusted the lamp so it shone right in my eyes. "I'm going to ask you some questions, Courtney. You need to think hard and tell the truth."

FIFTEEN

Something tickled my cheek. I opened my eyes, and the world spun around me in a slow circle before coming to a stop. Wherever I was, it was dark, and the floor was smooth and cool against my skin.

Water splashed my forehead. I tried to sit up, but my arms felt waterlogged and my head was too heavy. I reached down and touched my legs. They were dry. *Hmm?* Nothing was making sense.

Concentrating my energy, I rolled over and slowly lifted myself up onto my hands and knees. Cool air brushed my face. I crawled through the darkness toward the breeze until my head clunked against a wall. I collapsed onto the floor. Drops of water fell against the back of my neck. *Where am I?*

I reached down for my phone in my pocket, only I wasn't wearing my skirt. I was wearing some sort of dress. I rubbed my scalp, and my hand came away with a clump of gooey gel stuck to it—and suddenly I remembered Dr. Straka and Dr. Delmar, and changing into a hospital gown, and the tiny room with bars on the windows, and the nurse hooking wires up to my head and giving me horrible medicine, and then bright light in my eyes, and questions about my grandpa and my alien visitors, and then . . . nothing.

Oh no! What time is it? I sat up. Pressing my palms against the cinder-block wall, I moved my way up to the window. It was dark outside. I pushed my face against the metal bars and felt the cool night air. Whatever time it was, it was dark out.

I needed to find my phone and the plastic bag Dr. Delmar had given me to put my clothes in. I felt along the wall, bumped into the bed. Something dropped off the bed onto the floor. I reached under the bed and grabbed it. It was a Sharpie pen. I felt around some more, and my hand brushed against something else. The bag with my clothes in it. *Thank God!*

I dumped everything out on the bed and my phone lit up. 8:38 p.m. *Are you kidding me?* I'd been there since eleven in the morning—and I'd told them I had to leave by seven! I started to scroll through my missed calls, but seeing my hands, I realized that my fingers were covered in black marker. *What the hell?*

I turned on my phone's flashlight to inspect further. Ink was smudged all over my hands. Agatha's phone number was still on my palm, though. There was nothing on my gown, but when I shined the light down at my legs, I saw that drawn on my right knee, in black marker, were four dead insects—just like my tattoo. I gasped. *What kind of sick weirdo did this to me?*

I stood up and shined my light on the bed. *Oh. My. God.* The insects were drawn all over the wall. I looked down at my hands, smudged with ink, and then at the wall again— the way the insects were drawn—and I knew. No one could have done this but me. *I* was the sick weirdo.

Jesus. My darkest secret—the tattoo from my grandpa— was splashed across the wall for the whole world to see. *But why?* I remembered Agatha telling me how her brother had done the same thing in his dorm room—and how she'd said the aliens had made him do it. *Did the aliens make me draw this too? It had to be them!* Again though, *why?*

I climbed up onto the bed, licked my thumb, and rubbed

the wall. The ink didn't come off, of course. I spat on my hands and rubbed frantically. It barely smeared. I spat directly on the wall and rubbed as hard as I could. Nothing. I looked up at the wall again. It was no use anyway. The insects were everywhere.

I slumped down on the floor and covered my eyes in defeat.

From behind me came the sound of a metal deadbolt unlocking, and suddenly the room lit up. "She's awake. Damn! Look at the walls."

"Grab her!" someone else yelled.

I scooped up my clothes and scrambled toward the open door, but before I could get there, the male nurse with tattooed forearms lifted me off the floor.

"Hold her still!" a woman yelled, and seconds later I felt a sharp poke in my arm. *Ouch!* A hand grasped my jaw and forced something plastic into my mouth. Warm, thick liquid oozed over my tongue, and I could taste bitter medicine. I shook my head to try to spit it out, but the nurse with the tattooed arms held my jaw shut, and I had to swallow.

A dull thumping rose in my ears, tickling my brain. My breathing slowed, and I felt drool dripping from my mouth. The thumping sound blurred into a long echo. My head felt tingly and numb at the same time, but I didn't care. I collapsed against the nurse's shoulder. He plopped me down in a wheelchair. "Go to sleep," he whispered.

The wheelchair made a *click-clack* sound as he pushed me down the hallway.

"Where are you taking me?" I mumbled.

"Sleep."

"But . . ." My eyes drooped closed, and the world around me disappeared.

"Well, hello there, bright eyes." It was a woman's voice, with a slight singsongy Scandinavian accent.

I blinked. Red lipstick and blue eyeliner, and then a pretty blond lady, with an old-fashioned hairstyle and a nurse's ID badge, came into focus.

Where am I? I tried to jump to my feet but immediately fell off the bed onto the floor.

"Be careful, bright eyes." The nurse walked over and stood next to me in her squishy-looking white shoes. I glanced up at her red lipstick, and then around the room. I was in a hospital room. But not like before. This was a real hospital room, with clean walls and curtains, and a bed with buttons and wires, and fancy medical machines and touch screens everywhere. Like St. Ignatius.

I sat up and glanced at the nurse's ID badge again. "Solomon Grace Hospital," I read aloud. The nurse nodded her head.

"What time is it?" My voice sounded gruff.

"It's a little past nine thirty," she said.

"Nine thirty!" I climbed to my feet. "Where's my phone, and the bag with my clothes?"

"Right there. But—"

I grabbed my phone, and my skirt and T-shirt. As I pulled my skirt on, I glanced at my knee. The drawing was gone. My hands were clean too: the Sharpie smudges were all gone, and so was Agatha's phone number.

"Who scrubbed my hands?" I demanded. "And my knee?"

"Oh, sugar, you've been dreaming. But you need to get back in bed. I can't let you go until Dr. Delmar sees you."

"Yeah, right."

I stumbled out the door and almost crashed into a nurse pushing a big cart. There was a huge SOLOMON GRACE plaque on the wall. I was definitely in the real hospital. The nurse with the tattoos must've driven me over from the old psych building.

"Can I help you?" a young female doctor asked. I looked past her and saw the sign pointing to an exit.

"What? No." I hurried to the elevator and pressed the button, quickly, like fifty times.

I pushed through the revolving doors to exit the lobby. It must have rained when I was inside, because the air smelled like wet dirt and worms. I walked across Solomon Grace's huge parking lot, along a footpath through the field, and over to the bombed-out parking lot. Then I made my way to Dr. Straka's office. *How could he have done that to me? He tricked me! That's what he did.*

Unlocking my bike, I glanced over at the dark, crooked brick building that was the old mental hospital. There was only one light on in the whole building, about halfway up. I pictured Dr. Delmar standing at the window, surrounded by dead animal heads and creepy science things, staring out at me staring up at him, and I worked faster on my lock.

I climbed onto my bike. My head was still groggy, but anything was better than what I'd just gone through. I checked my phone. Seven text messages from Lauren wondering where I was. Two voice messages. The first was from my mom, letting me know that she was taking Kaelyn to the movies, and warning me to be home by eleven sharp or else.

The other message was from a number I didn't know. I listened to it.

"It's Agatha. Where are you?" That was all.

I called her back but it went to voice mail. *Ugh!* I left a message: "It's me, Courtney. I was in the hospital with Dr. Delmar, but I'm out now. They gave me a bunch of medicine that knocked me out, like, twice. I kinda need to talk to you about what happened. And about what happened to your brother. I'm on my bike, so I can meet you anywhere. It's nine fifty, though, and I have to be home at eleven. Call me. Please. Bye."

Five seconds later, my phone rang.

"Agatha?"

"Meet me behind the Holy Donut in two."

SIXTEEN

Agatha shoved my bike into the trunk of her car. Then she slid into the driver's seat next to me and tapped her dried blood–colored fingernails against the steering wheel.

"You were right about the aliens," I said, buckling up my seat belt. "Dr. Delmar told me they're real."

She glared over. "For someone as bright as you are, you're pretty stupid!"

"What do you mean?" I asked, hurt.

"You let Dr. Straka take you to Solomon Grace to visit that asshole Delmar after I told you it wasn't safe."

My blood boiled up. "Excuse me for not wanting to die!" I shouted. "Aliens were trying to take over my brain and teleport me to my grandpa's cottage and drown me. And Dr. Straka said this Delmar guy was an expert on that stuff. So it would've been pretty stupid of me not to go talk to him."

"Aliens were trying to kill you? Really?" Her voice dripped with sarcasm.

"Yeah, really!" I turned and stared out the window. "And Dr. Delmar said he might be able to fix me. So obviously you don't get it, Agatha."

"No? Well here's what I do get, Einstein. Before Delmar showed up from Budapest or wherever, Dr. Straka had had exactly one patient who'd claimed to be visited by aliens: my brother. But since Delmar set up shop across the parking lot, he's been sending Straka all kinds of new patients with wild stories about aliens abducting them."

"So what? He's an expert on that stuff," I said. I never should've called Agatha to pick me up. "Just take me home. 421 Chestnut Street, by the elementary school."

Agatha pulled out onto the road. "Expert or not, Delmar is up to something shady," she said. "I don't know if he finds the patients on the Internet or what. But he has Straka screen them in his office, then send the believable ones right over to Solomon Grace for admission into Delmar's so-called sleep clinic. You're lucky you got out of there when you did."

Drugging me in that little room was definitely shady. Agatha had a point there. But it was a test to see if I was a candidate for his special program—Delmar had told me as much.

"Even if Delmar is creepy and shady, he's still a doctor," I said. "I mean, he helps people who see aliens. He can't be that bad. Can he?"

Agatha laughed. "Unfortunately, I've seen a few of the patients after Delmar's treated them. They're different, Courtney. Messed up—traumatized, most likely." She turned onto my street. "So yeah, he can be that bad."

Traumatized? What if I was traumatized now? An image of the tattooed nurse shoving the medicine down my throat flashed into my head. *What kind of nurse does things like that to people? What if he's the nurse for the special program?*

Suddenly I felt nauseous and weak. "I don't want to talk about this anymore." I leaned forward and covered my ears.

Agatha pulled my hand away from my ear. "It gets shadier. I used Straka's password to log into the Solomon Grace records database this morning and ran some of the names of the patients we sent over, and guess what? There are no records of any of them having been treated, or even admitted, at Solomon Grace. It's like Delmar's operating completely under the radar."

"Wait." I sat up. "That's your big, shady conspiracy theory? No patient records?"

She raised an eyebrow. "Exactly."

"Well that's stupid, because what if Delmar didn't admit them into Solomon Grace, but instead took them to his office in the old mental-hospital building? Then there'd be no records, right? Sorry, Agatha, but mystery solved." And *she* was supposed to be helping *me*?

Agatha smirked. "That's not how it works. He's staff at Solomon Grace. He works in the sleep clinic on the eighth floor. So there should be records for his patients. Besides, even if his office is in the old psych building, he definitely doesn't treat patients in that rat-infested dungeon."

"Actually, that's where he took me," I said, barely loud enough for Agatha to hear.

"What?" Agatha stomped on the brakes, and my seat belt tightened, jerking me back against the seat. "Are you kidding me?"

"No." My voice crackled. "That's where I had my test. In the old psych building, in a little cement room with bars on the windows." Hearing myself say this aloud made me feel dirty.

"Dude, are you out of your mind?" Agatha pulled over to the side of the road, just a few houses down from mine. "You let a strange man take you into an empty building?"

"Nothing bad happened. So it's fine!" Tears streaked down my cheeks, though. She was right. It was stupid of me to have gone there.

"Do you have a death wish?" Agatha yelled. "You're fifteen years old! And these so-called doctors took you into an abandoned building and performed medical tests on you and gave you drugs without your parents' permission. That's really dangerous, not to mention *illegal*!"

"You're the one who told me that Dr. Straka could fix

me!" I yelled back. "And he said Dr. Delmar was the expert. Meanwhile, I was losing my *mind*. So I didn't really feel like I had much of a choice!"

Agatha turned off the car and rubbed her eyes. "I'm sorry. You're right. I might have done the same thing as you." The anger disappeared from her voice. "But you have to understand how dangerous that was."

"I get it," I admitted. "I hate those guys! I was so sick, but the nurse with the tattoos wouldn't let me sleep. He kept shaking me and asking me more questions. Finally I passed out. And when I woke up and I saw . . ." I couldn't say it. I started crying.

"Saw what? Courtney?"

I couldn't say it, it was too frightening. But I had to.

"Drawings of insects, just like my tattoo," I blurted out. "I'd scribbled them all over the wall with a Sharpie, but I didn't remember doing it. And when I tried to get out of there, the nurse came in and drugged me a second time. It was like a nightmare. When I woke up again, I was in a clean room in the real hospital."

I tried to stop crying, but my body was trembling.

"Hey. It's okay." Agatha squeezed my shoulder. "Look at me."

I couldn't look up.

"You drew the symbol from your tattoo on the wall? The four insects?"

I nodded my head. "That's why I called you," I muttered through sobs.

"Dude? Look at me."

"What?" I wiped my nose and glanced up.

A smile broke across Agatha's face.

"Why are you smiling?" I wiped my eyes, and then my nose again, this time on my arm. Totally gross, but whatever.

She kept staring at me and smiling. Like she'd suddenly

realized I was her long-lost sister or something. "I was right about you," she said.

"Right? Like how?" I asked. But she just kept staring at me. "You're creeping me out, Agatha."

"Dude, you drew the mark. Don't you see what's happening?" she asked.

I shook my head. *No, I do not see what's happening.*

"The drawing, Courtney. It was the aliens who gave you the idea to draw the marks on the wall. Like they entered your head and told you to do it. It's a message."

"Yeah . . ." I'd pretty much figured that out back in the hospital room. But how Agatha could possibly think this was a good thing, I had no idea. "So what's the message? That I'm going to go crazy and drown myself in a bathtub like my grandpa?"

"No, no, no. The aliens are trying to help you. This is huge, Courtney!"

"But—the aliens are evil. They tried to drown me, Agatha."

She shook her head. "If the aliens were trying to kill you, you'd be dead. Think about it. They've been trying to get your attention to convey some message to you, but you've been too closed minded to see it. They're friendly."

"Friendly? Oh really?" Anger boiled up in my chest again. "If you know so much, then tell me what their friendly message is!"

The excitement disappeared from her face.

"That part I'm not sure about," she said, starting the car again. "Where's your house?"

"Right up there—the one with the silver mailbox."

She pulled over by my driveway.

"Somebody out there knows what the insect symbol means," she said. "We just have to find them."

Suddenly exhausted, I leaned my head against the window and thought about my bed.

"Let's meet tomorrow morning," Agatha said. "Eight o'clock at the Holy Donut. I'll get my brother there, and we'll figure this out together. Sound good, dude?" She poked me in the shoulder. "Hey! Dude? You listening to me?"

"Yeah. Holy Donut, eight o'clock. I'll be there, Astra," I mumbled, but I was so sleepy I wasn't sure all the words made it past my lips.

"Astra? Dude! Wake up!"

I struggled to open my eyes.

Agatha clicked on the overhead light. "Look at me. How many fingers am I holding up?" The sassiness was fighting its way back into her voice.

I turned and gazed at her. "One," I said. Then I held up my hand and gave her the middle finger right back, and I felt myself smiling for the first time in forever.

"Ah, there we go." Agatha smiled too. Then she clicked the light off. "Now get out of my car and go to bed," she said, pushing me.

"Yeah, cool, I'm beat." I slowly climbed out. "Just put my bike up by the garage."

"Seriously, do I look like a chauffeur?"

"Thanks." I waved over my shoulder.

"Unbelievable." She climbed out and wrestled my bike from the trunk. "Don't be late tomorrow, Courtney! I mean it!"

SEVENTEEN

"Courtney?"

I raised my head off the floor to see Kaelyn's silhouette in the doorway. But it wasn't my bedroom doorway. I sat up.

For some reason, I was in our basement, next to the washing machine. In the middle of the night.

"Yuck. Why are you sleeping down here on the floor?" Kaelyn asked.

Good question. I was still wearing my clothes. *Did I come down here for something after Agatha dropped me off?* Whatever had happened, my head was pounding. "We'll talk in the morning," I muttered. "I need to go to bed."

Kaelyn flipped on the light. Shading my eyes, I gazed at my sister. She was dressed in her soccer uniform, which seemed odd for the middle of the night.

I heard Mom's footsteps on the kitchen floor above me. Then the coffeemaker hissing.

"Shit. What time is it?" I jumped up and brushed my skirt off. It was dry, at least.

"You're not supposed to say *shit*," Kaelyn said.

She was right. But obviously it was morning, and I couldn't let my mom see me in my clothes from last night.

I rushed past my sister and up the stairs, where I ran right into my mom.

"Do I need to be worried about you, Courtney?" My mom grabbed the railing so there was no way I could get past her.

"No."

"What time did you get home last night?"

"Just after eleven." It was true, but her look told me she didn't believe me.

"Was there alcohol at the party?"

"Probably, but I didn't have any."

"Okay. Let's keep it that way. And sleep in your bed from now on. In your pajamas. We'll call this strike one."

"Yeah, okay."

"Three strikes and you're out."

"I get it, Mom."

She stepped aside, and I raced up the stairs. The clock on the microwave said eight fifteen. Crap. I ran up to my bedroom, found my phone, and threw on my lime-green golf pants and red hoodie.

I had two missed calls. One from Agatha—no message. The other was from Dr. Delmar, who had left a voice mail. Apparently I had passed the test, and I had the same brain as my grandpa, so he wanted me to come into his office today at noon. *Yikes! Thanks but no thanks!*

Trying not to think about this, I pulled on my yellow sneakers and rushed out the door, shouting "Bye, Mom!" before slamming it shut. I hopped onto my bike. The seat and handlebars were still wet—*from dew?* I wondered. Then I felt a raindrop, and then another.

EIGHTEEN

By the time I got to the Holy Donut, I was soaking wet and very late. I yanked on the heavy-looking door, which was actually pretty light, and the all-season reindeer bells jingled violently against the glass. The whole restaurant turned to stare at me as I walked in.

Agatha was seated in a booth. Her hair was dry and perfect, and the red stones in the Gothic cross dangling from her choker were the same color as the trim stitch on her punky-mod dress. *How fashionably coordinated.* Apparently *she* hadn't woken up on her basement floor. Feeling self-conscious, I lowered my head and made my way over to her table.

Oh wow! This was the same diner that I'd seen in my head on my birthday, where I watched Astra scrawling in her notebook with red colored pencil.

"You're late," she grumbled.

"Sorry. Hey, where's your brother?"

"Well, he's not here." She grimaced at my red hoodie, green pants, and yellow shoes. "You supposed to be a traffic light?"

"Ha-ha." *So rude. But whatever. It's not like we're friends.* I had to remember that. I was there to hit her and her brother up for a serious alien info download. I wanted to know about the bug drawings on the wall and how to avoid a nervous breakdown. And whether Delmar was still an option. As long as I got what I came for, I could handle her being a jerk.

"I gotta pee," I murmured.

Just as I left the table, the reindeer bells jingled against the entrance door. But unlike the other five customers in the restaurant, I didn't feel the need to look over and see who was coming in. *Coffee shop weirdos.*

I checked myself out in the bathroom mirror. My hair was clumped together and sticking straight out on one side. I leaned my head under the dryer and tried to fix it, but it kept shutting off after five seconds. *Crap!*

I glanced in the mirror again. Lack of a hip hairdo was the least of my worries. I had huge, dark circles under my eyes, and my lips were dry and cracked. *How did I not notice this before I left the house?* I looked like an escaped lunatic who'd slept in a dumpster. I peeked at myself in the mirror one last time, and shrugged. Nothing I could do about it now. *Stick to the mission.*

Back at the table, I slipped into the seat across from Agatha and put on a smile. "Sorry again for being late. I love your necklace; it's really—"

"Don't talk." Agatha glanced over toward the counter. "We're leaving."

Confused, I followed her gaze. A man with tattoos covering his forearms was seated on a stool. He glanced up, and I hastily looked away. It was Dr. Delmar's nurse—the one who'd drugged me! My heart thudded in my chest.

Agatha covered her mouth with a menu. "I'm going to spill my coffee," she whispered. "I want you to jump up and yell, then run out the door. I'll run after you."

"Are you serious?" *Splash.* Warm coffee hit my knees. "Ahhh!" I jumped up and ran for the exit. Agatha was right behind me, then next to me, as I banged out the door.

"Around back!" she yelled. We ran around the side of the building and jumped into her car.

"That was Dr. Delmar's nurse," I said trying to catch my

breath. "He's the one who drugged me yesterday, and he stopped me when I tried to erase the insects I drew from the wall."

"Hold on." Agatha started the ignition and threw the car into drive. Radio blaring, we bounced over the curb and cut into an alley.

"Same guy was parked down the street from your house last night," Agatha yelled over the spooky horror music. "He must've followed you here."

I turned down the radio. "Why would he follow me?"

"Maybe he wants to ask you out for coffee?"

"Seriously? Gross! Wait, you're kidding, right?"

She pulled behind the library.

"Why are we stopping here? What if your brother shows up at the restaurant and we're not there?"

"He's at home. We'll go see him as soon as I know we're not being followed." She parked between two minivans, then checked her mirrors.

"So really, why do you think that nurse guy is following me?" I asked.

"Maybe Delmar's worried you'll tell someone what happened yesterday." She tapped her fingernails against the steering wheel, then turned and glared threateningly at me. "You're not working for the FBI or anyone like that, are you?"

"Me? The FBI?" The question was crazy, but Agatha looked serious. "No, course not. I'm fifteen. I don't even have a job. Why would you think . . . What's going on, Agatha?"

"I'm not sure." She checked her rearview mirror again. "They hooked the wires up to your head and drugged you, and you drew the insects on the wall in the old psych building. Then you woke up in the real hospital, and they just let you go home?"

"Not exactly."

She turned her mirror to catch my eyes. "Then what exactly did happen?"

"The Solomon Grace nurse said I had to wait for Dr. Delmar, but I just got up and left." I shifted uncomfortably in my seat. "And Dr. Delmar left me a voicemail this morning. He wants me to come back in at noon. But I'm totally not gonna go, obviously!"

"Oh, dude, they're not done with you." She slouched back in her seat. "That must be why they're following you. That's not good."

"Not good? Dr. Delmar said in his message that I passed the test, and that I had the same brain-anomaly thing as my grandpa, and that he could fix it." I swallowed. "I know you think he's shady, but what if he's telling the truth, and he really can fix me?"

"Brain-anomaly thing?" She stared at me. "You told Delmar about your grandpa who tattooed you?"

"Yeah. Well, no, not about the tattoo. And he was the one who brought up my grandpa Dahlen. He said he knew him from a long time ago." I bit my thumbnail. "Is that bad too?"

"Wait. Dahlen? Oh, dude."

"*Oh dude*, what?" I asked.

Deep in thought, she slowly nodded her head. "He did know your grandpa. When Straka called Delmar before your appointment, he kept referring to you as 'the Dahlen girl.' I thought it was a medical term or code. But Delmar already knew who you were. So that makes sense. But I don't understand the connection. Or Straka's big interest in your medical records." She wasn't even talking to me anymore, but trying to make sense of some puzzle in her head.

"You're losing me, Agatha."

"Unless? Oh, dude." She shut off her car.

"What are you doing now?" I said, getting more frustrated. "I thought we were going to meet your brother!"

"We are. But first tell me everything Delmar said about your grandpa and this brain anomaly."

"Oh, gosh." I put my feet up on the dashboard. "He said my grandpa had an alien center in his brain, and that I probably have one too. But he might be able to shut it off."

"Interesting." She fidgeted with the cross hanging from her neck, then put it between her front teeth and bit down. "He's definitely not dumb. He knows aliens. Secret stuff. Oh, man."

"He definitely knows something—"

"That's it!" She spat out her cross and sat up. "Delmar's not running a sleep clinic. Your so-called test . . . and all the new patients Delmar has Straka send over to his lab . . . He's not trying to fix anyone. He's trying to find a *bloodliner.*"

"What's a bloodliner?"

"Wow. This could be big!"

"Agatha! You're supposed to be helping me figure out the message about the bugs on the wall, not thinking about Delmar and this other stuff."

She shook her head. "This other stuff is exactly what the bugs are about. We're trying to figure out why your grandpa gave you that tattoo. And what the aliens want us to do about it. Now think! What else did Delmar say about your grandpa?"

"Agatha! I hate my grandpa!" I shouted. The word *hate* felt like a punch to my stomach, though, and I immediately wanted to take it back. Or to explain to Agatha that I hadn't always hated my grandpa, that he was the kindest person I'd ever known, and that he saw something in me, something special, when everyone else thought I was weird. But then—

"Tell me what Delmar said," Agatha demanded.

"Fine." I met her eyes. "He said my grandpa was one of the few people in the world who could talk to aliens." The words sent a shiver through me.

"Your grandpa could talk to the aliens?" Her tone totally shifted, from angry to confused. "And Delmar knew this?" She didn't wait for me to answer. "Dude! This changes everything!"

"What changes *what*?" I kicked the glove box. "You're making me crazy."

"Courtney?" She stared calmly at me, like I was a little kid whose trust she was trying to gain. "The aliens that visit you in your room. Can you talk to them?"

I fussed with the latch to my seat belt. "Sort of. Now are you gonna tell me—"

"The aliens speak to you?"

I nodded.

Agatha rested her hands on top of her head, like she was afraid it would float away. "And you can understand them?"

"Yeah. Not that they make a ton of sense." I tucked my hands under my knees. "Why? Wait! Am I in more danger now? You've got to tell me what's going on. This one-way conversation is not helping me!"

"This is unbelievable," Agatha said, still talking to herself. "A special bloodliner!"

"You're doing it again!" I yelled. I grabbed her arm. "What is a bloodliner? In English!"

"All right, all right. The theory goes that the only people who are visited by aliens are those who carry alien DNA. Supposedly it's passed down through their bloodline. So they're called bloodliners. I don't know all the science involved, but there's a whole mythology based on old writings and stories. But basically bloodliners like you and my brother have some unique powers or chemicals in their brains that allow aliens to come down and visit them."

"Oh, that." I slumped back. "Dr. Delmar told me something like that. But the aliens actually don't come down from space. He says they live in a universe that we can't see, and they crawl through wormholes and zap into a portal in my brain or something."

"Crawl through wormholes?" she asked. "What are you, like, twelve?"

"Well, zap through wormholes, then," I said. "Whatever."

"Okay, sorry. Listen, the point is, Delmar's not looking for an ordinary bloodliner like my brother, who sees the aliens but doesn't have the ability to communicate with them. He's looking for a *special* bloodliner—like your grandpa. Someone who's powerful enough to not just see the aliens, but talk to them. So that's why Straka was so excited about you coming into the office yesterday. He and Delmar knew about your grandpa's powers, and they wanted to see if you were a special bloodliner like your grandpa. Damn, dude, you could be the whole reason Delmar set up shop here in West Bridge."

"So wait . . ." I was still processing everything she'd just told me. "Delmar doesn't really fix people? He's just looking for a bloodliner?"

"Haven't you been listening? Delmar's not looking for *any* bloodliner; he's looking for a *special* bloodliner. And now he's found one—you!"

"Me?" My heart was pounding so loud I was sure Agatha could hear it. I buried my head in my hands. "So Delmar lied? He can't make the aliens go away?"

"Dude! Whether he can make them go away or not, he's not gonna. You have to stay away from him. Look at me!" She yanked my hand from my face. "You know that, don't you?"

"I'm not stupid."

"No one said you're stupid. You can talk to aliens, Courtney! You're like a one-in-a-billion member of the chosen few. You have to start being careful."

"I can't breathe!" I yanked on the door's handle and

pushed it open, but Agatha lunged across me and pulled the door shut.

"I know this is all crazy new to you because nobody talks about this stuff. But it didn't used to be that way. My aunt Ketti told me about ancient sanctuaries where bloodliners used to go and learn about their powers. And how to keep from losing their minds."

I rolled down my window and rested my head against the door. "Like the place you went to Norway to look for?" I asked.

"Yeah," Agatha said. "Wait, how did you know about that?"

I shrugged, and my brain tingled. "My imaginary friend told me. But you wouldn't know anything about that, would you?"

"Whatever, dude. There are other places. We just have to follow the clues. Starting with your tattoo."

I shoved my fingers through my hair, trying to stop the tingling. "You think my grandpa gave me my tattoo as a clue so I could find one of these places? Like he knew I'd need to know how to deal with aliens at some point?"

"I do."

I sighed. "So this is your plan, Agatha? That's how you think I'm going to fix myself?"

"Something like that. Yeah."

"Ugh! That's a horrible plan. You don't even know where to look!" My chest was tightening up again. "And besides, you don't get it. My grandpa tried to drown me." That was the first time I'd ever said it out loud. I didn't like how it sounded.

"Drown . . . as in *kill*?"

"Yeah, as in *he dunked me underwater to stop me from breathing*." I leaned forward and clenched my hands into fists. "And now the aliens are trying to take over where he left off.

So even if my grandpa left me a clue, I don't think I wanna follow it."

"You're probably right," she said. She fastened her seat belt.

"Really?" I sat up. She was agreeing with me? But about which part? "I'm probably right about what?"

"Buckle up. I'll take you back to your bike."

"Seriously? Just like that? We're giving up?"

"You're kind of a crybaby, Courtney. I think you should go and take a pill and forget about all this. You're not really cut out for hunting down the truth."

"What? I'm totally cut out for hunting down the truth! My grandpa always told me I was destined for great things." *Oh God, where did that come from? Just let her take you back to your bike, Courtney!*

Agatha started the car and turned up her Scandinavian death metal music. "Guess your grandpa was wrong. But hopefully Dr. Delmar can wave his magic wand and switch off the alien part of your brain, and all your problems will be solved."

I turned down the radio. "But no—he's horrible, you said so yourself. And your brother's waiting for us. Don't you think it could help him if he talked to me?"

"No idea." She shot me an inquisitive glance. "You tell me."

"Oh, wait a minute, I get it," I said. "This is like a reverse psychology thing. You're trying to trick me into thinking that it's my idea to go there, right? Well, that's not going to work on me." I folded my arms across my chest. I couldn't believe I'd almost fallen for that.

But, well . . . I bit the end of my fingernail off and spat it out. "Fine. I'll go see him." I clicked on my seat belt. "Can you turn the heat up, though? And put something better on the radio? I'm sure this music is huge in Norway or wherever, but it's making me carsick and we're not even moving yet."

"Welcome to the dark side, young Jedi." She turned up the volume, and a cacophony of torturous guitars and gurgling voices assaulted my eardrums.

"Whatever. I hate you too!" I yelled over the noise.

NINETEEN

We walked up onto the porch of a huge old house, blue with white trim.

"Wow, is this your house?" I asked.

"No, I don't live with my brother," she said.

"Well, I would. This place is enormous!"

"Hold on, Courtney." Agatha grabbed my arm and turned me toward her. "I didn't tell you before because I didn't want to freak you out. But my brother hasn't quite recovered from his breakdown. So this isn't exactly a normal house."

"What do you mean?"

"This is a group home for young adults with mental issues. Kinda like supervised living for people coming out of the hospital who might not be ready to live on their own."

"Oh. Wow. Okay. I get it."

I leaned against the railing while Agatha knocked.

A skinny chick with short black hair and super-thick blue eyeliner cracked open the door. "Hey, Zola. Danny around?" Agatha asked. Zola's glassy eyes shifted lazily between Agatha and me; then she swung the door open.

We followed Zola downstairs to Danny's bedroom. It was weird for a bedroom, though. There was no bed. Just a sad-looking green couch and a camping cooler covered in bumper stickers that appeared to serve as a coffee table.

"Where is he?" Agatha asked, looking around.

Zola nodded toward the closet.

"Ah, right. You mind leaving us alone?" Agatha asked Zola. "We kinda gotta talk serious."

Zola sat down on the couch, causing it to wobble, and pulled her knees up into her chest. "Nothing I haven't heard before. Trust me."

"Yeah, but—"

"It's cool, Danny," Zola called out. The closet doors pushed open, and a guy in his early twenties with a mop of curly brown hair and a scruffy beard stepped out.

"Hey, Danny," Agatha said, walking toward him. He met her halfway, and they hugged.

Danny glanced at me for a split second, then brushed past with his head down. "Sorry about the mess." He picked up two blue plastic milk crates, flipped them over, and set one down in front of me. "Sit, please," he told me.

"Thanks," I said shyly.

"So you see aliens, huh?" he asked. "They visit you?"

So much for small talk. I nodded my head, but he wasn't looking.

Agatha moved a pizza box off the camping cooler, then plopped down on it and stretched her legs out. Her Viking boots sank into the shaggy burgundy carpet, scattering dust into the air. I sneezed. Then I sat down on my milk crate.

"Courtney is a special bloodliner, Danny," Agatha said. "The aliens talk to her, and she communicates back, just like Aunt Ketti used to say could happen. She can help us figure out what they want. But we need to help her track down a clue."

"Oh, here we go again," Zola said sarcastically.

Agatha glared over at Zola, then turned back to Danny. "Tell Courtney all that stuff you found out about the knights who protect the bloodline. And the sanctuaries."

Danny sat down on the other milk crate, across from me. He scanned the floor. Then he looked up at me.

I held my breath. His eyes were the same beautiful green as Agatha's. But something was different about them. They were less fiery, maybe? And there was a sadness in them. I'd seen the same look in the mirror.

"It feels like they're taking over your mind sometimes," he said to me. "Doesn't it?"

"Yeah. Definitely." Tears streaked down my face, and I quickly wiped them away. "It does."

He nodded his head gently. "You can really talk to them? Like, understand them?"

"Yeah," I said. "You can't?"

"No. I see them, but I can't understand what they say." He lowered his eyes. "Did one of your parents have the curse?" he asked.

"The curse?" I felt a tightness in the pit of my stomach. "Agatha said it was a good thing."

"We got it from our great-aunt Kelli," he said.

We? I glanced at Agatha, but she quickly shook her head.

"There's no curse, Danny," she corrected her brother. "It's a gift. You know that."

"Quit with the bullshit already," Zola said. "He doesn't want to hear your fairy tales again."

Agatha spun around on the cooler and shoved a finger at Zola's chest. "Get out of here, or I'll pick your medicated ass up and throw you out!"

Zola rolled her eyes up at Agatha. "Call off your dog, Danny. Before I call Nurse Ratched and have her arrested."

"Be cool, Agatha," Danny said. "Zola's just trying to help me through stuff we've been working on in group."

Agatha turned back to her brother. "What kind of stuff?"

"Stuff like trying not to think about aliens," Danny said.

"No, no, no." Agatha shook her head. "That's not something to work on. That's not how we're gonna solve this. Show him the tattoo, Courtney."

"Really?" I balked. But Agatha's face was stone-cold serious, so I stood up and raised my shirt. Danny followed me with his eyes. I lifted my arm so he could see the ribs below my armpit.

He nodded, and I pulled my shirt down. "Those look more like flying beetles than birds," he said. He looked down at his dirty tennis shoes. "But it's the same kind of symbol our aunt Ketti wore. I used to see it in my head, everywhere, especially right after aliens visited me."

"Danny, enough already," Zola said.

"Shut up!" Agatha shouted at Zola. "Danny, that's why Courtney can help us. She drew that symbol all over the wall yesterday while she was sleeping. The aliens are giving us another clue. They want us to understand them."

He shook his head. "It's not good for me to think about that stuff, Agatha."

"Yes it is, Danny! You can't just sit in here numbed out on meds pretending this isn't happening to you. This is a once-in-a-lifetime chance to discover who you really are."

"Ha!" Zola let out a loud forced laugh.

"Stand up!" Agatha yelled at her. "You have something to say, stand up and say it to my face. Right now!"

"Take a chill pill, Agatha," Zola said.

I bounced my knees nervously. Obviously this wasn't going the way Agatha had planned. I glanced across at Danny and our eyes met.

"My aunt Ketti was wrong," he said. "There's no ancient order of protectors, or evil soldiers out to destroy our world. No secret book or place out there with all the answers. We're all alone."

I gasped.

"Truth hurts, don't it?" Zola sat up on the back of the couch. "My mom Freddy-Kruegered her wrists in the bathtub when I was fourteen because she thought little green men from Mars were going to take her away on their spaceship again."

"A bathtub?" I turned and stared at Zola. "My grandpa drowned in a bathtub. And now the aliens are trying to drown me!" I stood up. My head was spinning. "So what do I do?"

Danny gazed at me. "You need to be careful, Courtney. Get that tattoo covered up."

"Do it, sunshine," Zola said. "Then forget everything Agatha told you about aliens or your grandpa or the secret Mr. Spock bloodline." She stood up and walked toward me, holding her wrist up for me to see. "Otherwise your next tattoo's gonna look like this."

I stepped back, but not before I saw thick puffy scars and the trace of stitch marks running along the veins of Zola's wrist.

"Tattoo by razor blade," she said.

My stomach twisted. I turned and hurried out the door. Scrambled up the stairs, outside, and across the street.

"Let me explain," Agatha said, running after me.

"I can't believe you took me there!" I yelled. I kicked the back tire of her car. "You pretended like you were my friend, and you told me you were going to help me. But this was all about your brother."

"That's not true."

"Yes it is. You used me, Agatha."

"You're wrong." She rubbed her eyes and paced. "My brother's just really confused right now. So I thought meeting you would make him want to help us. But the truth is this is bigger than that. It's about you and me. Our destinies are intertwined, Courtney. I want to help you. And . . ." She stared over at me as if trying to decide if she should continue. In a softer voice, she finished her thought: "I need your help. We can help each other."

"Stop talking! Please. I can't think about this right now." I pulled at my hair. "I feel like my head's going to explode."

"Okay." Agatha unlocked her car. "Get in. I'll take you to your bike. No more talking, I promise."

I couldn't imagine what other options I had, so I got into the car.

Agatha watched me from her car as I unlocked my bike. I felt horrible for abandoning her, but I definitely couldn't risk spending the rest of my life hiding in the basement of a halfway house like her brother.

I pulled my phone out of my pocket. My appointment with Dr. Delmar was in fifteen minutes. *I can just make it.* My only hope was letting him shut off the alien part of my brain. Not a great plan, I knew, but it was the only one I had. So as soon as Agatha's car pulled out onto the main road, I turned my bike around and shot past the Holy Donut, the emergency entrance for Solomon Grace, and the field.

I turned between the construction barrels and into the bombed-out parking lot and then stomped on my brakes. There was one problem with my plan. What if Agatha was right? Even if she was wrong about the secret society of alien bloodliners, the tattoo could still have been a message from my grandpa. He'd always said I was destined for great things. And the way he'd said it, it was like he knew the future or something. *But that was just talk. I mean, he was crazy, right?*

I glanced along the cracks towards the old psych hospital. I was almost far enough away that the dilapidated building looked safe. The rusted yellow school bus along the side gave it away, though.

Oh man!

I pulled out my phone, flipped to my mom's number, and pressed call. She picked up on the first ring.

"Hey. It's me, Courtney."

"I know that, Courtney. Do you need something?"

I scraped the bottom of my shoe against my bike pedal. "I was just wondering if there was a chance we could talk about Grandpa."

"Courtney . . ." I could hear the disappointment in her voice.

"Well, not about Grandpa. Just about what happened at the cottage—to me. You know, when I got the tattoo and he disappeared."

"Do I need to call Dr. Anderson?" Her voice was calm, but definitely threatening.

"No." I got off my bike and laid it on the broken asphalt, then walked along a branch of the main crack.

"Good," my mom said. "Let's call this strike two, and agree never to bring up the subject again. Deal?"

"Yeah, okay. Deal. But it's just I'm having dreams about my tattoo. And so I have a quick little question I was hoping to ask you. Please, Mom."

There was a long silence. "If it would make you feel better to have that god-awful tattoo removed, I can call Dr. Anderson and get the name of a reliable cosmetic surgeon."

"No, that's not it."

"Then this conversation is over."

"Wait—just real quick, do you know what the tattoo is supposed to be? Like, what it means? I was thinking maybe it was a symbol for something. I mean, if I'm stuck with it, shouldn't I at least know what it means?"

"It means nothing."

"Well, not to you, but what if it meant something to Grandpa? Maybe about the bad people who took him away? Or like, what if I'm marked, and now the same people, or things, who drowned Grandpa are going to come for me?"

"I'm not going to frustrate myself with your nonsense."

"Okay, that was dumb. But . . ." I gouged my fingernail into the cuticle of my thumb. "Well, is there a chance the tattoo is a place that I'm supposed to find? Like a clue from Grandpa, maybe about how to fix my brain? Or why I'm so messed up? Or maybe what my destiny is?"

"Good-bye, Courtney."

Ugh! She's such a horrible mom. Seriously! She's worse than no help!

I thought about calling my dad, for a second anyway. But in his own way, he was just as bad as my mom when it came to talking about anything pre-divorce. I shoved my phone back into my pocket. Then I mounted my bike and pedaled toward the building.

I drove my bike around the corner of the building, past the service ramp and the old bus. Before I even stopped, the steel service door creaked open.

"Can I help you?" The security guard looked me up and down. "You're here to see Dr. Delmar, right?"

"I don't know," I said. "Well, yeah, that's me. But I have to make a call."

"Knock when you're ready." The door slammed shut.

I pulled my phone out again and called Agatha.

"What's going on?" she asked nonchalantly.

"Your brother said 'we' got the curse from 'our' aunt. 'We,' like more than one person. Does that mean you're a bloodliner too? Doomed to mental illness and all that?"

She laughed through the phone. "I don't know. From what I've heard, it's not like a normal gene that's passed down from generation to generation. It's rare. And it skips around. But if you're asking me if aliens visit me, the answer is no."

"So then why are you so obsessed with finding this secret society?"

The phone went silent, and I was sure she'd hung up. But then I heard her breathe.

"Two reasons," she said. "When I was little, my aunt Ketti was sure I'd inherited her bloodline, so she told me about the secret order. But I guess the aliens chose my brother instead, and by then my aunt had moved back to Norway. Once I realized what was happening to Danny, my aunt had passed away, and he was already traumatized."

"Oh, Agatha. That sucks." I glanced at the steel door. "So you think finding one of these secret places will help your brother?"

"I hope so."

"Yeah. So what's the other reason?"

"That's a little more complicated," she said.

"Tell me, Agatha. Please. Quickly! I've got like thirty seconds."

"It's my dreams," she said. "I've been having the same one, for years. Total end-of-the-world stuff. But—you know what, I'll tell you about it another time."

"No, tell me now, please!" I said. "What happens in the dream?"

"The ground crumbles apart, and the sky tears open and peels back. And there's another world behind it—an alien world—like it's been there the whole time," she said.

"Oh, wow!" *Just like the drawing in the sketchbook!* "Is it the end of the world?"

"The aliens aren't the bad guys, Courtney. In the dreams, they're as scared about what's happening as we are. I'll spare you the gory details, but both worlds are crumbling and everyone's in danger. It's evil that's winning."

"My grandpa used to talk about something like that. The world crumbling apart," I said. "But, well, you don't think it's really gonna happen, do you?"

"I don't know. Apparently it almost happened in Norway, like a hundred years ago."

"Oh, this is bad!" I dropped my bike and paced along a crack in the parking lot.

"It gets worse," she said. "Last night, in my dream, you were there with me."

"Are you serious?" I stopped and looked around me. I was surrounded by crumbling asphalt.

"I'm totally serious. I think you've always been there in the dream. But until last night, I never got a good look at you."

Holy shit! I was the girl! The one she had told that corpse guy Jorg about when he'd asked about her dreams about the apocalypse. I shot a quick look at the hospital door, half expecting the security guard to burst out of it. "So is that what you meant when you said our destinies were intertwined?"

"Yeah. So far it's just a dream. But I can't help thinking that the universe has a plan. Cosmic forces fighting to thwart evil. And that we all have a purpose and parts to play. I think the universe is trying to tell me something— about the path I'm supposed to take."

I took a deep breath. "So do I have a path that I'm supposed to take too?"

"I would think so. Where are you?"

"Outside the old psych building. Where are you?"

"Across the parking lot from you."

I looked around and spotted her car, parked way over by Dr. Straka's office.

"You're here to stop me from going to see Dr. Delmar, aren't you?"

"No."

"Really?"

"You've been through some shit, I get it. Thinking about your grandpa brings back bad feelings. I get that too. You're being stalked by aliens while your friends are making out with their boyfriends. I get it. You're pissed off. You just want to be normal."

"So what are you saying?" My stomach growled, and I rubbed it with my free hand.

"That maybe you're not ready to figure out what the aliens really want from you. Or to help me figure out my dream. So you're gonna try your luck with Dr. Delmar. See if he can patch up whatever figurative hole in your head the aliens are sneaking their way in through."

"Yeah, but what if it works?" I asked. "What if he shuts off the alien center in my brain and I'm not me anymore? Wouldn't that totally upset the cosmic forces and screw up my destiny?"

"I'm sure it would. Or worse."

"Crap!" My stomach growled again, even louder. "I'm starving," I said.

"You changing the subject?"

"No, seriously, I haven't eaten in like thirty hours."

"I know a super-cool taco bar," Agatha said. "My treat."

I gazed across the parking lot at her car. "Just like that, I'm supposed to forget about my appointment with Dr. Delmar and follow you to a taco bar where you can brainwash me with your end-of-the-world, secret-society conspiracy theories?"

"Or not," Agatha said. "Oh no. Behind you!"

"What?" I asked.

"There you are," someone called out.

I spun around.

Dr. Delmar held open the door. "Come on in." The security guard stood behind him.

"Not cool," I whispered into the phone.

"Give me two seconds," I told Dr. Delmar, holding up my finger.

I ran over to my bike and jumped on. "I'm coming your way, Agatha!"

It was almost four o'clock when Agatha dropped me off. Not that I was in any hurry to get home, but Agatha was going to some crazy Norwegian black metal concert in Berkeley, so she was in a mad dash to meet up with her rock 'n' roll friends.

I walked into the house and I could hear my mom in her office, talking on the phone. I shut the front door quietly and headed up the stairs.

"You're in trouble! You're in trouble!" Kaelyn sang out, dancing out of the family room.

"What? Why?" I said, turning around.

"Just kidding. But Mom's on the phone with Dr. Anderson, and I heard your name."

"Oh, great."

"Then they got all whispery and smoochy-smoochy. 'It's date night, sweetie.'"

Puke. "I'm going to take a shower. Then I'm gonna read my book. So don't bug me till dinner."

"Yeah, right. Enjoy your nap. Ha-ha. You slept in the basement last night, you slept in the basement . . ."

After a long shower, I wrapped a big fluffy towel around myself, walked into my bedroom, and shut the door. Then I crawled into bed. My head plopped against the pillow. I wanted to pull up my comforter, but it was too late. I was already asleep.

TWENTY

By the time I woke up, my room was pitch black. I glanced at my alarm clock. 8:33 p.m. I'd slept for almost four hours.

I walked over and flipped on the overhead light. *Yikes!* It was bright, and I was naked. I shielded my eyes, but not before I caught a glimpse of myself in the mirror—the blurry insects on the top of my rib cage. I ran my finger across them. Agatha's brother was right: they looked like winged beetles. *What were you thinking, Grandpa?*

Suddenly I remembered the shoe box filled with Grandpa's old photos in the storage room in the basement. If I was gonna look for clues about my tattoo, that box would be the place to start.

I threw on a pair of pink plaid Capri pants and my comfy yellow sweater. Then I peeked out my window. Parked in the driveway behind my mom's car was Dr. Anderson's old silver Mercedes. *Ugh!* And next to our front porch was a scooter just like Lauren's brother used to ride.

Crouching down on the floor by my closet, I put my ear next to the heat vent and heard muffled voices.

I fixed my hair in the mirror, and then I crept down the stairs.

Kaelyn was on the couch in the family room, and crouched down in front of her was a skinny girl with blond pigtails. Her back was to me, so I couldn't see her face. But she definitely wasn't Lauren. And she was drawing something on Kaelyn's arm with markers. Flying beetles?

"What are you doing?" I charged in. They both looked up at me, startled.

"I'm getting a tattoo," Kaelyn said. "It's Captain Huggy Face. From *WordGirl*."

"Hi, Courtney," the blond girl said. It was Haley from art class.

"Uh . . ." *What is she doing here?*

"I'm watching Kaelyn," she said, seeing my confusion.

Talk about awkward.

"So that's your scooter outside?" I asked, uncomfortably stating the obvious.

"Yeah. Keys are in it, if you wanna take it for a ride," she said.

"Yeah, maybe. Thanks." I tried to sound interested. Truth was, I'd ridden Lauren's brother's scooter around their neighborhood like a hundred times, so it wasn't like I wouldn't know how to ride Haley's scooter. You know, if I wanted to. "So where is everyone else?"

"Mr. and Mrs. Elliston picked up Mom and Dr. Anderson," Kaelyn said. "They went to a fancy party. And Mom didn't know if you'd be up to the responsibility. So Haley's babysitting."

Haley nodded and smiled, almost apologetically.

"Cool," I said. "I'll stay out of your way."

"Mom gave Haley money to order pizza for dinner, but we wanted to wait for you to wake up. I told her how you slept on the basement floor last night, so you're probably really tired."

"Yeah, funny," I said.

As cute as Kaelyn was, I was starting think that she took pleasure in watching me squirm. Something I was sure she'd picked up from Mom. Two peas in a pod. *Perfect.* I walked toward the basement steps. "I'll be downstairs."

For all my mom's obsessions over appearance, our basement storage room looked like it had been hit by a bomb. It always looked that way too. Boxes on top of boxes on top of storage bins, and stuff pouring out all over.

I kicked a stack of Mom's wooden lawn ducks. One smashed against the wall and its bill broke off. Somehow this made me feel good, and I laughed.

Finally I found the blue shoe box with Grandpa's photos in it. I sat down on a torn moving box overstuffed with lawn-chair cushions, and took the lid off the shoe box.

Score! It was still filled with photos. And an old key. I picked up the key and studied it. Something was stamped into its flat metal surface. A letter *K* for sure . . . and an *M*, maybe?

I dropped the key back into the box and pulled out a stack of photos. I twisted off the rubber band holding them together and began to sift through them. They were old black-and-white pictures of people standing along the side of a mountain road and sitting in a bar. I recognized my grandpa in some of the photos. His wide smile and sparkling eyes. But otherwise the photos were pretty unenlightening.

I grabbed another stack and pulled off the rubber band. The first photo was of Grandpa at his cottage. Nervousness shot through me. That was one place I never wanted to look at again. I quickly flipped through them, then twisted the rubber band back on and dropped them in the box.

"Hey."

Startled, I looked up to see Haley standing in the doorway.

"Pizza's here," she said.

"I'll be up in a little bit."

"Right on," she said. But she didn't leave. "So, you ready for school on Tuesday?"

"Not really," I muttered.

"Yeah. I hear you." She glanced back toward the stairs. A long, awkward silence followed, then she looked at me again. "I just want to say, I think it's really cool what you and Agatha Kirlich are doing."

My heart stopped. "What do you think we're doing?" I asked, defensively.

"You know, helping her brother, Danny."

"I'm not helping her brother with anything," I said quickly.

Haley looked sheepishly down at her feet. "Oh, okay. Sorry." She slowly glanced back up. "I just meant, well, it's cool you visited him."

"Who told you that?" I wasn't trying to be rude, but the last thing I needed was someone from school knowing my business with Agatha.

"Danny told me. My mom's a nurse, and I help her out at the group homes. I do cleaning and stuff; I was there this afternoon. Danny's really cool."

All right. I guess that makes sense.

"Yeah, he's nice," I said. I fit the lid back on the shoe box, then glanced over at Haley. She looked young for a junior in high school. Kinda pretty, in a mousy way. But her nail polish was jet black, and both her wrists were tattooed.

"Listen Haley, it would be better if you didn't tell anyone about me visiting Danny in that place."

"I swear I won't tell anyone, Courtney. Cross my heart."

"Thanks." I grabbed a box of Halloween costumes off the shelf and dug through them like I was looking for something. But Haley didn't leave.

"Can I ask you a question, Courtney?"

"Depends," I said, lowering my eyes.

"Do you think Agatha's prophecy of the apocalypse is going to come true?"

116

"What?" My eyes shot over to catch her expression. How did she know about Agatha's dream?

She bit her lip. "You know about it, right? That's why you're helping her brother?"

I shook my head, unwilling to give her any more information than she already had.

Her eyes flashed with excitement. "You had to hear about it! The earth and sky cracking apart and exposing the alien dimension—"

"No, never heard of it, sorry." *How does she know all this?*

"But you've heard about the prophecies of Aga Valkyrie, right?"

"Aga Valkyrie? I don't think so." I tried to sound uninterested, but I could feel my fear taking hold on my face, so I turned away.

"Aga Valkyrie is the name Agatha models under," she said. "It's from Nordic mythology. It means 'Chooser of the Slain,' and she was, like, a goddess of war who chose which soldiers would die in battle. Anyway, she's totally famous in the black metal scene in Scandinavia. Like some of her poems or whatever about her apocalyptic visions were made into black metal songs."

"Aga Valkyrie is famous?" I asked, confused.

"Agatha, not the goddess," Haley said. "Well, the goddess is totally famous too, but that's ancient stuff."

"Agatha . . . is famous?"

"Totally. She's on album covers and stuff. And she's in some totally gory metal videos. They're hard to find over here, but she's huge in Norway and Sweden."

"Oh, wow." This was interesting. The church in Norway and the horror makeup video shoot were starting to make sense. "How do you know all this stuff?" "I tried not to sound suspicious, or overly interested, for that matter.

"We moved here from Sweden when I was six," Haley said. "But my cousin Jorg is big in the Norwegian metal scene. And he's worked with Agatha over there."

"Jorg?"

"Yeah. Actually, he's over here now, with his band. They're playing a concert in Berkeley tonight! But—well, it's an eighteen-and-over show, and I don't have a fake ID. Agatha will definitely be there, though."

This was too much. I needed air. I started to stand up. But I couldn't leave the photos, and if Haley saw me grab the box, she'd ask about it.

"Don't worry, Courtney," she said as if reading my mind. "Your secrets are safe with me."

"What secrets?" I stared at her. The hairs on the back of my neck stood up.

She smiled. "Exactly." She twisted her dirty-blond pigtail around her finger. "That's what's cool about you. You keep to yourself."

"I keep to myself because everyone thinks I'm crazy." As soon as the words crossed my lips, I felt ashamed.

"You're not crazy," Haley said. "You're just different, in a cool way."

"Thanks." *Spend an hour in my head, and then tell me how cool I am.*

"Okay, pizza's getting cold." She turned and ran up the stairs.

I shoved the shoe box with Grandpa's photos into an old Halloween bag, then carried the bag upstairs to my bedroom.

Standing in front of my dresser, I glanced at myself in the mirror, at my silvery-blue eyes. "You're different," Haley had said. She was right about that. *Different how, though? Cursed, maybe? Damaged for sure. Doomed?* Tightness stretched up from my chest and squeezed my throat.

Doomed seemed to fit. My grandpa must have known that. Maybe that was why he tried to drown me? *Oh, wow. Of course!*

Agatha had it all wrong. Her dream was a prophecy of things to come. But what if it wasn't my destiny to help her? What if I was the one doomed to rip the hole in the sky and destroy the world with my broken mind?

OH GOD! I covered my mouth. It was a horrible thought. But it made sense. Grandpa, or his alien friends, must have seen the prophecy of my future and then tried to do the world a favor by stopping me dead in my tracks.

Why hadn't I figured this out before? My mind kept spinning. Maybe my mom knew about the prophecy too? That could be why she was so unwilling to talk about the cottage incident. As tragic as my drowning in the bathtub would've been, it would've been an out for her, too. Her chance to escape the darkness that surrounded me and have a normal, happy family.

It definitely made sense.

Staring at myself in the mirror, I yanked my shirt off, raised my arm, and turned sideways. *But what about this?*

It all made sense, except for the tattoo. If you were going to kill somebody, why would you tattoo them first? None of this made sense.

"Courtney! Hurry up!" Kaelyn yelled up the stairs. "Pizza's almost gone!"

I grabbed my phone and texted Agatha: *Found a box of old photos. Call me!*

"Courtney! Pizza!"

"I'm not hungry! So leave me alone!"

TWENTY-ONE

Something smelled rotten, like a zombie's breath. I rolled over and the smell grew stronger. Gagging, I sat up. It was morning! I was on the floor by my closet, next to the heat vent.

"Courtney! We're leaving for soccer!" Kaelyn yelled up the stairs.

I glanced around my room. Spread across my floor, organized in neat rows, were my grandpa's photos. I grabbed the shoe box off the closet floor, then scooped up one of the rows of photos, wrapped it in a rubber band, and tucked it in the box.

"Courtney! Wake up!" my sister yelled at the top of her lungs. Then I heard the *clip-clap* of plastic soccer cleats running up the stairs.

"Great!" I stood on my knees and swept up another row of photos, raking them into a pile. Then another. Scrambling around on my hands and knees, I shoved the loose photos back into the box.

"You're awake?" Kaelyn stood in the doorway, her arms crossed over her chest.

"Looks that way." I glanced down at floor. *Crap.* Right next to her foot was one last picture—and resting on top of it was the key with the engraving on it. I looked up at Kaelyn, hoping she hadn't noticed me staring at the floor.

"Mom's taking me to my soccer game if you want to come."

"Oh jeez—sorry, Kae, not today. But I'll go to your next game. I promise."

"Yeah, I doubt it. Later." She turned and ran off. Seconds later, the front door slammed shut, and then my mom's car beeped and backed down the driveway.

I'm a horrible sister.

I scooped up the key and the last photo. It was one of the old black-and-whites. It showed three men dressed in black suit coats sitting in a bar, drinking out of big metal beer steins. One of the men was my grandpa. When I'd come across the photo last night, something about it had bothered me, so I'd kept going back to it, like it was a clue. But a clue to what? I didn't know.

I studied it again. Nothing jumped out at me and screamed "clue." But staring at it gave me a strange, tingly feeling.

Holding the photo, I crawled over to my closet, dug out the box I kept my old stamp collection in, and pulled out the magnifying glass. Still not sure what I was looking for, I studied the photo under the lens.

No way!

Etched into the beer stein in my grandpa's hand was a design: four flying beetles, arranged in a square—the same design as my tattoo. Agatha was right: my tattoo meant something!

I grabbed my phone, my heart pounding. It was eight in the morning, and Agatha still hadn't responded to my text from the night before. In fact, I hadn't heard anything from her since she'd dropped me off yesterday. I called her, but it went to voice mail.

"Call me—quick! We need to meet. Now!"

I threw on a kinda hip yellow dress that I had bought last Halloween for my hippy costume, and a retro cardigan sweater, and then I checked my phone again. Still no word from Agatha. I left her another message: "Call me. Actually, meet me at the taco bar in twenty. I'm out of here."

Tucking the photo into the shoe box with the others, I ran downstairs—right into the zombie smell I'd gotten a whiff of earlier.

Uck. I gagged.

"Good morning, young lady." Sitting at our kitchen table, his hands wrapped around my mom's WORLD'S BEST MOM coffee mug, was Dr. Anderson. In his pajamas. *Really? Mom left me alone here with this weirdo?*

"What are you doing here?" I asked, gripping the shoe box at my side. "And what's that disgusting smell?"

"It's corpse-flower tea," Dr. Anderson said. "Keeps your insides regular. Sit down, I'll make you a cup."

"No thanks." I backed away from the table, covering my mouth and nose with my hand. "Why are you here?"

"Let's talk about you, Courtney. What's in the box that's so important?"

I locked the shoe box against my chest with both arms.

"They're love letters. From a boy I met on the psych ward in St. Ignatius." I had no idea why such a strange lie had popped into my head, but I rolled with it. "Hey! I never thanked you for locking me up in St. Ignatius. Thanks, Dr. Anderson. It was so much fun on the psych ward."

"Your sarcasm is a cry for help. Now sit down, please, and show me what's in the box."

"They're naked pictures of me and my boyfriend. I'd show you, but I wouldn't want you to get your fingerprints on them. My boyfriend's dad is a big-time lawyer who loves to sue doctors. Plus, my boyfriend gets crazy jealous, and he has a gun."

Dr. Anderson sipped his zombie tea and stared at me. Under his gaze, my skin felt dirty and gross.

"Something's troubling you," he said.

"You're a genius," I snarled.

"You're angry about me and your mother."

"Yeah. Too bad I didn't drown, huh?"

He looked almost startled by that one. "That's an unusual thing to say."

"Is it?" I glared at him. I hated him—for locking me up, and for dating my mom, and for being a crappy doctor who knew nothing about kids but acted like he knew everything. Turning away in disgust, I scanned the hallway. My backpack was hanging on its hook. *I should shut up, grab it, and leave.* I glanced back at Dr. Anderson, at the smug know-it-all look on his face. *No. I can't leave yet.*

"Maybe I'm unusual because unusual things have happened to me," I said. "Did you ever think about that?"

He rolled his eyes at me.

"How about before you guys locked me up? Did you stop to think that traumatic shit had happened to me as a kid? And that maybe it was coming back to haunt me, and that I was having a hard time with that? That hey, maybe the nightmares and taping tinfoil to my window were actually normal fucking reactions to crazy things that were happening in my head? You ever consider that?"

Dr. Anderson calmly sipped his zombie tea. "Somebody needs a stronger dose of medication," he said.

"Get out of our house before I call my boyfriend and have him throw you out!"

"Tsk, tsk, tsk." He tapped his ring against my mom's coffee mug. "There's no boyfriend. Just poor, tortured you and your little head full of secrets."

"You're sick!" I grabbed my backpack off its hook, zipped it up with the shoe box inside, and banged out the side door.

TWENTY-TWO

The waitress filled my water glass for the ninth time. Then she glanced down at the bill impatiently. I'd been there for almost two hours. I still hadn't heard back from Agatha, though, and I had no money to pay for my chips and guacamole.

I stared at my phone. *Come on, Agatha. Call!* I had to pee so bad my knees were bouncing on their own. But I couldn't leave my backpack at the table. And the way the manager was watching me, I knew that if I got up with my backpack, he would probably tackle me for trying to bolt without paying.

My phone vibrated against the tabletop. It was Agatha. "Where are you?" I whisper-yelled.

"I'm here."

The manager guy and two busboys stared over my shoulder.

I turned around.

"Agatha?" She looked like a rock star! Wearing a red velvety witch's dress, black stiletto boots with big silver skulls on the front, and fashionably torn stockings that only went halfway up her long, pale legs.

I glanced up at her hair. It was matted and tangled, which definitely wasn't fashionable. Or rock-starry. And she wasn't smiling, either. Then I saw the smudges of black eyeliner streaked down her cheeks. *Ew!* She looked rough.

"Love the makeup," I said mockingly.

She shook her head but couldn't help smiling. "Coffee, please," she said, waving to the waitress, and then she sat down across from me. *No snarky comment about my hippy dress. She must really not be feeling good.*

She also smelled like alcohol. "Wait. Have you been drinking?" I asked.

"No. I ran into some friends from out of town at the concert last night, and I still haven't been home. My dress is covered in beer and my head is pounding. I'm not in the mood for small talk. So show me what you got."

I bit my lip to keep from smiling.

Agatha took a long swig of coffee, then raised the magnifying glass again and stared down at the four black-and-white photos of my grandpa in the bar. She flipped each one over, checking the back. Then rearranged the order. Then looked at me.

"Well, what do you think?" I asked, bouncing my knee under the table.

She leaned her head against her hand. "You tell me."

"I think my grandpa was in a bar, and his beer stein had the beetle symbol on it."

"So?"

"So maybe he's telling me to find that bar. Or that mug?"

"That's brilliant," she said sarcastically.

"Excuse me if my brain doesn't work like a detective's. Just tell me what we gotta do, and we'll do it!"

She slid one of the photos over to me.

"Does that look like any bar you've ever been in?"

"No," I said. "But I've never been in a real bar."

"Look at the people in the background." She tapped her fingernail against the photo.

They were all dressed in robes, and several of them had crosses around their necks. "Are they monks?" I asked.

"I'd say so. Which means we're not looking for a bar; we're looking for a monastery. One that serves beer in metal steins."

"A monastery?" I pulled out the rest of the black-and-white photos, and quickly found the photo I was looking for: a bunch of old cars parked along the side of a mountain road. Next to the wooden railing was a sign that said TODAS LAS ALMAS MONASTERY, 2.2 MILES.

I pushed the photo over to Agatha. I was so excited, I wanted to scream.

She picked it up and studied it without taking her head out of her hand.

"So? Am I genius or what?" I drummed on the table.

"Bravo, dude! You are a detective," she said. "And look at the rows of grapevines. And the old California license plates on the cars. That was probably taken somewhere in Napa Valley."

I quickly typed *Todas las Almas* into the search engine on my phone. I clicked on an article about monks making beer. "Found it," I said, handing Agatha my phone. I was getting good at this!

"Dude, wow," she said. "It's in Napa. Right off Highway 121. This place is less than two hours away."

"Let's go!" I jumped up.

Agatha glanced across the table at me and squinted her eyes. "Sit down."

Aw, man. What now?

She slid my phone back over to me. "We'll go tomorrow."

"But I have school tomorrow. It's the first day. I can't skip."

"Oh, I bet you can," she said.

"Seriously? Skip the first day of the school year? When they make the seating chart and hand out the syllabus?"

"I'll forge you a doctor's note. For excessive whining disorder." She pulled twenty bucks from her wallet and slapped it on the table next to the bill. Then she stood up.

"Really? Skip school? You're a horrible role model," I said. "Plus, my mom will kill me if she catches me."

"I'm going home to bed," Agatha said. "Call me before six a.m. tomorrow and you're dead. I mean it, Courtney!"

"Hey, wait." I held up my phone. Agatha turned around, scowling, and I snapped a picture. "Perfect. Thanks, Chooser of the Slain."

"I'd smash your phone if my head didn't hurt so much."

"Give me twenty bucks and I'll delete it right now," I said.

Agatha laughed. "So now you're blackmailing me?"

"It's not blackmail. I'll pay you back. I need to buy some new shoes. It's all part of the plan for tomorrow, I swear. Pleasey-please?"

She pulled out her wallet again and handed me a twenty.

"You rock!" I said. "Oh—and here," I said, handing her the shoe box. "You have to keep this safe."

She shoved it under her arm and walked out.

I smiled all the way to my bike.

My mom and Kaelyn were eating dinner when I got home. I slammed the front door, loudly, then pretended to creep up the stairs with my backpack slung over my shoulder and the stand-in shoe box under my arm.

"Courtney. Get back here now!" Mom yelled. I turned around, and she was already standing by the bottom of the stairs. It was amazing how quickly she could move when she thought I was about to get away with something. "Hand over the shoe box."

"But it's mine."

"Give it to me."

"Fine, but this is a total invasion of my privacy," I said.

"You have no privacy rights," she said. She opened the box, then looked up at me with suspicion. "This is what you were hiding from Dr. Anderson?"

"I wouldn't say hiding. But whatever. He's the doctor."

She pulled my newly purchased, slightly used pink Adidas running shoes out of the dented Kenneth Cole shoe box they'd given me at the resale shop. "Why would you need to hide something like this from Dr. Anderson?"

"Because they're *my* shoes. And Dr. Anderson looks at me creepy, Mom. And I didn't want him touching them and getting his zombie-smelling DNA all over them. If you know what I mean."

"That's enough, young lady." She handed them back to me. "You've got way too much anger bouncing around in that head of yours."

I looked down at my feet. *Oh, you have no idea how much anger I have.*

"Look at me when I'm talking to you."

I glared up, and I could feel the hate beaming out of my eyes.

"Life is unfair, and good guys don't always wear the white capes," she said. I had no idea what she was talking about, nor did I care. "You better figure out which team you're on, Courtney, or you could find yourself in a world of trouble."

Still no idea.

"Okay, Mom. I'll be sure to do that." *Thanks for absolutely NOTHING!* I so wanted to scream. But instead I trudged upstairs and flopped down on my bed. *Ugh!*

TWENTY-THREE

So, first day of school. Apparently no one took the bus anymore, because I was practically the only one on it. *Fine by me.*

The bus groaned to a halt in the circular drive in front of the school.

Avoiding eye contact with the cool crowd loitering by the parking lot, I bolted straight through the front door and down the hall to my first-period class, AP Biology with Ms. Shramner.

I sat down at a lab table in the back row and opened my notebook. One by one, the rest of the kids trickled in and took their seats. These were the AP serious types, so no need for me to make small talk about how lousy my summer was.

Ms. Shramner walked in and plunked down her shoulder bag, and everyone picked up their pens.

Before I knew it, the bell was ringing. *Time to go.* After leaving Ms. Shramner's room, I bolted out a side door, put my head down, and walked across the faculty parking lot like I knew what I was doing.

Agatha was right where she'd said she'd be. I jumped in her car and slouched down in the seat just in case anyone happened to look our way. "Hey," I said, looking up at her. "Feeling better?"

Agatha glanced down at my new-used shoes, then at my light blue chinos, and then up at my pink V-neck sweater. "You supposed to be *Miami Vice* or something?" she asked.

"No idea what that means," I said.

She reached behind her seat, grabbed my shoe box with the photos in it, and put it on my lap. "Figured we should bring this."

"Thanks for keeping it safe," I said.

She nodded curtly, then pulled out on the road and cranked up the volume on what sounded like a herd of sheep being tortured. I pushed myself up into a normal sitting position, buckled my seat belt, and shoved the shoe box into my backpack. Then I reached over and turned down the radio.

"And FYI, I got like three compliments on this outfit." Which was a lie, but still, who died and made her Miss Fashion?

She glanced over at me for a second. "You look like a hot chick trapped inside a bad yachting outfit."

"Ha-ha," I turned toward the window. Then I twisted back around. "Wait, you think I'm a hot chick?" This was the closest thing to a compliment I'd ever heard come out of Agatha's mouth.

"You're a hot chick for sure," she said, eyes on the road.

"Wow, thanks." I decided to press my luck. "Would you say I'm a *cool* hot chick? Not like Norwegian Goddess cool. But like normal, kind-of-hip cool?" I crossed my fingers.

"Cool? Hmm? I guess—in a too-smart-for-your-own-good kinda way."

A huge smile broke across my face. "Thanks!" Then I sat up straight. "Wait. Okay, listen," I said. "Can I ask you another question?"

She ignored me. Not that I cared.

"What if this is a trap?" I asked. "Like, my grandpa gave me the tattoo so I'd find the photo and go to this monastery place, but the whole thing is a setup?"

"We'll find out soon enough, won't we?"

"Oh jeez." I bounced my knees and bit my thumbnail. I really wanted to ask her if there was a chance that I might cause the ground-splitting apocalypse. "But—"

"But nothing. You've got a tattoo on your ribs left by your grandpa, two days ago aliens made you draw it all over the wall, and now you found a photo with the same mark on it. This is destiny: the universe is calling. It's time for action, not time to squirm around second-guessing yourself."

"Well, let's say my destiny is to go to this place. It could still turn out really bad. I mean, people die every day, and maybe that's *their* destiny. So what if you're wrong, and the aliens are bad? Or what if the monks think I'm destined for horrible things and they decide to kill me?"

"Dude, take it easy." Agatha rolled down the window and shut the radio off. "What's the worst that can happen? We walk into a room full of evil aliens and angry monks drinking beer? Big deal."

"How about I *die*?"

"Yeah, well, we all gotta die sometime," Agatha said. "That said, I agree, it would suck if it happened today. But it won't. 'Cause let's say this does somehow turn out to be a brilliant trap set up by evil aliens or bad-guy monks. That's still nothing we can't handle. We'll just kick some bad-guy ass and get the hell out of there. End of story."

"I can't kick ass, Agatha, in case you haven't noticed. I suck at being brave. My brain isn't like yours—it gets over-whelmed. I totally panic and freeze up and cry when I'm scared." As if on cue, I felt tears welling up in my eyes. "And I'm scared right now. Like, really scared!"

"There's nothing wrong with being afraid."

"Yes there is!" I wiped my eyes.

"No, there isn't. But the trick is, if you get scared, you fight through it."

"I don't know how to fight through it."

"Yes you do. You've talked to aliens and survived a mental hospital! You're a badass. So whatever happens from here on out, you can handle it."

"I guess." I *had* been through a ton lately, and I hadn't gone crazy or died from fear yet. "Maybe you're right."

"Good. Now pull a map up on your phone. We're heading north up 80, and at some point we gotta cut over to Highway 29 and then take 121 to Napa."

"Okay. And thanks. For everything. I mean it, Agatha. I don't know what I would've done without you."

"Oh, hey, don't go all emo on me." She cranked up the radio again.

"Wake up, fancy pants." Agatha shook me, and I sat up. How I'd managed to fall asleep with the sounds of hell on fire blaring in my ears, I wasn't sure. But I had, because we were parked next to the wooden sign from the photo: TODAS LAS ALMAS MONASTERY, 2.2 MILES.

A rush of nervousness surged through me, and I threw off my seat belt. "What exactly are we gonna say to these people, Agatha?" With all the worrying I had done about things going horribly wrong, I'd never really thought about what the plan would be if things went well.

"No idea." Agatha cracked her window and blew a stream of smoke out.

"Oh my God, you're smoking pot? Right now? And right in front of me?"

"Close your eyes if it bugs you so much," Agatha said.

"You're, like, the world's worst role model. Seriously . . . you know that, right?"

"Yep. And you're the pillar of all things pure." She kicked open her door. "Now let's go talk to some monks about extraterrestrials. Maybe they'll wanna see your bad-girl tattoo."

132

"Yeah? You're pretty funny." I grabbed my backpack and climbed out.

Next to the signpost was a muddy path that dipped quickly down to a giant slab of rock. Agatha and I grabbed on to a wilted bush and carefully slid down onto the rock. I didn't know much about monks—whether they lived in the woods to get away from normal people or what—but if this path was the only way to their home, I couldn't imagine they got too many visitors. From where we stood, we could see for miles, and there was no sign of a building of any type—just rows and rows and rows and rows of grapes.

"Now what?" Agatha said.

Sticking out of the ground to my right was a wooden sign shaped like an arrow. "Over here." I grabbed the sign and peeked over the edge. Carved into the side of the rock was a steep set of stairs barely visible under the moss and dirt covering them. Holding on to each other, we made our way down to the floor of the valley.

"You see the next sign?" Agatha stomped the mud off her boots.

"No." I adjusted the straps on my backpack. "It's all over-grown. You'd think they'd have a shuttle bus or horse and carriage or something, wouldn't you?"

Agatha laughed. "These are monks in a monastery. It's not an Amish village with buggy rides and a gift shop to buy driftwood furniture in."

I pulled out my phone. Zero signal. "So how do we know this place is even still around?"

Agatha glared at me. "You're the one who found it online."

"Yeah . . . but it was an old article," I admitted. "But you said you knew where it was, so I thought—"

"All right, let's not get worked up." Agatha stood up on

tiptoes and glanced around. "My Spidey sense tells me to go . . . that way." She pointed.

"Okay. Let's go," I said. It all looked the same to me, but we had to go somewhere. I cut in front of her and started in the direction she'd indicated. "Should we sing a Norwegian hiking song?" I asked.

"Shut up."

After what seemed like an hour of walking through armies of grapevines propped up on wooden crosses, we reached an old wall made of stacked-up stones. I sat down on a stone that had fallen off the wall and wiped the sweat from my eyes.

"Check this out," Agatha said.

I walked over. There was a gap in the wall—an entrance-way, with crumbling stone pillars marking each side.

"Oh wow. Look." I pointed to a clump of trees a few hundred yards ahead, and the stone steeple rising out of it. "That's a church. Come on!"

The front door to the church was locked. We walked around to the side and pulled on the door. Locked. Same with the back door.

"Shit." I kicked the big wooden door. "What kind of church locks people out?"

"Can we help you?"

I spun around to see five men in brown frocks standing behind us, all of them holding sharp shovels and rakes in their hands. *Like they just finished burying a body,* I thought, swallowing hard.

"I'm Courtney. She's Agatha. We walked here." I made a walking motion with my fingers.

"I'm pretty sure they speak English, Courtney," Agatha whispered. She nodded to the monks. "You guys know of a place around here where we can get a drink?"

The monks looked at one another. "The monastery's closed to the public," one of them said.

"Closed?" I asked in a sheepish voice.

A younger monk with bushy sideburns looked at me and nodded like he could feel my pain. "We can offer you water," he said.

"Okay. But, well, we're not really the public," I said. "I mean, we kinda want to go to your bar, and maybe talk to people."

The monks gaped at me like I was the devil, then whispered between themselves.

Agatha shot me a concerned look. "Show them the picture," she whispered.

"Oh, right." I dug the shoe box out of my backpack and pulled out the photo of my grandpa with the beer stein. I offered it to the monk with the cool sideburns.

He looked confused, but finally he took the photo from my hand.

"That's my grandpa, holding the beer stein with the bugs on it," I said. "We were hoping we could go to that bar. Is it around here?"

"I'll take that." One of the older monks grabbed the photo from Sideburn Monk. He studied it. "Which one is your grandfather?" he asked.

"Him." I pointed my grandpa out.

"You two wait here." He walked off with the photo. I tried to peek around Sideburn Monk to see where Old Monk was going, but he'd already disappeared from sight.

Great. He had my only photo of the stein with the tattoo mark on it. My only proof. I kicked at the ground, then glared up at the monks.

After ten minutes of us standing there in silence, Old Monk appeared again. "I'll give you a tour. Follow me."

We followed Old Monk across the courtyard from the church to an ancient stone building complex with a mossy brick roof and cross-shaped windows. It reminded me of a castle or a fortress, except that it was sunken into the ground and didn't have a moat or tall towers like a real castle would. Still, for a random building in the middle of nowhere, it looked pretty cool. But instead of taking us inside, Old Monk led us around the side of the building and kept walking.

"Where exactly are we going?" I asked.

Ignoring me, Old Monk trudged on. For what felt like a long while, the only sound I heard was the clomping of our feet on the dirt. Finally, we came to another courtyard, and a stone patio. I heard voices. And then I saw a doorway on the other end of the patio, and a sign for a café. *Oh wow!*

Old Monk trudged across the patio with us in tow and led us through the café doors—then stopped so suddenly that Agatha and I both ran into him. "Sorry."

A group of monks in black frocks glanced up at us from the wooden picnic table they were crowded around. I recognized the stone wall behind them from the photos. *This is it!* I took a deep breath. My chest tingled with nervous excitement.

Old Monk pointed to two giant copper igloo-shaped things with pipes running up to the ceiling. "Those are the brew kettles, where the beer is made," he said. "And over there is the bar. That concludes the tour. Brother Luke can service your oder at the bar." He handed my photo back.

"Thanks," I said. "Does—"

But he was already walking back out the door. *Guess this tour doesn't end with a Q&A.* The monks at the table were staring now.

"Awkward," Agatha whispered.

"This totally is the place in the picture, though," I said, also in a whisper.

Agatha nodded toward the bar, behind which a guy in his early twenties was standing. He was wearing an apron over his brown monk's frock. I followed Agatha over and we sat down on two high stools.

"Hi." I half waved at the bartender monk. "Are you Luke?"

"It's Brother Luke," he said.

"Oh, cool, and I'm Sister Courtney," I said. I couldn't help myself.

Agatha's Viking boot struck my shin and I grimaced.

"Two beers, please," Agatha said, her voice sounding unnaturally deep. The monks at the picnic table looked over again.

"How about water?" Brother Luke asked, grinning slightly.

"That's cool," I said. I set my backpack on the counter and shoved my picture in the small pocket.

On the wall behind the bar were rows of shoebox–size storage lockers, each one with a padlock on it. I could see big, silvery beer steins inside some of them. We were definitely in the right place!

"Here you go, ladies." Brother Luke set two plain glass mugs on the counter in front of us. Not quite the fancy beer stein I'd been hoping for. I peered down into it. For water it looked kind of brownish-yellow. *Gross.*

Agatha apparently had the same thought, because she pushed her mug away.

An old man, tall and slender with stark white hair, came through the door and sat down a few stools over from us. He was probably in his seventies, judging by the wrinkles on his face, but his jaw was strong and square, and he sat with his back perfectly straight, like someone in the military.

Brother Luke walked over to the tall man, and I watched them whisper back and forth until the tall man turned his piercing black eyes on us. I took a quick breath. He was wearing a priest's collar. I looked down to avoid his gaze.

"That's a priest," Agatha whispered.

"I can see that," I hissed back.

"Dude, look at him!" Agatha said.

"Shh." Slowly, I glanced up. The priest now had a silvery beer stein in his hand—with four beetles on it, just like the one from the photos! Just like my tattoo!

"Holy crap!" I blurted out, louder than intended.

Brother Luke shot me a disapproving look and came over to us. "Everything okay?"

"Oh yeah, totally. Sorry. So wait." I leaned forward and lowered my voice. "Any way we could get fancy steins like that guy has?" I discreetly motioned toward the priest.

Brother Luke narrowed his eyes. "What exactly are you girls doing here?"

"Nothing. Why?" I quickly leaned back from the bar.

"We're just sightseeing," Agatha said. "Her grandpa used come here. Show him the picture, Courtney."

I began to pull out the photo.

"Brother Thomas already showed me your picture," Brother Luke said. He grabbed our mugs and dumped them into the sink behind the bar. "Time to go, ladies. Sightseeing is over."

"What if we're not really sightseeing?" I said.

Brother Luke glanced over at the priest, then back at us, one eyebrow raised. "I'm listening."

I took a deep breath. "I think my grandpa left me clues so I'd come here," I whispered. "But I'm not sure. If I could figure out what the beetle symbol on your beer steins means, I might know more. Does that make sense?"

He turned his focus on Agatha. "And what's your story?"

Agatha pulled a medallion out of her pocket and set it on the bar.

"What's that?" I asked. But she ignored me.

I leaned forward to study it. Engraved on the medallion were four birds. *What the hell?* She'd never shown it to me . . . or even mentioned its existence, for that matter.

"Interesting," someone said in a thick Irish accent.

It was the priest—who was somehow standing right behind us now. Without asking permission, he grabbed the medallion. He took off his glasses and flipped the metal coin over in his long, bony fingers.

I glanced at Agatha, but her eyes were fixed on the priest. After a long ten seconds, he looked up. "The Legion of Saint Mary Magdalene the Apostle," he said.

"What's the Legion of Saint Mary Magdalene?" Agatha asked. She sounded nervous, which made me feel nervous.

The priest studied her face.

"Like most questions, the answer depends on who you ask," he said. "But if you're asking me, it's an agnostic cult founded on the heretical lost gospel of Mary Magdalene." He looked down at the medallion again. "This is from the Legion of Mary Magdalene Monastic Church in Ustka, Poland. It's an old nunnery infamous for harboring religious outlaws and worshipping gods from the outer heavens."

"Outer heavens?" I asked, too loudly. The table of monks gawked.

The priest slid his glasses back on, and the monks quickly turned away. "Where did you get this?" he asked Agatha.

"My great-aunt," Agatha said, her voice shaking. "My dad's aunt. She lived in Norway. She took me to Sweden once, and then on the ferry to Poland, across the Baltic Sea. Maybe that's where she got it."

"How come the Legion of Mary Magdalene has the same sort of symbol on it as your beer stein?" I asked.

Agatha's face went pale, but the priest smiled at me. "You look a little young to be out on a school day," he said. "What's your name, child?"

Child? Whatever. "Courtney Hoffman."

"Courtney Hoffman. I'm Father O'Brien." He held out his hand, so I shook it.

"I'm Agatha." They shook hands too.

Father O'Brien picked up my grandpa's photo and studied it. "Your grandfather was Samuel Dahlen?"

"Yeah! Did you know him?"

Father O'Brien looked me over. "I did," he said. "Now, where's your grandfather's key?"

"Key? I don't know. What key?"

He continued staring at me, and I squirmed on my stool. "You want to drink out of a big girl's cup, Courtney, you'll need the key to unlock your stein locker."

Then it struck me. "Oh, wow, right. My grandpa's key!" I fished the key with the initials carved into it out of the shoe box and handed it to him.

"Brother Luke!" he called out. "Miss Hoffman here would like to sample the harvest ale. Get her stein down, please." He tossed my key to Brother Luke. "And fill one of mine for Miss Kirlich."

"Hey!" Agatha whipped around. "How do you know my last name?"

Father O'Brien smiled. "KLK. The initials on the back of your aunt Ketti's medallion."

"You knew my aunt?"

"I know a great deal."

Agatha and I locked eyes. She winked, and I bit my lip to contain my excitement. We were definitely in the right place!

Brother Luke slid a ladder along the lockers, then climbed up and opened what must have been my grandpa's locker.

He pulled a dusty stein down and carefully washed it in the sink, then filled it up, along with another stein, and set them both in front of us.

I stared at mine. I was afraid to touch it, but I wanted to so badly. I carefully grabbed the handle and turned it counterclockwise until I could see the four beetles. Smiling, I ran my finger across the engraving, and the skin along my ribs tingled.

"The scarab beetle," Father O'Brien said. "Beautiful design, isn't it?"

I couldn't take my eyes off it. It was so much cooler than my blurry tattoo.

"'K of M,'" I said, reading the letters underneath the beetles. Like on the locker key. "What does it stand for?"

"Nothing anymore. Or everything, possibly, depending," he said. "Come on, grab your cups. Let's go out to the garden. I want to show you a painting your grandfather used to enjoy."

We followed Father O'Brien across the room. "Don't even take a sip of beer," Agatha whispered. "It might be drugged."

"You serious?" I whispered.

She nodded her head ever so slightly.

"You're so paranoid. No wonder you don't have a boyfriend."

"Shh. Seriously. This is not a time for your comedy act."

I was so excited I couldn't help being goofy. I held my beer up for Agatha to see, and then I sipped it. It was apple cider, with bubbles. But I didn't tell Agatha that. "Ah. Poison." I cut in front of her.

At the far end of the room was a thick wooden door, barred and chained shut. Father O'Brien dug a ring of keys out of his pocket and fussed with the metal padlock holding the chains together until it popped open. He unraveled the chain and slipped the heavy board from its brackets.

"Pardon our mess, girls. We don't use the garden much anymore."

The door swung open.

The garden was an overgrown courtyard covered by a roof—except for the middle, where a tree stretched up and out.

"Whoa!" I said under my breath. I pulled on the bottom of Agatha's shirt. To our left was a long picnic table, and hanging on the wall above it was a huge metal plaque with the beetle design on it and K OF M written just underneath.

Seeing the emblem, Agatha smiled.

"Welcome to the Todas las Almas beer garden," Father O'Brien said.

"So wait. What does K of M mean?" I asked.

Father O'Brien narrowed his eyes, like he was disappointed that I hadn't figured it out since the last time I asked him. "It's the sacred order of the Knights of Magi. This was their meeting place when your grandfather was alive."

The Knights of Magi! My tattoo really did mean something! "What do the Knights of Magi do?" I asked.

Father O'Brien chuckled. "Well, in your grandfather's time, they mostly talked—about science and religion and everything in between. And they filled up on ale."

"That's all?" I felt like I'd been punched in the gut.

Father O'Brien walked past the beetle plaque and pulled open two big storm shutters. Behind the shutters was a huge oil painting—taller than me, and as wide as it was tall.

"One of their favorite topics of conversation was this painting," he said.

I studied the painting. It was dark—a night scene with a bunch of people and animals outside a cave. *Creepy!*

"*Il Dono dei Magi,*" Father O'Brien said. "Or, in English, *The Gift of the Magi.* It was supposedly painted by the famous Renaissance artist Giovanni Bellini."

"So is that supposed to be baby Jesus in the manger?" Agatha asked.

I shot her a quick, nervous glance. If she was wrong, Father O'Brien might think we were atheists—or maybe something worse? And I didn't want to do anything to make him angry. Not until he'd given us the information we were looking for.

"That's right," he said.

Phew!

Father O'Brien pointed to the men with crowns on their heads in the middle of the painting. "These are the three wise men, the magi who traveled from the East guided by a star to bestow precious gifts upon the newborn king."

Oh, I see it now. There were the donkey and the sheep, and the glowing baby and the mom and dad, and the wise men and their camels. It was a painting of a nativity scene. Pretty run-of-the-mill. The only weird part was a lady with a long robe and glowing eyes standing next to the wise men.

"This was my grandpa's favorite painting?" I asked. "I didn't even know that he, you know, believed in God."

Father O'Brien pointed to the lady with the glowing eyes, and suddenly she seemed to be staring right at me. He turned and looked at me.

"Do you know who this woman is, Courtney?"

Agatha was busy staring at the painting, so I was alone with Father O'Brien's piercing gaze.

"No." I shook my head.

"Some people, like your grandfather Dahlen and Agatha's aunt Ketti, believed that this woman was the fourth wise man. And that she was responsible for bringing the Christ child the true gift of the magi: the knowledge that he descended from an alien bloodline."

I felt the blood drain from my face, and I must've been white as a ghost. I wanted to see Agatha's expression to make sure I'd heard that correctly. But Father O'Brien's eyes were pinned on mine, and there was no way I could look away.

Agatha cleared her throat. "So, uh, Father. Are you saying that my aunt Ketti and Courtney's grandpa believed that Jesus knew about aliens? And that they thought Jesus was a descendent of aliens?" She shot a quick glance skyward as if she were expecting to be struck by lightning.

"Your aunt believed in a secret alien bloodline. That alien visitors came down to earth long ago and conducted blood-letting ceremonies, during which they transfused alien blood into selected humans, forever after altering their DNA. And that this alien bloodline allowed its carriers to communicate with their extraterrestrial relations."

A priest is totally talking to us about alien bloodlines. This can't really be happening!

"Every secret has its believers and its protectors." Father O'Brien made the sign of the cross on his chin. "The Knights of Magi claim that their sacred order dates back to early biblical times, and that they are the protectors of the secret alien bloodline and those who were born into it."

"So was my grandpa a protector?" I asked. "He used to tell me about evil forces that were out to get him. But . . ." I looked down at my pink shoes. "Well, my mom said he was just crazy. So which was it?"

Father O'Brien rubbed his temples. "We all have demons, Courtney. Our proverbial cross to bear."

I shook my head. "That doesn't answer my question."

"Unfortunately, that question is not for me to answer. When your grandfather passed on, many secrets died with him. That's when Ketti Kirlich moved back to Norway to join with the Legion of Saint Mary Magdalene."

"So my aunt Ketti and Courtney's grandpa were protectors of the secrets of how to communicate with the aliens?"

Father O'Brien shook his head. "I don't know what they were, girls—knights, or fools parading as philosophers. I just left them to their meetings."

"No! You have to know more," I blurted out. "You were here; you still have the painting. You knew them. So you must know something about the aliens!"

"Bite your tongue!" Father O'Brien lurched forward, and I backed up against the tree. He yanked his glasses off like he was getting ready to fight me. "I'm a man of the cloth. I've dedicated my life to upholding and defending the doctrine of Almighty God. Fantastical stories about aliens and bloodlines are not mine to defend."

I felt a lump grow in my throat, and then tears well up in my eyes.

Father O'Brien kept staring at me. Like he was testing me, waiting for me to break.

I swallowed hard and stared back. "Please," I said. "I need to know the truth about my grandpa. And, you know, about me."

Shoving his glasses back on, Father O'Brien walked over and pulled back one of the shutters, uncovering the last four feet of the painting. It showed a swarm of bats spiraling into the night air. And climbing the mountain toward baby Jesus and the wise men, an army of grotesque-looking men with torches and swords. They were shooting burning arrows up into the sky. It was ghastly.

"Oh, dude!" Agatha moved toward the painting. "Those are the bad guys, aren't they? The old stories were true. The Knights of Magi fighting against the evil soldiers out to destroy the bloodline!"

I glanced at Agatha and vaguely recalled her brother mentioning something about soldiers when we visited him, but what exactly, I hadn't a clue.

"Look at me, Courtney," Father O'Brien said. Biting my lip, I turned my eyes upward to meet his stare, but there was a softness in his eyes now. "Agatha's right. Some stories are more than just stories. Every protector has a force of opposition whose purpose is to destroy them and the secret they protect!"

"I don't know what that means," I said, my voice shaking.

"I'm talking about the Soldiers of Bilim," Father O'Brien said.

"Soldiers of what?" I shook my head at him. Why did everyone assume I knew about this stuff?

"Courtney, show me your grandfather's badge," Father O'Brien said. "Is it in your backpack?"

"I don't have any badge."

"What? Oh dear." Father O'Brien plunked down on the picnic table under the giant Magi emblem and rubbed his head. "Then why are you here, child?" he asked.

"My tattoo. Before he died, my grandpa gave it to me. I was seven years old, so I don't really remember a lot. But it's a tattoo of the Knights of Magi emblem. It's right here on my ribs." I pulled up my shirt.

"Pull your shirt down," Father O'Brien said, scowling.

"Sorry." I quickly did.

"You told me about the tattoo. I don't need to see it."

"But that's not all," I said. "I'm being visited by aliens. I know aliens aren't in the Bible, and I don't know anything about the Knights of Magi being protectors, or about opposition forces or any of that stuff. I'm not super knowledgeable like Agatha. But my grandpa talked about aliens. He told me I was special, and destined for great things, and that it would all make sense one day. Well, now the aliens are visiting me. Only none of it makes sense. So when I found those old photos and saw my tattoo on the beer steins, I thought that maybe if I came here, someone could tell me what's happening to me. And, you know, what I'm supposed to do about it."

I wiped my eyes, but it was too late. Tears streaked down my cheeks.

"Are you able to communicate with these so-called aliens?" he asked.

"Yes," I said. "They tell me that I'm connected with them, and they keep trying to take me to my grandpa's cottage. But bad things happened there, and I'm afraid."

"Bad things like what?"

"I don't want to say."

"Take her home, Agatha." He started shuttering up the painting. "You come back when you're ready, child."

"Wait, please!" I said. "Just—"

"We came all this way," Agatha said. "There are things we need to know."

"I'm sorry, Agatha. But now is not the time," he said. He strode over to the door that led back to the café. "There are dark forces out there, girls. They're trying to expose the alien bloodline and destroy all things sacred. That much of the story I know is real. The rest I'll tell you when you're ready. Now go!" he said, pulling the door open.

"Okay, we're leaving," I said, hurrying over to the exit. "But how will I know when I'm ready?"

Father O'Brien rubbed his temples. "If you can do what you say you can, Courtney—communicate with the aliens— then they've already told you where you need to go."

"But they sent me here," I said.

"And I'm telling you you're not ready for this place."

"So what? . . . Oh no. The cottage?" I asked. "You want me to go there?"

Father O'Brien rested his hands on my shoulders. "You bring me back your grandfather's badge, and I'll help you with the truth."

Before Agatha walked through the door, he handed her an envelope. "Your aunt Ketti would want you to have this."

Agatha looked at the envelope with curiosity. "What—"

"No more questions," Father O'Brien said curtly. "Go!"

Brother Thomas was waiting for us inside the café. He grabbed our beer steins and ran them over to Brother Luke, then herded us out the door and back the way we'd come. I thought he'd stop following us when we reached the courtyard with the church, but he stayed with us—out the crumbled stone gate, all the way back through the armies of grapevines, and to the moss-covered stairs we'd come down earlier that day.

He stayed long enough to watch us climb up the steep path to where Agatha's car was parked. Then he disappeared.

TWENTY-FOUR

As soon as we were in the car, Agatha opened up the envelope from Father O'Brien. She pulled out a letter and started reading it.

"What is it?" I asked.

"A letter my aunt Ketti wrote to Sister Mary Cordelia— Commander of the Knights of Magi."

"Whoa! What does it say?"

Ignoring me, Agatha continued reading.

"Whatever." I took off my right shoe. *Ouch!* I had blisters on my heel and the side of my foot. I pulled off my other shoe. *Ouchy-ouchy! More blisters. Guess I should've broken my shoes in a little before wearing them on a ten-mile hike.*

"It's about the damaging psychological effects of being visited by aliens," Agatha said.

Oh, great. Definitely not the kind of stuff I needed to be thinking about. I leaned back, and she kept reading to herself. But after a few minutes, my curiosity got the best of me.

"Is it bad?" I asked, sitting up.

"Your grandpa theorized that each bloodliner shares consciousness with those aliens carrying a close DNA match to his or her own, which allows for communications."

"My grandpa?"

"Yeah. My aunt's referring to a report he wrote."

A report?

"According to your grandpa, as intelligent as Evolarian aliens are," Agatha continued, "they're completely clueless when it comes to human psychology. They don't get how traumatic it is for a human to wake up in their bed with strange creatures standing over them."

"Yeah, well, I could have told you that," I said. "Wait, so, 'Evolarians'? That's what they're called?"

"Yeah." Agatha held up the letter. "You want to read it?"

"Do I have to?"

"The last paragraph mentions you."

"What?" I grabbed the letter from her and read the paragraph out loud: "As to the missing Solomon-Trondheim helmet, in his last communications with me Samuel Dahlen spoke highly of his granddaughter, CH. Despite his granddaughter's young age, Dahlen was already certain of her unprecedented capabilities. Based on my conversation with Dahlen, I am confident that when CH comes of age, not only will she be able to use her talents to locate her grandfather's missing portal machine, but she will possess the ability to reestablish communications with the missing Solomon-Trondheim helmet and aid our Evolarian allies in stopping the Bilim from destroying the delicate boundaries between our worlds."

It was signed *Ketti Kirlich, agent of the Knights of Magi.*

I flipped the letter back to the first page and stared at the Magi crest.

"This doesn't make sense," I said.

Agatha snatched the pages from my hand.

"It makes perfect sense. Your grandpa left you a tattoo so you could find your way to the Magi. And now the Magi need your help!"

"But Father O'Brien said I wasn't ready. You heard him."

"No." She started the car. "He said you needed to go to the cottage and find your grandpa's badge—to prove you're ready to know the truth. In other words, you're no good to the Magi until you get your shit together."

"Oh. Really?" I slumped back in my seat. It was a lot to take in. But I could feel in my gut that Agatha was right.

"So where's the cottage?" she asked.

My blood ran cold just thinking about going there. "I don't know," I said, refusing to meet her eyes. "Somewhere up near Clear Lake."

"Could you be a little more specific?"

"I was almost killed at that cottage, Agatha. Sorry if I'm not excited to go back there."

"Listen. For the last two months you've obsessed over how you just want your life back to normal. Well, this is your chance to meet your new normal. Nothing's going to get better until you do something about all this. So where's the cottage?"

I bit my thumbnail. "I really don't know. I was seven the last time I went there! But my mom has a file with all my grandpa's estate stuff in it in her desk at home. If the address to his cottage is anywhere, it'd probably be in there."

"Great," Agatha said, already buckling her seat belt. "Let's go get it."

"It's been like eight years since he died," I reminded her. "Who knows who owns the cottage now, or if it's even still standing?"

Agatha put the car in drive and pulled out onto the windy mountain road. "We'll worry about that later. For now, first things first: we get to your house and snag your grandpa's file. Cool?"

"Yeah, all right, cool." I buckled my seat belt. I could not think of a single place on Earth that I'd less like to go to than my grandpa's cottage.

Agatha pulled over at the end of my street and looked at me. "You're up."

I grabbed my shoes off the floor and slid them on as

gently as possible. It didn't help; the blisters were on fire. "Ouch!"

"Let's go," she said. "And hurry back. Two minutes, in and out. Go!"

I climbed out and half limped, half jogged down the street.

Dr. Anderson's Mercedes was parked at top of our drive-way. *Ugh.* And in the circle part of the driveway was a long black car I didn't recognize. An airport limo or something? A lady sat in the driver's seat, but the rest of the car was empty. I hurried past it to our front porch.

Soon as I stepped into the house, the smell of Dr. Anderson's zombie tea made my stomach curdle.

"Well, hello, Courtney."

I froze in my tracks. *What is* he *doing here?*

Dr. Delmar was sitting at the kitchen table. He was dressed almost normal, in a sweater from this decade, at least. And his hair was combed.

Kaelyn was sitting across from him, coloring on a piece of manila construction paper with her colored pencils.

"Kaelyn? Where's Mom?" This was too crazy for my brain to make sense out of.

"She's still at work—jeez, take a pill," Kaelyn said.

"At work?" I didn't even look at Dr. Delmar. "So who's watching you?"

"Well, it *is* Tuesday," Kaelyn said. "Dr. Anderson's watching me. But he's in the shower."

Yuck! I didn't know if it was the zombie tea smell, or the thought of Dr. Anderson naked in our house, or the fact that Dr. Delmar was staring at me, but I felt sick. Like, really sick.

I ran to the kitchen sink and threw up.

"Eww, disgusting," Kaelyn said. "She has a weak stom-ach," she said to Dr. Delmar in a pitying tone.

"Yes, I know. Everything okay, Courtney?" Dr. Delmar asked.

"No!" I yelled, my head still in the sink. "Who let you in?"

"Thank you for the drawing of the space man, Kaelyn," Dr. Delmar said.

"It's an alien!" Kaelyn said.

"Yes, of course, it is," Dr. Delmar said. "Walk me out, Courtney?"

I wiped my mouth and shot past him and out the front door. The second he stepped onto the porch, I yanked Kaelyn's drawing from his hand and slammed the front door shut so she couldn't hear us.

"What do you think you're doing?" I asked. "You have no idea how much trouble you can get me in with my mom and Dr. Anderson."

"I'm sure you can understand that I was concerned when you disappeared on your bicycle before your appointment Sunday," he said.

"Oh, that," I said, calming down a bit. "Something came up. I meant to call you and reschedule, but my mom is always watching me, and she'd kill me if she found out I went to you and Dr. Straka without telling her."

"Dear me. We wouldn't want that." He scratched his chin. "Why don't you come by Solomon Grace tomorrow after school?"

"Yeah, sure. Okay." No way was I doing that. But I was willing to say anything at this point to get him to leave.

"The big hospital. Three o'clock. I'll have a nurse meet you outside the gift shop near the east entrance."

"East entrance. Got it," I said.

He climbed into the back of the black car, and his driver reversed quickly down the driveway. *Oh no!* What if he drove by Agatha and recognized her car? That would screw everything up! Panic gripped my throat—but the black car sped north on our street, the opposite direction of Agatha's car. *Phew!* I ran back inside and straight to my mom's study.

The file with my grandpa's papers in it was exactly where I remembered it being. I tucked it under my arm and bolted toward the door. "Tell Mom I'm sleeping over at Lauren's house."

"Mom's gonna be mad!" Kaelyn called after me.

I hesitated for a second, but there was no time to deal with her right now.

"Bye." I slammed the door and took off running.

"Well?" I asked. "What does it say?" I turned up the heat and rubbed my hands together.

Agatha turned the page. "411 Lake Portage Trail. Your mom still pays the taxes."

"Our family still owns it?" I asked, surprised. I would have thought my mom would've gotten rid of it the first chance she got.

"Actually, according to the other papers, your grandpa left the cottage to you."

"Me? Weird."

"Well . . . not *that* weird, considering everything," Agatha said, giving me a sideways glance. "Anyway, we've got three hours until it gets dark, and it's at least two and a half hours away. So buckle up!"

"Ten-four." I fastened my seat belt and gripped the sides of my seat. *Here goes nothing.* As nervous as I was, I was also kind of excited. Almost hyper.

TWENTY-FIVE

"**There.**" I pointed to a rusty mailbox hidden in the snarl of bushes alongside the road. The address stickers had peeled off, but the name s. DAHLEN was still legible. Nervous electricity rushed through my gut.

Agatha turned the car into what used to be a driveway, and we crept along slowly. "Apparently your mom didn't budget for lawn care."

Definitely not. Trees and weeds had totally taken over. But there it was, rising up out of the tangle of plants: the cottage. It was still standing.

"Oh jeez," I said. I took a deep breath, but the air didn't come close to penetrating the tightness inside my chest.

I put my fingers on my throat and stared at the cottage. It was just like I remembered it. Old and brown with green shutters. Only now it was practically falling apart. I wondered if my mom had even bothered to visit the place since my grandpa died. At least the crazy ham-radio antenna was still standing tall next to the woodpile. And the giant metal rain collection drum on the side of the house looked to be okay too.

Suddenly I missed my grandpa. I remembered our nature walks along the lake. The way he knew the name of every plant, every rock, every bird and insect—and knew what made them special, and how long they lived, and what made them die.

"It's gonna be dark soon, and I doubt there's electricity." Agatha climbed out of the car.

I followed her up to the front porch. The screen door had been torn off, probably by the wind, and was now leaning against the bushes. The front door itself still looked strong. Agatha turned the knob and pushed it open.

"Are you kidding?" I said. "It wasn't even locked?"

Agatha glanced back at me. "You first," she said.

I shook my head. "Agatha, I don't even know why we're here. I mean, what are we even looking for? Seriously?" My mind started racing. "An old priest gives you a paper supposedly written by your dead aunt that says the future safety of the Magi depends on me, and you think bringing me here, a place where I almost died, is gonna somehow help us do . . . what, exactly? Rise up and conquer the evil forces of opposition before my first-period class tomorrow morning?"

"Whoa! You need to chill out!"

"I can't!" My heart hammered in my chest.

"Fine. Then wait on the porch and cry into your elbow. I'll go look for the badge." She disappeared into the cottage.

"Slow down!" I called after her.

I caught up to her in the family room. Dead leaves and wads of stuffing from the couch cushions were strewn across the floor. My grandpa's reading chair was torn apart and covered with soot from the fireplace. His bookshelf was empty too. No ham-radio/alien-transport machine. No books, or musty old-book smell.

Looking around the room, I realized that almost everything was gone. "Oh my God. Someone stole all his stuff."

Agatha poked her head into my grandpa's bedroom. "Someone was here looking for something, that's for sure."

I walked over to the doorway. My grandpa's desk was tipped over, and the drawers lay smashed on the floor. *Who would do this?* My mom probably didn't even care that the place was unlocked and trashed. I glanced down the short hallway to the bathroom door. It was shut.

"We should go, Agatha. I'm getting a bad feeling."

"When don't you have a bad feeling?" she said sarcastically. "Go search the other bedroom. Chop-chop."

"Fine, but this is stupid." I pushed the door open to the guest bedroom, and it creaked on its hinges. The mattress was cut open and flipped up against the wall, and the drawers I'd kept my things in were piled up on the floor. I inched my way into the room. The closet was empty. Everything was gone.

While Agatha went through the pantry and the laundry-room closets, I checked the kitchen. My grandpa's metal coffee cups and his camping plates were still there. Picking up a metal plate, I remembered sitting at that table with my grandpa eating burnt toast and eggs. I opened the rest of the cupboards, but there was nothing there. No badge. No drawings of flying saucers or maps of alien wormholes.

Agatha stomped across the family room. "Any secret panel or loose floorboard that you can remember?"

"No."

"I'm gonna go outside and look around before it gets dark," she said. "You check the bathroom."

"The bathroom?" My heart sped up again. "I don't feel well, Agatha."

"All right. Settle down. We'll do it together." She walked toward the bathroom, and I followed ten feet behind her. When she reached the door, I suddenly felt light-headed, like I was going to pass out.

"I think I need to go wait in the car," I said.

"You're fine. Just take deep breaths." She opened the bathroom door and peeked in. "Interesting."

"I bet." My mind rushed with visions and sounds of me drowning.

"This is where he supposedly tried to drown you in the tub?" Agatha asked.

"Yeah." I could taste the rusty bathwater in my mouth and see myself being shoved violently under the water, then floating dead still. "Wait! Why? Is there a dead girl in the bathtub or something? It's me, isn't it?"

"Not quite." She laughed. "But you should take a look."

I took a few quick, shallow breaths, but I couldn't get enough air. The inside of my chest was on fire, and my heart felt like it was going to explode. "Agatha! You gotta take me to a hospital. I'm having a heart attack!"

She grabbed my arm. "No, you're not," she said matter-of-factly. "You're having a panic attack because you think this is where your grandpa tried to drown you."

"I *think* this is where he tried to drown me?" I yelled, holding my chest. "He dragged me in there and shoved me in the bathtub and held me under the water."

"Yeah, well, that's not happening now, is it?"

"No, but—fine!" I pushed my way around Agatha. And couldn't believe my eyes. What the hell? There was no bathtub. Just the old walk-in shower with the red-and-blue-plaid shower curtain. I remembered it now. But how was this possible?

"Agatha, I swear, he carried me in here and lifted me up against the window and then—" I looked at the window. "He lifted me *out* the window."

Agatha pressed her face to the glass and looked out. "There's a cistern right outside. Like a water storage tank or something."

I pushed her aside and stared out. "That's the rainwater tank. He lifted me out the window and dumped me into the tank."

Suddenly my memory came flooding back. Me plunging into the dark water, screaming for my life. But then realizing I could stand up—that the water was only up to my chest. I wasn't drowning at all.

I sat down on the floor to catch my breath. "There were men coming for him. So he dragged me in here, pushed me through the open window into the tank, and then told me to get in and shut the lid and stay quiet. And that's what I did. I stayed in there for hours. By the time I came back inside, my grandpa was gone."

"He was trying to protect you," she said.

I glanced over at the shower and wiped tears from my eyes. Then I let out an awkward laugh. "All this time I thought my grandpa had tried to kill me. I thought he must have seen something horrible inside me that he had to stop."

"That's probably why the aliens wanted to take you here, so you'd remember the truth."

"Oh Jesus." I glanced at Agatha. My heart was slowing back to normal, and the butterflies in my stomach were totally gone. "All these years, I felt so messed up."

"We're all messed up, dude. That's what makes us who we are."

"I'm so glad we came here, I can't even tell you," I said.

Agatha reached her hand down for mine and pulled me to my feet.

"Now kibosh the tears," she said. "We still got a badge to find."

"Maybe it's tucked underneath the rainwater tank?" I said, hurrying to the back door. "Wouldn't that be perfect?"

Agatha walked the perimeter of the cottage while I searched around the water tank.

"Find anything?" she asked.

"Nothing." I leaned back against the water tank.

"Me neither," she said. "Maybe it's inside the tank?"

"It's worth a shot! I'll drain it." I opened the spigot, and water came rushing out, hitting the ground with such pressure that it tore through the leaves and made a deep indentation in the soil. I scraped at the wet ground with my shoe and opened up a path for the water to run down to the woodpile, then walked back over to the tank, climbed up the side, and pulled myself up onto the top. The cover was made of heavy plastic and had a hinge down the middle of it. I flipped back one side so I could look down into the tank at the draining water.

"What do you see?" Agatha asked.

"Not much. Rust? I don't know. When the water gets down a little farther I'll jump inside." I leaned over the outside edge and glanced down at the wet ground next to Agatha. A deep rut was forming where the water flowing from the spigot had washed away the dirt. It looked like there was something shiny under the dirt. "What is that?"

"What?" Agatha looked up at me.

"Look where the dirt's washed away," I said, pointing. "Is that something metal under there?"

Agatha kicked at the mud, and her boot made a scraping sound. She jumped up and down, and the ground boomed like thunder.

"Dude, it's hollow!" she said. "There's a trapdoor or something under here." She kneeled and starting scooping away the dirt covering the door.

I jumped off the tank, got down next to her, and helped her dig. After a minute of that, as I was scraping away another handful, my fingers caught on a metal loop.

"Here's the handle!" I said.

Agatha grinned. "Well, get up, and let's open it!"

We stood and kicked away the dirt along the edges of

the hatch, then grabbed the handle and tugged. It took both of us pulling, but we managed to lift the door open.

Below it was a storage box about the size of a fridge. Inside were an old leather briefcase and my grandpa's ham-radio/alien-transport machine.

I stared at the machine and felt my skull tingle. He must have hidden it before he'd disappeared.

I leaned down and, careful not to touch the machine, grabbed the briefcase and stood up. "Maybe the badge is in here." I unfastened the two buckles and opened the front flap. A manila envelope with the Knights of Magi crest stamped across the front stared out at me. "Oh wow!" I took the envelope out. It was tied shut with a string.

I quickly tried to untwist the string holding the envelope closed.

"Courtney. Look at this thing." Agatha was on her stomach, leaning into the box in the ground, her hand stretched out toward the ham-radio machine still inside the box.

"Don't touch that!" I yelled. I grabbed Agatha's shoulder and tried to pull her up, but she wouldn't budge.

"Why? What is it?"

"It's my grandpa's ham-radio-slash-alien-transport machine. That's what he called it, anyway. But—"

"Dude. This must be the missing portal machine my aunt Ketti wrote about in her letter!"

"Probably," I said. "But Jesus, it could be super dangerous, Agatha. We have no idea what it does. Let's just cover it back up. I got my grandpa's briefcase. We can take it to Father O'Brien. He'll know what to do."

"No way! We gotta get this machine into the car."

"Yeah. I knew you were gonna say that," I said.

"Hold my legs. I'll pull it up," she said.

"No. I'll get it." I jumped down into the metal box and lifted the machine up to ground level—immediately a siren started blaring, and a security light mounted some-where in the tree above us flashed bright red in every direction.

"What the hell?" Agatha yelled.

"See! I told you. It's booby-trapped!" I yelled over the earsplitting siren.

Agatha snatched the machine from my hands and started running toward her car.

But suddenly she stopped. She turned back toward me, her face frozen with fear. The machine was pulsing, emit-ting strobes of bright white light, and vibrating in her clenched hands.

"What's wrong? Why are you stopping?" I said.

She didn't answer.

I grabbed the machine from her, and a vision of explod-ing metal flashed in my mind. I dropped down onto my knees.

"Did you see it?" Agatha asked.

Nodding my head, I let go of the machine and scurried away from it. "We've gotta get it back in the ground before it explodes," I said.

"I know," she said, staring into its flashing white light.

"It doesn't trust us," I said.

My grandpa's alarm siren was still blaring, and red light flashed on the treetops. In any second a neighbor or the cops would show up, and we'd have to explain to them how the alien-transport machine we were trying to steal was about to explode.

"Quick. Grab a side," Agatha said.

We lifted the machine up, hurried over, and dropped it back into the metal box. It stopped flashing.

"Whoa!" I said. "That's a good sign, right?"

Agatha shut the lid on the metal box. But the siren and the security light kept going.

"Oh this is bad!" I said. "We gotta cover this up so no one finds the hatch."

We kicked mud onto the steel door, and Agatha crawled around spreading the dirt out just perfectly as I collected a huge pile of pine needles. When she was done, we scattered pine needles around on top so it wouldn't look like anything had been disturbed.

Standing up, Agatha surveyed our work and nodded once. "It's good. Let's go! Now!"

Hugging the briefcase to my chest, I dashed to the car and we both jumped in.

"Hey. Listen," I said. The siren was quiet. And the security light had turned off.

"Dude, your grandpa was crazy smart."

I smiled. "I know."

She revved her car down the driveway and then peeled out onto the dirt road, leaving a cloud of dust behind us.

TWENTY-SIX

After going about a mile on the dirt road, we turned onto a paved street. Agatha pulled into the first gas station we saw and parked alongside the pumps.

"Let me see that," she said. I handed her the envelope I was still trying to unwind the string from.

She untied the string in two seconds. Then she carefully shook out a piece of paper and a thick black-and-white photo.

"No badge?" I asked.

"No." She picked up the piece of paper. It looked like another letter with the Magi crest on it.

While Agatha studied that, I set the empty briefcase upright on my lap and ran my fingers across the smooth leather. As I did, my hands tingled and the hairs on my arms stood up. *What the hell?* I pulled my hand away and the tingling stopped. Moving my hand over the briefcase again, I felt electricity!

I turned the briefcase over and shook it, but nothing fell out. It was totally empty. I flipped it right side up and shook it in front of my face—and a burst of light blinded me.

"Did you see that?" I asked.

"See what?" Agatha glanced up from the letter.

"I don't know—a flash of light, maybe? It came from the briefcase!"

Agatha shrugged and went back to reading.

I gripped the front flap of the briefcase and tried to bend

it backward, but it wouldn't give. "I don't know why the leather is so thick here." I tried bending the flap forward— and a seam opened up. I slipped my hand inside the seam. *Bingo!* It was a secret pocket. And there was something in it.

"Agatha!"

She looked up again. *"What?"*

I pulled my hand out, and sparkly blue light bounced off the windshield. I was holding an antique pendant the size of my palm. It was made of silvery metal with tiny blue stones embedded in it. It was shaped like a police badge.

"It's your grandpa's badge!" Agatha said, grinning. "And it's glowing!"

I rotated it in my hand, and the blue stones appeared to grow bigger. "Whoa! We gotta take this to Father O'Brien."

"Dude, that's so cool," Agatha said. "It must be alien technology."

"Look!" I said. Etched into the badge was the scarab-beetle crest of the Knights of Magi. I held it out so Agatha could see, and suddenly the crest appeared like a hologram between me and the windshield.

"Hey! Easy, Skywalker!" Agatha pushed my arm down. "Put that away till we figure it out. For all we know, you could be calling in a spaceship or something."

"You're so paranoid," I said. But the light *was* getting brighter and brighter. I slipped the badge back inside the secret pouch, and its light went dim. "I guess my grandpa really was someone important, huh?"

"You have no idea."

"What do you mean?" I asked, glancing over at her—but just then, my phone vibrated. We must have been out of range at the cottage, because suddenly I had five voice mails. And seven texts. I started to check them, but Agatha grabbed my wrist and shook her head.

"Focus. When did your grandpa disappear?"

"Eight years ago in June. June first. Why?"

"Because this was his last assignment." She handed me the letter from the envelope.

It was a "memorandum of mission" from Sister Mary Cordelia, Commander of the Knights of Magi, and it was addressed to "Chief Special Agent Dahlen."

My grandpa was a special agent. The chief special agent! *My mom is so clueless it's not even funny.*

I read it aloud: "The Evolarian transport helmet recovered in the 1912 Trondheim, Norway expedition was recently stolen from its safe house in Stockholm by agents of the Soldiers of Bilim. Per our Evolarian allies, in the wrong hands the helmet could be used to reopen any of the now-dormant wormholes between the two universes. While Evolarian command informs us that few, if any, humans possess the brain center required to operate the helmet, there are two known bloodlines whose direct descendants could possess such power: the Dahlen bloodline present in our own Chief Special Agent Samuel Dahlen, and the Skoglund bloodline last exhibited a hundred years ago by Chief High Priest Joakim Skoglund of Trondheim, Norway, before his unfortunate break with the Magi. High-ranking Soldiers of Bilim have recently been seen traveling between Turkey and the US. The helmet must be recovered. The Bilim must be stopped."

"This is crazy!" I said. "Evolarian aliens, helmets, wormholes, and Soldiers of Bilim? It's crazy, isn't it?"

"Yeah, that's one way to put. It explains a lot about my friend Jorg, too. His great-grandfather broke from the Magi after they took the helmet and other artifacts from Trondheim."

"Wait. Norway Goth guy Jorg is Haley's cousin?" I asked, remembering the conversation Haley and I'd had in my basement about the apocalypse.

Agatha shot me a menacing look. "Stay away from that Haley chick. Till I figure out her game, at least. All right?"

"Yeah. Okay, whatever," I said. "It's not like we're friends."

"Good. Now look at this." She handed me the photo from the envelope. It was of a group of men with beards leaning against an army tank, palm trees in the background. They were dressed in white collared shirts, which seemed kind of formal for the desert. Draped over the big cannon barrel on front of the tank was a banner of a snake wrapped around a thorny branch.

"I don't get it," I said.

"Flip it over."

Written in marker across the back was *Soldiers of Bilim, Istanbul, Turkey.*

"Oh, okay. So those are the bad guys." I still wasn't quite sure what I was supposed to get.

I flipped the photo back over. One by one, I studied the faces. "Oh no way! Is that Dr. Delmar?"

"Yup. Doesn't that totally make sense?"

"Oh my God—Agatha, he was at my house today!"

"What do you mean, *he* was at *your* house?"

"Yeah, when I went in to get the file from my mom's desk. He was just . . . there. Sitting at the table with my little sister."

"Jesus, Courtney! That's the kind of shit you might want to tell me!"

My phone started ringing. It was my mom. *Oh no!* I canceled it.

I flipped through my texts. All seven were from Lauren. Apparently my mom had called her looking for me. Things went downhill from there. Her last message read: *Please don't do anything stupid, Courtney. No matter how bad things seem, they're not really that bad. Call me!*

I grabbed two fistfuls of my hair and squeezed.

"That bad?" Agatha asked.

"Yeah." I exhaled loudly. "My mom knows I'm not at my friend Lauren's house. And it seems that Lauren thinks I'm having a nervous breakdown. And I'm sure she told my mom all about it."

"Well, dude, call your mom."

"And tell her what?"

"That you're fine, and you'll be home in two hours."

"You don't know my mom. She'll ask a million questions and then track me on GPS."

"Seriously?"

"Maybe. I don't know. I'll text her."

Sorry, Mom. At movies. Can't talk. B home at 10:45.

I was definitely in trouble now.

It was just before eleven o'clock when Agatha pulled off at the end of my street. "Pick me up tomorrow morning at school?" I asked.

"Will do. And by the way, you were brave tonight. Father O'Brien will be impressed."

I smiled. "Thanks." I set my mom's estate file on top of my grandpa's briefcase. "You better hold on to those."

"I got it. Got your back, dude."

"Wait." I pulled the picture of the Soldiers of Bilim in the desert out of the envelope. "I'm keeping this one in case Delmar shows up at my house again." I folded it up and shoved it into my pocket, then climbed out of the car. Time to face the music.

TWENTY-SEVEN

Dr. Anderson's car was still in the driveway. *Ugh.*

I tilted back the concrete frog on our porch and snatched up the key. Then, as quietly as I could, I opened the door and crept toward the stairway.

"Courtney," my mom's voice rang out. "In the kitchen, sweetie."

"Oh. Hi, Mom. I'm super tired. I'm just gonna go to my room and crash."

"In here. Now." She didn't sound angry, but she definitely meant business.

I walked into the kitchen. My mom and Dr. Anderson were sitting at the table, sharing a bowl of popcorn. *Puke.*

"Sit down, Courtney," Dr. Anderson said.

"No thanks."

They exchanged *I-told-you-so* looks. I glanced down at my hands and knees, caked with dirt. My mom stood up from the table.

"Let's go in my office," she said. She took me by the arm—not hard, but firmly—and guided me out of the kitchen and through her study door. Then she flipped on the light and shut the door behind us.

"I'm worried about you, Courtney." Her eyes looked puffy, like she'd been crying. I had to be seeing things, though, because my mom never cried. "Your friends are worried about you," she said. "Dr. Anderson is worried about you. We're all very worried."

"I'm so sorry, Mom. I should've told Kaelyn I was going to the movies, but I was totally in a hurry. It won't happen again."

She studied my muddy pants, then glanced over at her desk. Then back at me. "There's a file missing from my drawer."

"Really? Wow. Bummer." How the hell had she noticed that already?

"I know where you were," she said, raising her eyebrows.

"I was at the movies. I swear!"

"The Lake County Sheriff's Department called. One of the neighbors reported that someone had tripped your grandfather's homemade burglar alarm at the cottage."

"What cottage?"

"Courtney! This is no joke. You're throwing your life away for delusions of Martian visitors and secret tattoo conspiracies."

"No, it's not like that." I took a deep breath. I was her daughter. Whether she liked it or not, she had to know the truth about me.

"Yes, it is! And I can't just stand by and watch. I will not have you end up crazy like your grandfather."

"Mom, listen. You got it all wrong. Grandpa and me—"

"No, young lady! You have it all wrong. Your grandfather threw away his family to chase his delusions. His irresponsibility cost him his life, and nearly cost you yours!"

"Mom, Grandpa didn't try to drown me. He was trying to protect me from bad men."

"Courtney, stop it! Your grandfather tried to drown you in his bathtub, and that's all there is to it."

Bathtub? She'd been to the cottage a hundred times. She had to know there was no bathtub. Had she let me believe that story all this time to turn me against my grandpa?

I pulled at my hair in frustration. *No, she wouldn't do that*

170

to me. I was her daughter. Even if she had, it was for my own good. She was never close to her father. She didn't know him like I did. She thought he was crazy. With all his alien talk, who wouldn't think that? But I needed her to know I wasn't crazy. I needed her to know the truth about her daughter.

"Mom, just listen to me once, please. I know it sounds crazy, but what if Grandpa wasn't making up all that stuff about aliens? What if he was an agent for the Knights of Magi and his job was to protect a secret alien-human bloodline? And what if I inherited that bloodline, and that's why I see aliens?"

"That's it. I've heard enough," She pushed past me and yanked open the door. "Roger! I need you! Now!"

"Mom?"

All of a sudden, Dr. Anderson was standing in the doorway.

My mom grabbed me from behind.

"Get off me!" As I tried to jerk away from her, I felt a sharp sting in my left bicep. "Oww! What was that?"

Then I saw the syringe in Dr. Anderson's hand. "Wait. What did you just do?" I rubbed my arm. "Mom? He stuck me with a needle."

"Courtney, I've administered a sedative to calm you down," Dr. Anderson said.

"You'll thank me for this later, sweetie," my mom said.

I can't believe this! I stared at my mom and shook my head. "I need air." I moved toward the door. Dr. Anderson started to block me from leaving, but my mom put a hand on his arm.

"Let her go, Roger."

My duffel bag was next to the front door. I opened it up. It was my things—pajamas and comfy sweatshirts, my toothbrush and shampoo . . . *This can't be happening, they're sending me to the loony bin again!* I walked out onto the drive-way, pulled out my phone, dialed Agatha. Luckily, she picked up on the first ring.

"Agatha! Listen, this is bad. My mom's going crazy. I think she's putting me back in the hospital. She drugged me with something and I can feel it making things slow. You gotta come get me."

"Dude. Get out of there. Run! And keep moving! I'll call you in ten."

"All right." I felt dizzy, but I started down the driveway.

"Courtney?" It was my mom. She and Dr. Anderson were following me.

I didn't know where I was going, but I had to keep moving. Nothing was making sense. I was sitting on the grass. I needed to get somewhere, but I couldn't remember why.

TWENTY-EIGHT

A strange thumping sound was coming from somewhere. And I could smell perfume.

My eyes opened and the thumping grew louder.

"Ouch." I groaned and my eyes fell shut. The thumping was coming from inside my head. And it totally killed.

I forced my eyes open again. A pretty lady with an old-fashioned updo and red lipstick leaned over me. She looked familiar, but I couldn't remember where I knew her from.

My wrist throbbed. I tried to lift my arm, but something stopped it. I tried to sit up, but couldn't. Looking down at my arms and legs, I realized why: there were thick leather cuffs wrapped around my wrists and ankles and belted to the side of the bed frame. I was completely strapped down. In a hospital.

I was in a normal hospital room, though. With a TV, and an electric bed, and a machine monitoring my heart rate and blood pressure.

But why was I strapped down? *Oh no.* It all came flooding back to me. Mom and Dr. Anderson. The syringe. The duffel bag. They'd had me committed!

I looked at the blond nurse again, who was now fiddling with some equipment on the other side of the room. I definitely remembered her. I was back at Solomon Grace. Where Delmar worked.

"MOM!" I yelled as loud as I could, kicking my legs and trying to jerk my body free of the straps. "HELP. MOM! YOU

CAN'T LEAVE ME HERE! YOU DON'T UNDERSTAND WHO THESE PEOPLE ARE!"

"Oh, bright eyes." The nurse rushed over and put her hand on my shoulder like she was afraid I'd break the straps. "You can't yell like that. This is a hospital."

"I'm on the psych ward, aren't I?"

She nodded her head.

"Listen to me, please." I tried to sit up again, forgetting about the straps holding me down, then collapsed back onto the bed. "This is a huge mistake. My mom's crazy, and her doctor boyfriend's an idiot. There's nothing wrong with me. They're just trying to punish me."

The nurse glanced nervously at the door, then back at me—almost like she wanted to say something. But she didn't.

"Please. You have to believe me," I said. "I need to get out of here. Right now! Just undo these straps and give me my phone so I can call my dad. He'll explain everything and come pick me up. He'll thank you, I swear to God!"

The nurse grabbed a syringe off the tray. "Time for rest."

"No. I can't rest! I have to get out of here."

She leaned over me and injected the needle into the IV tube attached to my arm. "Nighty-night, bright eyes."

"Nooooo!"

I rubbed my eyes as I came to, then immediately kicked my feet. And they moved! No straps were holding me down. I lifted my head off the pillow. I was in a different bed from before. In a totally different room.

Sitting up, I gazed at the closed door. Steel with a metal lock. *Oh no!* I knew exactly where I was. I swiveled my head toward the wall behind me, already knowing what I'd see . . . my insect drawings. Covering most of the wall. I was back in the old psych hospital.

This is not good. How long had I been in here? A nervous feeling rushed into my gut. And why? What was Dr. Delmar planning to do to me?

I carefully climbed off the bed and stepped onto the cool tile floor. I needed my phone so I could call Agatha. She could come break me the hell out and take me to see Father O'Brien. We needed to get that badge to him and tell him about the portal machine.

I lay on the floor and looked under the bed, but this time I was out of luck. No plastic bag with my clothes and phone in it. No way to communicate with the outside world.

I paced the tiny room. Knowing Agatha, I was pretty sure she was running around somewhere, working on a plan. I just wished I could talk to her—hear her voice. She'd tell me this was nothing we couldn't handle. I tried to conjure up an image of her in my mind, hoping somehow to connect. But it didn't work. *Right!* I needed a phone . . . now!

I ran to the door, grabbed the handle, and shook it back and forth against the lock.

"Hello! Anyone?" I pounded against the steel door. "Somebody help me, please!"

"Shhh! Quiet." It was a girl's voice, muffled and echoey, coming from somewhere behind me. My eyes darted around my empty room. No one there . . . but I was certain I'd heard a voice. Maybe it was the aliens? Had they come to rescue me?

"Where are you guys?" I called out. "You have to beam me out of here, or whatever it is you do. I've been to the monastery and the cottage, and I get it. I'm totally on my grandpa's side—your side—now!"

"Courtney, be quiet!" said the muffled voice.

Where is it coming from? I crouched down and searched under the bed again. Nothing. But there was a heat vent in the wall next to the foot of the bed.

I hurried over and kneeled down next to it. "Hello?" I said, keeping my voice low. "Anyone there?"

"Courtney! It's me, Haley. From school." The vent distorted her voice a little bit, but it was definitely her. "I'm in the next room."

I lay flat on my stomach. "What are you doing in here, Haley?"

"My mom's a nurse over at the real hospital with Dr. Delmar. I was visiting her, and I saw them wheel you past me!"

I pressed my face against the vent. "Can you get me out of here?"

"Not now. Not when Nurse Aaron's working. You have to be careful."

"I need to get out, Haley."

"I know. I called Agatha and told her they had you locked up in here."

"You talked—Wait. You have a phone on you? I gotta borrow it. I'm in danger!"

"Agatha told me to give you a message. She said, 'No matter what happens, don't tell them about the machine.'"

"What else did she say?" I asked, my voice rising. "Is she coming to break me out?"

"Shh," she hissed. "You're too loud! All she said was that no matter what happens, don't tell them about the machine."

"I got it. Jesus. But what about getting me out of here? You have to help me, Haley!"

"Oh crap," Haley muttered. I could hear shuffling. "They're coming! Get in bed, Courtney! Quick!"

The metal bolt unlocked behind me and I jumped up and scrambled to my bed just before the door creaked open.

"Hello again, Courtney."

I squinted up from my pillow. It was the mean nurse from Holy Donut—the one with the tattoos on his forearms.

He pushed a medicine cart into the room, and a female nurse with short brown hair walked in behind him. She shut the door and leaned back against it. She was muscular like a bodybuilder, but her face looked friendly enough, so I tried to get her attention—to make eye contact with her and somehow communicate that this whole thing was a big mistake, that I was normal and didn't belong in there. But she wouldn't look at me.

There was a medical file in her hand—mine, I guessed. My eyes wandered up from her hand, and that's when I saw it: a tattoo of a snake wrapped around a thorny branch, right there on her left forearm. The same symbol that was on the banner in the Soldiers of Bilim photo from my grandpa's briefcase. I sucked in my breath and looked up at Tattoo Nurse. *Does he have it too?* I scanned his arms and immediately found it. *They're Soldiers of Bilim, just like Dr. Delmar!*

Tattoo Nurse must have noticed me staring at him, because he glared down at me and shook his head.

I gulped. "So wait, you're Nurse Aaron, right?" I asked him, trying to sound friendly and not scared.

"No." He nodded at the female nurse. "She's Nurse Erin. And you don't want her to get angry."

I looked at Nurse Erin and started to smile all friendly, but there was something about her eyes that made my smile fade. It wasn't the color, which was a soft brown; it was the dead look in them. If a person's eyes were the window to the soul, then she had no soul.

"Get the patient some water," Nurse Erin barked. Tattoo Nurse quickly grabbed a gallon jug of water off the bottom shelf of the cart and tipped some of its contents into a plastic cup. He tried to hand the cup to me.

"No thank you," I said.

Nurse Erin opened the file in her hand and pulled out

a piece of paper in a clear plastic cover. She handed it to Tattoo Nurse, and Tattoo Nurse set it on the bed next to me.

I glanced down. It was a sketch of the my grandpa's machine. The machine Agatha had warned me not to tell anyone about.

"Recognize that?" Tattoo Nurse asked. His voice was almost casual, like he didn't care one way or another how I answered. So I was about to tell him I'd never seen it. But then I looked over at Nurse Erin. Her beady eyes locked on mine like she could read my mind.

I felt the blood drain from my face, and the air escaped my lungs. I was shaking. No matter what I said, I'd sound totally guilty.

Looking down at the drawing, I kept my mouth shut and shook my head no.

"We're going to ask you once more, nicely." Nurse Erin stepped toward me. "Where is Samuel Dahlen's portal machine?"

"I don't know. I swear!" I said. "I don't know what that is."

"Then where is his transponder badge?"

"Badge? I don't remember anything about a badge. He's been dead since I was seven. I barely remember him."

"Let's see if we can jog your memory," Nurse Erin said. "Grab her shoulders!"

"No, wait! This is a mistake!" I scrambled to the other end of the bed. But Tattoo Nurse lunged at me, grabbed my wrist, and yanked me back to the other end of the bed.

"Ouch! You're hurting me!"

He grabbed my hair with his other hand.

"OWWWW!" I yelled.

He pulled me by my hair until I was lying down on my back, staring up at the ceiling, my head hanging off the bed. I felt a strap tighten around my legs, then another cinch down across my chest. *They know I'm lying. What are they going to do to me?*

I heard a glug-glug sound. Out of the corner of my eye, I could see Nurse Erin pouring water from the gallon jug onto something red. She leaned over me with a dripping-wet red washcloth in her hand.

"Let me go, please!" I begged her, my voice coated with fear. "I don't know anything! I'm just a kid!"

Smirking, Nurse Erin dropped the washcloth over my eyes and mouth.

I couldn't see; the washcloth was pressed against my face. My heart pounded in my throat. I couldn't get any air. "I can't breathe!" I shouted, but my voice was muffled by the cloth. I jerked my head and tried to shake it off, but one of them grabbed my head with both hands and held it still.

Oh God . . . they're gonna kill me!

I heard the glug-glug sound again.

"Stop, please, I—"

Water gushed down over my face, rushing into my mouth and nose. I gagged, and then heaved, but the water kept pouring into my mouth and against the back of my throat. I couldn't swallow. Or breathe. I gagged again, and again. The screen in my mind began to dim. They were drowning me! I tried to fight, but they were so strong, I didn't have the strength.

Then, just as suddenly as it had begun, the water stopped. The cloth was yanked off my face.

Gulping in huge lungfuls of breath, I stared up at Tattoo Nurse in horror.

Nurse Erin leaned in. "Where's your grandfather's portal machine, Courtney?" she asked.

I have to tell her where it is. But Agatha said not to tell them, no matter what.

I shook my head. "I don't know."

Nurse Erin stared down at me. The look in her eyes was slightly less menacing now. Maybe she believed me? My heart was pounding so fast I thought it might explode.

Tattoo Nurse tossed the wet cloth over my whole face again.

"AHHH! PLEASE!" I yelled. "I'll tell you anything I know, I swear. Just don't kill me."

"We know your grandpa left you encrypted instructions on how to operate the helmet," Nurse Erin asked. "So where is the file saved? Is it encoded into the portal machine? Or is it in the badge?"

WHAT? "I don't know anything about instructions or a helmet. I swear on my life." I tried to turn in the direction of her voice, but Tattoo Nurse grabbed my hair and yanked my head back down. I screamed, but that only made him tighten his grip.

Glug-glug. Water rushed over my face. I gagged again and again, my chest jerking violently. I couldn't breathe. The darkness started to creep in again.

"Stop!" Nurse Erin commanded.

The rush of water stopped. I tried to spit the water in my mouth out, but the cloth blocked it, and I started choking again. Tattoo Nurse turned my head, and I coughed out the rest of the water. When I finally stopped gagging, they yanked the cloth off of my head.

I started to sit up, except Tattoo Nurse pulled me back down by my hair. "Ouch!" Nurse Erin walked around the side of the bed and stared down at me as I gasped for breath and tried to regain my bearings. In her hand was the water jug. She held it up to the light.

It was still half full.

"Any last words, Courtney?" she asked.

Last words? She had to be bluffing, didn't she? Shaking with fear, I stared up at her. "I swear on my life, I don't know about any instructions, and I've never seen that in my life!"

She shook her head, then raised the water jug over my mouth. "Open up."

I locked my lips shut and tried to twist my head away, but Tattoo Nurse still had me in his viselike grip.

"Open up!" Nurse Erin grinned down at me.

I shook my head.

She set the jug down, jabbed her thumb under my chin, and forced my mouth open. There was something plastic in her other hand. A big plastic syringe.

"Sweet dreams," she said, and thick, medicinal-tasting liquid warmed my tongue and the back of my throat. Tattoo Nurse clamped my jaw shut. I had no choice but to swallow.

Nurse Erin patted me on the cheek. "You're a tough little bitch," she said, "that's for sure."

She unstrapped my legs and my chest. I flipped over onto my stomach and spat what little medicine I hadn't swallowed out onto the floor. "You guys could have killed me!"

"Not really. Felt like it, though, didn't it?" she asked.

Tattoo Nurse unlocked the door, and Nurse Erin pushed the cart out. Once they were both outside, they slammed my door shut, and I heard the deadbolt lock.

I was soaking wet and shaking. But I was alive!

Is Haley still there? Did she hear everything that just happened?

I slid off my bed onto the floor. The medicine Nurse Erin had made me swallow was settling in, because I was too dizzy to stand up. I crawled over to the heat vent. "Haley? Are you there?"

Gravity was working against me. I lay down on the floor. "Haley?" I reached my hand up to toward the vent, but my arm was too heavy. It fell to the floor.

Then I saw it: a tiny piece of rolled up paper sticking

out of the vent. Mustering up the last of my strength, I pulled the paper out and unrolled it. It was a gum wrapper. Written on the back in red ink was a message:

Talk to you tomorrow night. Later. —Haley

"Talk to you tomorrow night? Later?" *Seriously, Haley? I mean, seriously!* I read it again, then shoved it back through the vent in disgust. *I almost drown in my bed, and those are her parting words of wisdom? Ugh!*

Exhausted, I glanced over at the bed. It might as well have been miles away. The floor would have to do. I closed my eyes.

TWENTY-NINE

Something smelled good. Like pancakes. I opened my eyes to darkness.

"Well, good afternoon."

"Who's there?" I quickly sat up from the floor and stared around me like a wild animal, waiting for my eyes to adjust to the dark.

"No need to be frightened, Courtney." Dr. Delmar was sitting on the bed, looking down at me. He stood and pulled a filthy plastic curtain back from the window, and sunlight shimmered across my Magi beetle drawings on the wall behind him. I shaded my eyes. They looked like the cave drawings of a lunatic.

"You must be hungry. Come on over." He slid a cafeteria tray across the bed toward me.

I shook my head, but the smell of maple syrup made my mouth water. I crawled over and was about to grab the tray when I saw the medical cart. It was just like the one Nurse Erin had.

I scurried back to the heat vent, my pulse racing.

"Don't be frightened," he said. "Please. We're on the same team. I came to get you out of here."

"You did?" I wanted to believe him. But the way his eyes were shifting back and forth told me I probably shouldn't.

"Eat some dinner. I brought your favorites—pancakes and bacon."

He was right about pancakes and bacon being my

favorites. But how the hell did he know that? And was it really dinnertime already? *I must've slept all night and day.*

I didn't trust Dr. Delmar. But I hadn't eaten in days, and I was starving. So I scampered back over, pulled the tray down onto the floor, and shoved an entire pancake in my mouth. Then I drained the plastic cup of orange juice in two big gulps.

"I need to go home, Dr. Delmar. This whole thing's a mistake. My mom and her idiot boyfriend think I'm crazy, but I'm not."

Dr. Delmar reached down to the bottom shelf of the cart and pulled out a clear plastic bag. I recognized my clothes. *Is he really gonna let me get dressed? Is he gonna let me leave?* I could see my phone in the bottom of the bag too. I really wanted that phone. I shoved a piece of bacon into my mouth and tried not to stare too hard at my stuff.

"I have something for you." He unfolded a thick piece of paper and held it up for me to see. It was the photo of the Soldiers of Bilim that I'd shoved in my pocket: the army tank with the snake banner and the bearded men.

I stopped chewing and set the pancake I was holding back on the plate.

"Five days ago you were a frightened child running from imaginary alien monsters in your bedroom," he said. "Now you're a sworn agent of the Magi, on a mission to stop the ruthless Dr. Delmar and the Soldiers of Bilim. Isn't that right?"

"What? No!" I shook my head. "I'm not a sworn anything. I'm just here because my mom thinks I'm crazy."

Dr. Delmar reached down, grabbed a piece of bacon off my plate, and dipped it into a puddle of maple syrup. He took a bite and stared down at me. "The reason your mother suspects that you're crazy is because you set the alarm off at your grandfather's cottage while you were retrieving the radio portal machine for your Magi friends. Isn't that right? She thinks you're chasing imaginary aliens, poking around where you don't belong. But we know what you're really up to, don't we?"

My mouth went dry. *He knows about the cottage.* I tried not to reveal my panic. "I don't have any machine," I said, careful to keep my voice level. "I just went to the cottage because I haven't been there since I was a kid. When my grandpa tried to drown me. I was, you know . . . trying to face my fears and stuff."

He took one more bite of his bacon and then tossed what was left onto my stack of pancakes.

Puke! I kicked the tray away, though my stomach was still growling.

"I'm sure your priestly friends at the monastery told you all about the evil Soldiers of Bilim?"

My throat tightened.

He knows about the monastery, too? This was exactly the kind of danger Father O'Brien had been trying to protect himself and the Monastery against. And I'd probably led them right to them!

"And no doubt, they gave you a speech about our sinister plans to expose the sacred alien bloodline and destroy the foundations of all things sacred?" he asked.

Yeah, pretty much, I thought. But I needed to keep that secret. I glanced up at him and tried not to look guilty. "I don't know anything about priests or soldiers."

"Yes you do. You're working with the Magi."

"No, I'm not. That's the truth!"

"Let me tell you about truth, Courtney." Dr. Delmar pulled off his glasses and stared at me. "The Soldiers of Bilim have no interest in your biblical gods. Or your ancient witchcraft sanctuaries. Or the location of Father O'Brien's secret beer garden. Or about three wise men, or the alien origin of Jesus's blood."

"You don't?" I asked, sounding surprised. *Oh shit!* The words had slipped out. And the way I'd asked, I might as well have just admitted that I knew all about the Magi and their evil ways.

Delmar grinned. Then shook his head. "The Bilim are men of science, Courtney. We're the good guys. We always have been. It's truth we serve."

Now I was more confused than scared. But one thing was certain: I needed to get the hell out of there. "If you're really the good guys, then tell my mom I'm all better and let me go home."

Dr. Delmar chuckled. "I'm afraid it's not that simple, Courtney." He stood up from his chair and glanced out the barred window. "I don't blame you for siding with the Magi. Sworn agent or not, it's in your blood. But you have something I need. And I plan to get it."

My stomach clenched. "If this is still about that stupid portal machine, I already told you, I've never seen it before in my life!"

"I'm sorry you had to go through all that questioning with Nurse Erin." He turned from the window and looked down at me. "As it turns out, we don't even need your grandfather's portal machine."

"You don't?"

"No. Because we've got you!"

I shifted nervously on the floor. "What's that supposed to mean?"

"Come over here and look out the window with me," he said.

Shit. Shit. Shit. I stood up and walked over next to Dr. Delmar. There was no plate of glass, or even a screen, in the window. Just old metal bars across an opening to the outside.

He gazed up at the sky. "It's astonishing, isn't it?" I felt his hand on the back of my neck. "Two universes right outside our window: ours and the aliens'. Two worlds conjoined in time and space, yet each completely undetectable by the other. It's mind-boggling to think about, isn't it?"

"More like creepy." I glanced down at the floor. "To me, anyway."

His breathing got heavier, and I could smell stale coffee on his breath.

"You're a bloodliner, Courtney. I'm just a humble servant of science. Tell me, how is it that for thousands of years the bloodliners have allowed their alien brethren full access to our universe, yet the human race still knows nothing of *their* world?" The veins were protruding from his forehead now.

I shrugged, and I felt the weight of his hand encircling my neck. "I just found out aliens were real the other day, from you, I swear." It was hard to think with his thumb resting against my throat.

"I'll tell you why we know nothing of the aliens' universe, or their species, or their philosophies, or their biological makeup, or their technology or plans." He pulled me by the neck, forcing me to shuffle my feet over so we were standing shoulder to shoulder. His thumb tightened against my throat as he spoke. "It's because the Magi stand around with their hands in their holy pockets and let the aliens travel freely between the two universes, and yet they ask for nothing from them in return!"

"You're hurting me, Dr. Delmar."

He let go of my neck and pushed his glasses back on, then wiped his hands on his sweater, over and over, like he was embarrassed. "You still don't get it. No one does." He pulled off his glasses again, tried to clean them on his scratchy sweater. "There's an entire alien universe out there, filled with incredible species and unimaginable civilizations. Yet the Magi treat it like some sacred mystery instead of the invaluable source of scientific knowledge and technological advances that it is!"

"I get your frustration. I do," I said.

"Do you?" Dr. Delmar banged a fist against the window bars, and I flinched. Little pieces of cement fell from around the window to the floor.

"Do you hear me out there?" he yelled through the metal bars, his voice going up in pitch. "We're coming for you!"

Oh man! He's officially crazy! I slid along the wall away from the window.

Catching sight of my movement, Dr. Delmar pivoted toward me, his eyes flashing wildly. "You're trying to escape?"

I quickly shook my head. "No! I'm listening to you. How could I escape? I'm locked in here."

"You want to go home, Courtney, don't you?" he said. His voice was gentler now, but the unstable look was still in his eyes.

I nodded. "Yeah, I really do."

He marched over and pushed his face close into mine. "Then tell me you understand that the Soldiers of Bilim are not the enemy!" he said. "It's the Magi who've hidden the alien presence and kept mankind in darkness for thousands of years!"

I wiped his spit from my cheeks. "I'm not sure—"

"Courtney, think! What kind of allies can these Evolarian creatures possibly be if we open our world to them and they give us nothing in return? What is it they're hiding?"

"I don't know. I swear! I've never thought about it that way," I said.

He closed his eyes and took a loud, deep breath.

I glanced at the door. Then at the window. I was trapped

in hell. Where were my so-called alien friends when I needed them? *Wait!*

"Okay. Listen, Dr. Delmar," I said, looking up at him. "There's one thing I do know, and that's how to talk to the aliens. For whatever reason, though, they refuse to visit me here in the hospital. But if you tell my mom I'm all better, and you let me out of here, I'll go home and talk to the aliens for you. Tonight in my bedroom. I'll tell them how you're pissed off about the Magi controlling everything, and how you want to know stuff about science and technology, and they'll tell me the answers, or how to find them. Then I'll write everything down and bring it to you. I want to help you, I swear. You just have to let me out of here!"

Dr. Delmar laughed. Then he moved over to the bed and sat down. Resting his chin in his hands, he stared straight ahead. "I'll tell your mother you're all better," he said.

"You will?"

"Yes." He continued staring at the wall. "Right after you do something for me."

"Okay." I bounced on my toes a little. "Just tell me what to do."

"You're not going to talk to your alien friends for me, Courtney. It's too late for that. You're going to open up a wormhole into their world for me. And I'm going to invite their Drazgorn foes into our world for a little sit-down."

"Huh? What's a Drazgorn?" I shook my head. "And open a wormhole? That's . . . What makes you think I can do that?"

He locked eyes with me.

"Oh, I think there are lots of neat tricks that little mind of yours can do. Things that would surprise us both." He pulled the medical cart over so that it was pressed up against his knees, then, grabbed the handles and lifted himself up to his feet. "Get your beauty sleep, young lady." I watched him push the cart, and along with it, the clear plastic bag with my phone and my clothing in it, over to the door. He slipped the key on his belt into the lock. "Tomorrow you're going to help me make history."

After shoving the cart into the hallway, he hurried out of my room after it. The door slammed shut with a bang. I heard the deadbolt slide into place, and then nothing.

I fell back onto the bed. *Whether he's evil or not, he's definitely crazy, and totally dangerous!* I pulled at my hair. *How do you open up a wormhole to another universe? What does that even mean? This is insane!*

A shiver of electricity trickled down my neck. I sprang up.

But the room was empty. Then I saw her in my head. Agatha! She was at the monastery, in the beer garden, talking to Father O'Brien. She was showing him the badge. Behind them, the shutters were open and I could see the *Gift of the Magi* painting. The burning sky and evil men climbing up the mountain.

"Agatha!" I whispered loudly.

Agatha jerked her head around so she was staring right at me. "Courtney?" she mouthed.

It worked! "Yeah! It's me! I'm in the hospital!" I yelled.

But before she could respond, she was gone from my head, and I was alone in my barred cell again.

Ugh! I fell back on my bed and kicked my legs in frustration.

I couldn't sleep. Or sit still. No matter how hard I tried.

I sat up on my bed, and my whole chest tingled with nervous electricity. *No!* I jammed the tips of my fingers into my guts, just below my sternum, and tried to poke at whatever nerves or trapped energy were causing the dreadful tingle, but it didn't work. My body was on fire.

Standing up, I paced the tiny room. The insects on the walls stared down at me. It was getting harder to breathe. I needed to get the hell out. Right now. I had to get to Father O'Brien and warn him about Dr. Delmar and his crazy plans to open a wormhole. And save myself from whatever he had planned for me!

I ran over to the window and pressed my face against the metal bars. The sun was setting, and the sky was orange and purple. I stared out at the parking lot and breathed in the cool air. I tilted my head so I was looking straight down the building. I was only two stories up. And I could see the huge garbage dumpster right below my window. If I could just dislodge a few of the bars, I could get a better look. And maybe squeeze out and drop down onto the dumpster?

I took a look at what I was working with. *You gotta be kidding me!* Just two rusty screws were holding the whole crisscross of bars in place. I grabbed the bars and shook them as hard as I could. The screws moved a little. Still holding the bars, I wiggled them back and forth until the top half pulled out from the cement. *Almost there!* I grabbed the topmost bar with both hands and pulled down with all my weight—and with a *creaaak, snap!* the whole crisscross pulled out from the cement.

I can't believe that worked! I set the bars on the floor and leaned out the window. The top of the dumpster was flipped back, and piled up inside were those white ceiling tiles I'd seen the construction guys pulling down the first time I came there. *Are you really thinking about doing this, Courtney?*

I dragged the bed over to the window and used it to climb up onto the windowsill, then sat down with my feet hanging out and stared down at the dumpster. *No way.* I'd never be able to jump facing forward. So I twisted around until I was on my stomach, and my legs and feet were hanging down against the brick outside of the building. Then, gripping the edge of the sill, I slowly lowered myself down until I was dangling.

Within seconds, my hands and the muscles in my arms ached. I let go.

Ahhhhhh!

My feet hit first, and my knees buckled. Before I could recover from the impact, something cracked beneath me, and I fell backward. I tried to get my hands behind me to catch myself. My head got there first.

THIRTY

A strange buzzing roused me out of a dream about floating in bright light. My mouth tasted like blood, and the back of my head hurt. But when I opened my eyes, I saw sky—starless and black, except for a sliver of the moon. *Wait.* I was free!

I sat up. It was hard to guess how long I had been outside, knocked out or whatever—it had still been light out when I jumped—but at least my body was in one piece. I rubbed the back of my head and, wincing, felt a bump.

But I didn't care. I was away from Dr. Delmar. Now I just needed to find Agatha so we could warn Father O'Brien about his plans.

I climbed to my feet, and a buzzing rose up in my ears, and my legs felt wobbly and my head dizzy. I grabbed the wall and was lowering myself down onto an old mattress when warm light struck my face.

Huh? I squinted my eyes and glanced up. "Whoa!" The aliens from my bedroom were standing inside the dumpster with me, five feet away.

A smile broke across my face. "Hey." I stepped toward them, but lost my balance on an uneven stack of ceiling tiles and fell over. Undaunted, I climbed to my feet again, still smiling. "Where have you guys been?"

The female alien glanced at the others, then back at me, but said nothing.

I carefully stepped over the ceiling tiles that had tripped

me up and made it safely past them onto an old, smelly mattress.

"I've been wanting to talk to you guys," I said. "I was at the monastery. And my grandpa's cottage. We found his badge and the secret-mission memo. I totally get it about you guys now; I know I don't have to be afraid of you. I'm supposed to help the Magi get my grandpa's transport machine so they can stop the Soldiers of Bilim." I reached the end of the mattress and, leaning forward, tried to wrap my arms around the female alien.

She disappeared as I grasped at her, and I fell forward and landed on an old light fixture.

"Ouch. Hey, where did you guys go?" I rolled over. All three of them were behind me now.

We need your help. The female alien's voice crackled in my head. *The stolen helmet is close by. It creates a great danger; it must be recovered.*

I stared at her, and the fogginess began to clear from my mind. "So you guys need your helmet back? The one Agatha's aunt talked about in the memo?"

They glanced at each other, then nodded their heads.

"Okay. But listen, we've got bigger problems than your lost helmet," I said. "The Soldiers of Bilim are really pissed at you guys. Dr. Delmar wants me to open up a wormhole to your universe—he says he doesn't even need my grandpa's machine if he has me. That's why I had to escape. So look, you gotta zap me to the monastery so I can tell Father O'Brien." Closing my eyes, I held out my arms and waited for them to send me back. "Ready when you are!"

We cannot teleport you, the female alien said.

I opened my eyes. "What are you talking about? You did it before. You lifted me out of my bed and zapped me to my grandpa's cottage, and then you almost did it again in Dr. Straka's office."

That was only in your mind, Courtney. This was a new voice. A male one. Somehow I knew it was coming from the tallest alien, so I focused my eyes on him. *We don't have the ability to teleport you,* he said. *We directed you back to your memory of the cottage, but you never left your bed.*

We're running out of time, the female alien said. *Your grandfather's badge will take you to the Point Utterly Between, Courtney. Secure the helmet, and we'll meet you there.*

"But I don't have his badge." I held my hands out for them to see. "And how am I supposed to find the helmet?" I glanced at the shorter alien, hoping he might be the quiet but brilliant voice of reason that our conversation was missing. But he just gazed at me.

"Do you even talk?" I asked him.

He shook his head.

"Great," I said.

There's a wormhole located in the tunnels underneath the old hospital, the tall alien said. *It's been inactive for thousands of years, but the Bilim are trying to use the helmet to open it up. And if they do, it could have devastating consequences for the universes. So you need to recover that helmet. Now.*

"Okay. Wow." I jammed a hand through my hair as I tried to process this new information. "Wait! If the helmet's in the tunnels, why don't you guys just beam in there and grab it? That would be much easier than me trying to break in and steal it."

Unfortunately, it doesn't work like that, the female alien said. *This is your universe to protect, Courtney.*

We have no actual presence in the physical dimension of your universe, the tall alien explained.

I shook my head, then pointed at the female alien. "But she stabbed me in the eye with that needle in my bed—"

That was only in your mind.

The female alien touched my shoulder, and her hand passed right through me.

"Oh man! You're like a hologram," I said.

We're here in light only, Courtney, she said. *That's why we need you to recover the helmet and meet us at the Point Utterly Between.*

I stared at her, and her giant eyes suddenly made me feel sad.

It's time for you to pick up where your grandfather left off and find the helmet, she said. *Only your bloodline has the power to control it. You'll know what to do.*

"I will?" *I never know what to do!* I thought. But something in the way she said it made me believe her. I ignored the fear building in the pit of my stomach. "Okay. I'll do it."

There's a gate protecting the wormhole, the female said. *It's invisible to normal humans, but you'll be able to see it. As long as the gate's still closed, you will be able to procure the helmet and follow the blue light to the Point Utterly Between. We will meet you there.*

"Point Utterly Between? Blue light?" More confused than ever, my eyes bounced from the female alien to the tall alien and back again. "And wait, what if the gate's open?" I asked.

Shut it, the tall alien said. *Then throw the helmet over and into the wormhole. That will collapse the passageway for good. And Courtney: stay away from the red tunnel. It's the mouth of the wormhole, and it will try to draw you in.*

"Okay." I bit my thumbnail. "But can you explain the blue—"

They were gone.

Seriously?

The hairs on my arms suddenly stood up. Something else was out there! I stood on my tiptoes and peeked over the side of the dumpster.

Oh wow! A new crack, at least a foot wide, had twisted its way through the middle of the parking lot. *Is the wormhole making that happen?* Whatever dizziness had been left over from bumping my head was now totally gone. I needed to get that helmet before Dr. Delmar did something seriously bad.

"Courtney?"

I whipped my head left. Haley was sitting on her scooter, over by the corner of the building closest to the service door.

"What are you doing in there?" She hopped off the scooter and started walking over to me. "Wait . . . how . . . ?" She looked up at the brick building. "Did you *jump*?"

I stared out at the crack in the parking lot and the back of my skull tingled. "Do you see that huge crack?"

She turned and looked at the parking lot. "Course I do. I know what's making it too."

"You do? What?"

"Dr. Delmar and Nurse Erin and the others. They've got a helmet down in the tunnels that came from alien astronauts."

The helmet!

I guess the aliens knew what they were talking about. But how did Haley know all this? *Doesn't matter.* I filled my lungs with a long, deliberate breath, then slowly exhaled, and I felt my mind relax. Things—my past, my grandpa's stories, the tattoo—were finally making sense. And I had a mission: find the helmet and stop Dr. Delmar from opening up the wormhole. And now I had someone who could show me where the helmet was!

At least, someone who *claimed* she could.

"An alien astronaut helmet?" I asked, trying to sound doubtful. "Are you sure?"

"Totally sure. I've seen it. It's insanely old-looking."

This felt like destiny.

Suddenly energized, I slung my legs over the rim of the dumpster and dropped down onto the pavement.

"Ouch. You cut your chin," Haley said, studying my face. "I can take you home on my scooter. Or we can go to my house, if you're worried about your mom?"

I looked her in the eyes. "Forget all that. I need you to get me back inside the old hospital and show me the helmet."

"You serious?" She twisted one of her pigtails around her finger.

"Totally serious."

"It's super gross down there. And if you get caught . . ."

"I get it. Still want to go."

"Cool!" she said, grinning. "I was hoping you would ask!" She dug her wool ski hat out of her backpack and pulled it on. "We'll have to sneak in through the service entrance and take the back elevator down to the old laundry area, because there's always a guard by the two main elevators. But we gotta be quick, before the night watch comes on duty. They'll totally kill us if we get caught."

"Then let's not get caught."

THIRTY-ONE

"**F**orty years ago, this place used to hold over a thousand year-round patients," Haley said, pulling open the service door.

Year-round? I glanced back at the school bus. Then at Haley. "Wait, is it Thursday? Or Friday?"

"Thursday," Haley said.

So I had only been in there two days, but that was plenty enough for me.

I followed her into the building, and we tiptoed down the bombed-out hallway.

"So how come you know so much about this place?" I asked, trying to hide the suspicion in my voice. "And, you know, Dr. Delmar and all that?"

"My mom works over in the main hospital, and she's interested in that kind of stuff." Haley stopped at a corner and poked her head around. "It's clear," she said. "Come on!"

We ducked under a strand of yellow caution tape, and then booked it along the back of the old gymnasium, past the *Helter Skelter* graffiti wall.

"Your mom doesn't have a snake-and-thorn tattoo on her arm by any chance, does she?" I had to ask.

"My mom? No."

I followed her into a rickety elevator. She flipped a lever and then pressed B for basement, like she'd done it a hundred times.

"So, hey." I pretended to study my chewed-up fingernails. "*You* don't have a snake-and-thorn tattoo, do you?" I peeked over at her.

"Funny." She locked eyes with me. "I hate the Soldiers of Bilim. They're worse than the Magi, even though the Magi are the ones who raided the Scandinavian holy sites and severed the people's communications with their alien ancestors. That's according to my cousin Jorg, anyway."

The elevator door opened, but I didn't budge.

"Relax, Courtney." Haley grabbed my hand. "I'm totally gonna help you and Agatha stop the apocalypse. Even Jorg's on your side for that. Now come on! This way!"

Jorg—what?

We ran past a row of huge washing machines and ironing presses the size of Ping-Pong tables. Then we cut into a dark tunnel. The floor was wet and the walls smelled like worms and dirt. I didn't know if it was the darkness playing tricks on me or what, but suddenly I could feel the ceiling closing down on us.

"Stop!" I yanked Haley's hand. "You sure you know where we're going?"

"Totally. To the old shower room. There's a closet there where the electrical wires come in. We can climb up into the ventilation and get to ground zero."

"Ground zero?"

"Come on!"

We hurried through the narrow tunnel, and the mud on the floor squished through my bare toes. Up ahead, I could hear a whirring sound, like a super-loud fan or some kind of electric motor. There was light coming from farther down, too.

Haley stopped and, looking at me raised eyebrows, she covered her lips with her finger. Then she crept on. I followed her, my shoulder rubbing against the tunnel wall.

Finally we came to a fork. Haley grabbed my hand again and pulled me left through a doorway.

The old shower room smelled like a dead animal. But there were lights on the walls, and although the white tiles were grimy and cracked, the room was clean compared to the tunnels.

"On the other side of this wall is what they call the staging room," Haley said. "There's usually a guard in there." She caught my eyes. "The guards aren't nice, Courtney. They have guns, and I don't even think they speak English. So we cannot get caught! Understand?"

I swallowed hard. "I understand." *What have I gotten myself into?*

"Cool!" Haley, at least, was unfazed by the danger. She tiptoed across the tile floor, and I followed her into a toilet stall. Near the top of the wall was a hole with light coming in from the next room. Haley motioned for me to stay still; then she carefully climbed up on the toilet seat and looked through the hole. Crouching back down, she nodded her head, the whites of her eyes glowing in the light.

I took a deep breath. Then I stood up and peeked through.

Two guards were seated at a wooden table in what looked like an old locker room, playing cards. Their machine guns rested next to them on the table. *Seriously? Machine guns?*

I scanned the room for anything looking like a space helmet. The place must have been a locker room for the doctors, back in the old days, because it was super nice. Like the locker rooms at my dad's country club, it had wide wooden benches and comfortable chairs, and framed photos all over the walls. Only these photos weren't of golfers. Or golf courses. Instead they showed men in suits and robes. And tanks. And strange technical drawings, and old maps. *No way! This must be the Bilim's headquarters!*

I was sweeping the room with my eyes when the guards

stood up. I froze as I saw why they were standing at attention: Tattoo Nurse had just walked into the room.

Memories of the red washcloth, and of water blocking my airway, flooded my head. I squatted down and took a few quick breaths.

Haley crept out of the toilet stall, and I followed her to the far end of the shower room, then into a closet with electrical wires and breakers all over the walls.

"I didn't see any helmet," I whispered. My heart was pounding.

"No. That's just the staging room. You want to see ground zero, we need to climb up there, into the air duct."

I followed her gaze to a big metal grate near the ceiling.

"See if you can get it down," she said. "I'll keep watch."

Careful not to bump any electrical wires, I rested my foot on top of a metal box attached to the closet wall and, grabbing an exposed pipe, hoisted myself up. I slid the grate out and handed it down to Haley.

"Perfect!" she whispered. "Can you climb in?"

I glanced out the closet door and back at the toilet stall, thirty feet away. Then down at Haley. The chick was either super brave or super stupid. Or maybe both?

I grabbed the lip of the duct and pulled myself up and in. Then I helped Haley.

The air duct was dark. And dusty. After crawling fifty feet on our hands and knees, we finally reached the end. Haley laid herself flat on her stomach.

I stared through the slats of the grate into what was, apparently, ground zero. It was a room not much larger than the one I'd just escaped from, with cracked cement walls and a muddy floor. An electrical wire, as thick as a garden hose and with jumper cable-type clamps on the end of it, stretched across the room to the base of what looked to me like an electrocution chair, complete with leather straps.

Holy shit!

Even creepier, there was a life-size mannequin sitting in the chair! And the top of its bald head was melted and charred black. Staring at it, my skin crawled. *What the heck do they need that thing for?*

"What is this place, Haley?"

"It's horrible, isn't it?"

"Definitely."

The cement wall that the electric chair faced had what looked like a bomb hole right in the middle of it. "What's through there?" I asked, pointing.

"I don't know . . . I've never actually gone down there." She glanced at me. "But I saw a drawing of ground zero in Dr. Delmar's office one time, and his notes said that the hole is the opening of a tunnel that leads to an old dormant wormhole, that's like a passageway to the alien world. According to my cousin, it's got something to do with the apocalypse and stuff, but I don't know what. He only tells me bits and pieces when he needs my help."

She stared at me like she wanted to measure my reaction.

I smiled politely. "Yeah. That's kind of crazy."

I scoped out the room again, through the grate, for anything extraterrestrial-looking. I didn't see any sort of gate, open or closed. Or anything that I might call a wormhole. The only real way in or out of the place, other than the hole in the wall, was through a rusty steel door, and that was shut tight. Next to the electric chair was a black cargo trunk and two metal coolers with big red-and-white stickers that said "HUMAN ORGAN. FOR TRANSPLANT."

I shuddered. I didn't want to think about what those were for.

"Where's the helmet, Haley?" *Please don't say through the bomb hole!*

"They keep it in the trunk next to the chair."

Phew! "Okay, look out."

"Courtney! What are you doing?"

I twisted around so my legs were facing the grate and kicked hard, sending it flying. It fell against the damp floor with a dull thud. *Good thing for mud floors.*

"I'm going down to get the helmet."

Before Haley could protest, I jumped. Thump! I landed on the floor feet-first and caught myself against the wall. I was following instructions from three aliens who'd visited me in a trash dumpster. *This is insane. I'm insane.*

"Courtney! How are you going to get back up?"

"I'll bring the trunk over and climb up on it; then you can pull me up." It would work. I could almost reach the bottom edge of the vent with the tips of my fingers even without the trunk.

Haley started to say something, but I turned my back on her and hurried over to the trunk. Without opening it, I dragged it into the center of the room, away from the jumper cables and puddled water. *Let's not get electrocuted.*

The tall alien had said that as long as the gate wasn't open, I could take the helmet with me. But there was no gate at all . . . was there?

I glanced over at the hole in the wall behind the electric chair. My pulse quickened. *Just get the helmet and get out, Courtney,* I told myself. But I couldn't. I had to see what was through that hole.

I crept toward the hole. The closer I got, the more my brain tingled with a magnetic pull, like it did when I felt an alien presence. But there was something different about this feeling—something dark and unfamiliar. Closing my eyes, I leaned my head in through the hole in the cement. *Please don't let there be an alien monster in here!*

I opened my eyes.

"What's in there?" Haley whisper-yelled at me from the vent.

"Nothing." I wasn't lying; in fact, the bomb hole wasn't even a hole—it was just a deep indent. It really did seem like a bomb or something had gone off. But the wall was so thick that the blast hadn't gone all the way through.

"There's just concrete here." I reached my hand out and touched the rough edge. Something shocked my fingers, and I jerked my hand back. "Ouch!"

"What is it?" Haley whispered.

"I don't know. It stung me, though."

"Grab the helmet and let's get out of here!" she said, sounding a bit panicked.

I turned back around, clicked the latch on the trunk, and swung open the lid. *Jackpot.* Resting in an old wool army blanket was what could only be the alien space helmet I was looking for. It was beautiful in a funky kind of way—shaped like a bike helmet, but with no visor, and it was made out of hundreds of strands of twisted metal. Sort of like my grandpa's badge, but even more complex-looking.

"Do you have it?" Haley asked. I was blocking her view. "Courtney. Hey!"

"It's powerful," I said without taking my eyes off the helmet. I could feel myself being pulled down toward it.

"Grab it and let's go!"

Ignoring her, I ran my fingers along the helmet's metal surface and turned it over. There were two burn spots on the back of it. I glanced down at the jumper cable clamps, then back at the helmet. The cables weren't for the chair; they were for the helmet. Dr. Delmar must have put the helmet on the mannequin and run electricity through it—probably to try to activate it?

I picked the helmet up. I could barely feel its weight in my hands. I raised it up over my head.

"Don't put it on!" Haley whispered loudly. "It's not safe!"

"It looks safe to me." I felt a tickle in my hands. And the top of my head felt warm, like it wanted the helmet on it.

"Seriously!" Haley hissed loudly. "Look at the mannequin; its head is fried! You don't even know what that thing is capable of."

"That's from the jumper cables. It's not hooked up to any electricity now." Leaning forward slightly, I gently slid the helmet down over the top of my head. *Whoa.* It fit perfectly.

But I didn't get to enjoy the sensation for long—the helmet suddenly made a high-pitched screeching noise and tightened onto my head.

"What the heck?" I said, grabbing my head. I couldn't get it off. I turned and glanced at Haley, and I realized that the helmet was messing with my vision. Haley had a bluish glow to her. Everything had its own color now, and I was sensing what I could only guess were waves of energy. I took a deep breath and felt electricity tingle down through my legs.

I turned around in a circle and smiled at the swirls of color.

"Get out of there," Haley whispered.

"This is so cool!" I said.

I moved toward the electric chair. Even with the colors streaking through my vision, everything looked clearer now. The bomb hole wasn't just a jagged dent in the concrete wall after all; I could see where the layer of concrete ended and another wall, this one made of black bricks, began. And embedded in the bricks were blue gemstones the size of pennies! They formed a perfect circle.

I reached my hand out and ran my fingers over one of

the gemstones. It lit up, and I could feel its energy seeping in through my fingers.

Suddenly the brick surrounding the glowing gem crumbled away, and a small hole opened up.

No way! I pulled my hand back. *Did I do that?*

"Haley! Are you seeing this?" I shouted back.

"I don't see anything but you staring at the wall. Now come on."

I touched one gemstone, then another. I couldn't help myself; they felt warm and alive against my fingertips. With every touch, a stone lit up and a portion of the brick wall crumbled and disappeared, until there was a jagged hole the size of a soccer ball before me. All of the gemstones were glowing now.

"What are you *doing*?" Haley hissed.

What am *I doing?* I stepped back. The gemstones disappeared through the hole behind them, and warm light burst out and lit up my bare knees.

I crouched down and peeked through the hole. On the other side of the wall was a long room made of the same blackish bricks, and in the middle of it was an enormous silvery gate. *The gate to the wormhole! And it's closed!* I grinned. I could take the helmet and go!

I started to turn around, but something beyond the gate caught my eye. Narrowing my eyes, I peered beyond the gate's twisty, antler-like pickets and saw the glowing red tunnel the tall alien had spoken of. It was like a spiraling vortex of breathing red light and flashing energy. This was it: the wormhole. He'd warned me to stay away from it. But he hadn't told me how beautiful it would be.

Moving closer, I reached my hand in through the hole in the wall and stretched my fingers toward the metal gate. I wanted to touch the red tunnel, more than I'd ever wanted anything before.

"Courtney!" Haley's voice pierced through my entrancement. "I can tell that wall is super interesting, but we need to go! Get back up here. Now!"

"Can't you see the gate, and the spiraling light? It's a wormhole, Haley!"

"All I see is you staring at a wall. Can we please go? You're freaking me out!"

That's right. The female alien had said that normal people wouldn't be able to see the gate. So Haley was normal. *Well, normal-ish.*

I stretched my fingers out farther toward the gate. My desire to touch it now felt more like a need. The helmet was vibrating on my head. I stretched farther—and suddenly the gate creaked open. It felt like the helmet, or my brain, was controlling it. Slowly the gate's twisted pickets swung toward my open hand.

Oh gosh! What had I done?

My body jerked forward, slamming my shoulder and chest against the edge of the soccer ball-sized hole. It felt like a giant magnet was trying to pull the helmet and me through, squishing me against the wall so I couldn't breathe.

"Courtney! Quit screwing around," Haley whispered loudly.

I needed to shut the gate before the wormhole pulled me in!

Okay. The tall alien had said to throw the helmet into the wormhole if the gate was open. That's what I had to do!

I reached my hand up and grabbed the back of the helmet to yank it off. But it wouldn't budge.

"Courtney!" Haley called, raising her voice louder than before. "I hear someone coming!"

I turned toward Haley's voice, my heart pounding wildly. But I couldn't see Haley or the vent.

"Hurry up!"

"Just give me a second." Something wasn't right. I was definitely still in the room with the electric chair, but there was a tunnel of blue light in front of me now. It was between me and where Haley was supposed to be.

Blue is good. That's what the tall alien had told me. He might have been wrong about taking the helmet off. Actually, he'd never told me to put it on. Either way, at this point, I had no option but to trust him.

I took a small step forward, toward the blue tunnel, then another, bigger step. One more step—and the floor fell away from under me.

For a moment, I was floating. Then I heard a loud *WWOOOOOOSSSHHH!* And suddenly I was falling forward at the speed of a roller-coaster car. I squeezed my eyes shut, and seconds later—*bang!*—my knees slammed against a hard floor. I flew forward. My right wrist slammed into something hard; my chin landed on my left arm.

I opened my eyes, and the room rotated around me. Gradually, the rotations slowed, and the wooden leg of a chair came into focus. I grabbed the horizontal bar below the chair and pulled myself up to my knees. But it wasn't a chair; it was a bar stool. Standing up, I looked around the room. I was in the monastery bar. *What the hell?*

Everything was the same as it had been the last time I was there, except that all the tables were empty. No monks talking and laughing. Or staring at me. The whole place was empty, and quiet. Like, eerily quiet.

I dusted off my knees and straightened my hospital gown.

"Here, this will help."

"Ahh!" I spun around. Brother Luke stood behind the bar, holding a silver beer stein with the Magi beetle crest on it.

He set it down on the counter for me. *Where the heck did he come from?*

"You startled me," I said. I took a deep breath and tried to smile. Then I glanced down at the spot on the floor where I'd just crash-landed. "I was just in the hospital. Now I'm here. I followed the blue light. They told me to meet . . ."

My eyes shot over to Brother Luke again. He raised his eyebrows expectantly.

"Am I in the alien universe?" I asked. "This is their world, isn't it? Where are they?" I looked around, then back at Luke. "Are you an alien?"

He smiled. "I'm definitely not an alien. And this most definitely isn't an alien universe."

"Then where is everybody?"

"You're in the pub, Courtney. Drink that. It will help your mind adjust."

"No. I know I'm at the monastery. But how exactly did I get here?"

"Ah, right. Guess that's a little confusing," he said. He nodded toward the beer stein like he wanted me to take a drink.

I picked it up and took a sip. It was apple cider, but bitter and thick and strange. *Yuck!* I coughed. "You sure this isn't the alien universe?"

Brother Luke laughed again. "I'm totally sure. This is the pub. It's an acronym. PUB. Point Utterly Between. You're safe here."

"PUB. Okay. Yeah. The Point Utterly Between. That's what the aliens called it too." I sat down on a stool and took another, much more tentative sip of my cider. It still tasted awful, but Brother Luke was right: it was making me feel better. I squinted up at him. "So what exactly is the Point Utterly Between?"

"I'm just an intern with the Magi, so I can't officially

answer that," Brother Luke said, wiping the bar down with a towel, "but unofficially, the PUB is a hyperspace, or a molecularly neutral ground, between the alien universe and the human universe."

"You guys made a bar to hang out in between the universes?" I asked.

He smiled. "Yeah, sort of. It's a buffer zone where inhabitants from both universes can meet without upsetting the magnetic polarity of either one."

"Oh, wow. Okay." Brother Luke was super smart for a monk bartender. Not that monks or bartenders weren't usually smart. But this was fringe-science-smart stuff. "And so you work here in the PUB?"

"Basically. Tending the bar is part of my apprenticeship." He pointed at my chest. "You've got some dried blood on your hospital gown, by the way."

"Oh, I know. I must look horrible." I scraped at the patch of red with my fingernail. "I've been locked up in a mental hospital. And I had to jump out of a window into a dumpster. I hit my head." I looked up and caught him staring at me like he didn't know what to think. "You think I'm weird?"

He laughed and leaned against the counter. "I'm a monk, working in the PUB, training for a position with the Knights of Magi. Two years ago I was studying astrophysics at MIT and serving twenty-dollar craft cocktails on Newbury Street. Nothing strikes me as weird anymore."

"Yeah, I know what you mean." My definition of *weird* had definitely morphed over the past few days. I took a deep breath. I didn't know if it was the cider, or if my nerves were just calming down, but my anxiety was gone; I felt super relaxed. I slouched on the bar stool and gently rocked my legs back and forth.

"Hey! Don't get too relaxed." He nudged my elbow. "You need to go through that door and meet with the others."

I glanced in the direction he'd nodded toward. The wooden door to the beer garden was cracked open.

"The others?" I spun back to look at Brother Luke. "Who are the 'others'? My alien friends? Is that what you call them?"

"I don't know who you're meeting with. But if you're here, you're in the big leagues now, Space Girl."

Space Girl, huh? I liked the sound of that.

Brother Luke grabbed my beer stein from my hand. "You gotta go!"

"Oh, right! Thanks." I stood up from my seat and hurried toward the door.

THIRTY-TWO

I poked my head through the door. My alien friends were nowhere in sight. And the beer garden looked exactly the same as last time, except that the tree in the middle of the courtyard was totally gone.

"There she is." Father O'Brien stood up from the picnic table holding what looked like a television remote control.

I gazed up through the big hole in the roof where the tree used to be. The sky was a swirl of bright silver with bursts of deep red. "Wow!"

"Wow, indeed," Father O'Brien said. "Nothing quite like the glow of the multiverse sky."

I squinted my eyes, and the sky glowed brighter.

"It's beautiful," I said. "But why's it so different? What's a multiverse?"

"You have a lot to learn if you want to be a sworn agent of the Magi," Father O'Brien said.

"A sworn agent?" I smiled at the sound of it. "Really?"

"There are two known universes traversing Earth's home galaxy," he said, ignoring my questions. "The universe we live in and an alien universe. Two worlds conjoined in time and space, as your grandfather would say, but fated to remain physically separated and hidden from each other."

"Somebody else mentioned that," I said, biting my thumb-nail. "But the part that I still don't get is, if the universes are totally separated, then how do the aliens get here?"

"Other than to the PUB, which is neutral ground, the

Evolarians don't physically travel to our universe anymore. They navigate interdimensional channels and visit blood-liners with their minds."

He typed something into his remote control, then pointed it at an old, boxy TV sitting on a shelf next to the Magi crest. It was totally antique, with metal antennas sticking out the top, and it definitely hadn't been there last time I was in the garden.

Father O'Brien pressed a button, clearly expecting that it would do something, but the picture didn't change from static. "Bollocks!" He banged the top of the TV, twice, but nothing happened. "Take a seat," he said curtly. "We don't have much time before your meeting with command."

"Command?" Hurrying over to the picnic table, I glanced up toward the sky again. There was something up there; I could feel it tickling under my skin.

"Sit, child!"

"Okay, sorry!" I dropped to the bench.

He sat down across from me. "I take it you know about the wormholes and why you're here?" he asked.

I bit my lip. "I know a little."

"Wormholes link the universes," he said. "That's how the Evolarians first traveled from their universe to ours. They came through wormholes. Or 'star gates,' if you like. But when they discovered that the universes were molecularly incompatible, the passageways had to be closed and all access to their gates buried over."

Molecularly incompatible? Dr. Delmar hadn't mentioned that. Neither had the aliens in the dumpster. "But so—"

Father O'Brien held his remote up. The TV beeped twice, and the screen turned white.

"Ahh, there we go." He turned back and stared at me. "Now, where is this badge of yours?"

"Badge?" I asked.

"That *is* what transported you here, isn't it? Your grand-father's badge?"

"No. I don't have the badge. Agatha does." Suddenly, I really missed Agatha. "Wait. Do you guys have a phone I can use? I really need to call her."

"Agatha didn't sneak the badge into the hospital and deliver it to you?"

I shook my head.

Father O'Brien narrowed his eye in suspicion. "If you don't have the badge, then how in God's name did you transport into the PUB?"

In all the confusion, I'd forgotten about the helmet. *What happened to it?* I reached up to touch my head, hoping it was still there but knowing it wasn't. "I had a helmet . . ."

"The missing Solomon-Trondheim helmet?" Father O'Brien's voice held a mix of excitement and anger.

"Yeah, I guess so. The aliens visited me in the dumpster, and they told me to find the missing helmet and bring it here. So I snuck down into the tunnels and found it, and it zapped me here." I quickly looked around. "I don't understand why the aliens aren't here."

"Child!" His eyes were as black as his priest shirt. "I'm getting a bad feeling about you."

"About me?" I swallowed hard. "You serious?"

He raised his remote control to his mouth like a phone. "OB to command, I need Special Agent One Who Drinks and Dances to transport to the PUB, immediately."

Setting the remote down, he pressed the palms of his hands together, like he was praying, then glared at me. "You've been locked up for two days under the psychiatric care of a ranking officer of the Soldiers of Bilim."

I couldn't tell if it was a question or not, but everything he was saying was making me uncomfortable. "Yeah. Dr. Delmar. And some nurses."

Brady G. Stefani

"You've got blood on your shirt and you're covered in dirt, as if you've been tortured. But here you are." I tried to smile at him. "Did they send you here? Are you working for them?"

"What?" My smile vanished. "No! I cut my chin when I fell, and the dirt's from the tunnels. How can you think that about me, Father O'Brien? I went to the cottage and found the badge like you told me to. How can I be bad?"

"The Bilim are trained paramilitary soldiers. Yet somehow you managed not only to escape the Bilim's capture but also to recover the missing Solomon-Trondheim helmet and use it to transport to the PUB?"

Hearing his logic made me realize I didn't have a very believable story. I felt tears welling up in my eyes.

His eyes narrowed. "Tell me, why I should believe you?"

"Because I'm telling the truth." I wiped my eyes.

"That's not good enough!" he shouted. He sounded like my soccer coach when he got angry. "I don't believe it!"

"I don't know what to believe either!" I yelled back. "Last week I didn't even believe aliens were real, and I thought my grandpa was crazy. Then I found my grandpa's badge, and I was thrown into a dirty hospital, and Dr. Delmar wants me to help him open up a wormhole. But I jumped out the window to escape and hit my head. And when I woke up in the dumpster, the aliens were there, and they told me it was my mission to go back into the hospital and steal the helmet. So I did it!"

Father O'Brien's expression softened, and he reached across the table and patted me on the shoulder. "Your grandfather would be proud of you."

"Really?" I felt my cheeks flush with warmth.

He nodded. "You're a brave one. You dug deep and found the truth. And you've chosen to fight for the just cause."

"For the just cause?" *Oh God!* I suddenly remembered

what Dr. Delmar had told me about not trusting the aliens—how convincing some of what he'd said had been—and before I knew what was happening, I jumped up from my seat and slammed my hands on the tabletop. "What if you're wrong? What if the aliens are the bad guys?"

He shot me a perturbed look.

"I mean," I rushed on, "what if they're using us? I mean, they told me they'd meet me here and they didn't. They told me to steal back the helmet for them because our universe was in danger, but how do we know that's even true? Dr. Delmar says the Magi help the aliens stay hidden, but the aliens give you guys nothing in return. So maybe we shouldn't give the helmet back?"

Father O'Brien grinned and patted my hand. "You're right to ask these questions. But I assure you, God as my witness, the Evolarians are proven allies of the human race."

"Proven how? Because it seems like they just show up and tell me what to do. They're kinda bossy."

Father O'Brien chuckled. "Our relationship with the Evolarians dates back centuries to before the time of Christ. They came to us with gifts, and seeds of knowledge. And when they discovered that the wormholes they'd opened were causing the universes to tear each other apart at the seams, they closed them and returned home, taking nothing with them."

Tear each other apart at the seams? Dr. Delmar definitely hadn't mentioned that.

"Before they left," he continued, "the aliens conducted bloodletting ceremonies and infused a scattering of humans with the sacred bloodline. It's this bloodline that allows us to remain in communication with the alien universe. We all work together now to keep the universes safe and the wormholes closed off."

"So then the aliens are totally on our side," I said.

"The Evolarians are indeed on our side."

"Okay, but when you say the wormholes had to be closed because the universes were tearing each other apart, do you mean that literally? Or is that just, like, a figure of speech?" I bit my lip.

"Unfortunately, the universes are as opposite as light and darkness. An opened wormhole between them would cause both worlds to tear each other apart—literally. That's why the gates must remain closed."

An image of the opened gate in ground zero flashed into my mind, and stuck. "Oh no!"

"It's ghastly, but true. For thousands of years, seers like Agatha and her aunt Ketti have been prophesying about the reopening of the wormholes and a fiery bridge between earth and sky ending all life. It's an often-repeated prophecy, rumored to have been foretold in the gospel of Mary Magdalene."

My throat tightened. "I have to tell you something, Father O'Brien. When I transported out of the tunnel under the hospital, the gate to the wormhole was open. Because I opened it! I didn't mean to . . . it just happened. And now the universes are going to tear each other apart at the seams, and it's going to be my fault!"

"Jesus, Mary and Joseph!" Father O'Brien scratched his head. Then he shook it.

"Fear not, child," he said. "You came to the right place. The Bilim have been trying to reopen wormholes and unlock alien secrets since long before your grandfather and I were born. It's the Magi's job to stop them"—he clapped his hands together—"and one way or another, that's exactly what we'll do!"

"But how?"

"I don't know." Standing up, he ran his fingers through his gray hair, then started pacing. "It's been over a hundred years since a wormhole was opened using a helmet. These helmets practically have minds of their own. So how we go about closing this wormhole, and how we deal with what could come crawling out of it, are questions for agents to answer. This is not my area of expertise."

"*Crawling* out?" I asked. My skin suddenly itched.

"Let's not worry about that now." Father O'Brien glanced over at the door to the café. "Our best agent should be transporting in through that door any minute now. He's a special bloodliner like you, which means he'll have access to information I don't have. He'll know how to close the wormhole."

"Any minute?" I asked. My pulse picked up. "But that could mean lots of minutes. What if the world is already crumbling apart right now?" I pictured the red tunnel of light and the opened gate back at ground zero. Was Haley still there, waiting for me to come back? What if something happened to her? I needed to do something!

"Maybe the helmet fell off when I landed here," I said. That was it! My heart raced even faster. If I could find the helmet, I could go back to the tunnel and close the gate to the wormhole, and everything would be okay! I started toward the door.

"That's not what happened, Courtney," Father O'Brien said, stopping me in my tracks. "You transported here physically without a badge. The helmet is back at the hospital with the ghost copy of your body."

I whipped back around. "I'm still at the hospital? In ground zero?" A new wave of panic burned through my gut, and I pulled at my hair.

"Not entirely. Just sit down, Courtney. You're making me nervous."

"I can't! I have to go back to the hospital, Father O'Brien. I'm in serious danger! If the Bilim guards find me, they'll strap me in the electric chair and steal the helmet back. Then I'll never be able to shut the wormhole!"

A loud beeping sound pierced the air.

"What's that?" I looked over at the TV.

"It's command center." Father O'Brien rushed over and adjusted the antennae on the TV until the beeping stopped.

An older woman's face appeared on the screen. "Father Seamus O'Brien," her voice crackled.

"Commander Cordelia. Good evening to you," Father O'Brien said.

Commander Cordelia? That was the name on the letter from Agatha's aunt. And the person who had signed my grandpa's last memorandum of mission. She was the one in charge of the Knights of Magi!

"What's our situation, Seamus?" Commander Cordelia asked.

"I'm here with the Hoffman girl. Samuel Dahlen's granddaughter."

"Ah, the One Who Cries," Commander Cordelia said, sounding almost happy.

The One Who Cries? I glared at the TV screen. *Not cool.*

"Yes, that's her." Father O'Brien winked at me. "She located the missing helmet in the tunnels underneath the old Solomon Grace mental hospital. However, she is *not* in possession of her grandfather's badge. Apparently her friend Agatha was unable to deliver it to her in the hospital through the nurse's daughter. So she somehow used the helmet to transport her physical self here, leaving her ghost and the helmet back in the hospital. Now she's worried that she might be captured at any second. And last but not least, she believes that the helmet has already opened up the gate to the wormhole."

"Oh dear," Commander Cordelia said. "The clock is ticking. If we don't shut the wormhole and get the helmet out of there . . ." Her voice trailed off like she couldn't bear to say it.

"We understand the gravity of the situation, Commander," Father O'Brien said. He glanced at the café door. "We're still waiting for Special Agent One Who Drinks and Dances."

"Lovely," the commander said, a hint of sarcasm in her voice. "How is the One Who Cries holding up?"

There was no way *the One Who Cries* was going to be my code name.

"Listen, Commander," I said. "If you guys can zap me back there, I can shut the gate and then sneak the helmet out and bring it to the monastery. But about my name—"

"Oh my, she's a chip off her grandfather's old block. Ready to take on the world!" Commander Cordelia laughed.

Father O'Brien gave me a cautious look. "Only a special bloodliner with a badge can transport another bloodliner in or out of the PUB," he said. "Unfortunately, I'm not a bloodliner, and you don't have a badge."

"So I'm stuck here?" I asked.

"Special Agent One Who Drinks and Dances will have his badge," Father O'Brien said.

"Stand where I can see you, One Who Cries," Commander Cordelia said through the TV.

Father O'Brien grabbed my shoulders and moved me right in front of the TV.

"Ahh. Last time I saw you, young lady, we were tattooing the Magi crest onto your torso, and you were crying for all the world to hear. How old are you now?"

I stared at the TV screen. I'd thought she was wearing a scarf around her head—but no, it was a habit. She was the nun from my grandpa's cottage! *This is getting weirder by the second.*

"I'm fifteen," I said. "But, Commander, I don't cry any-more." *Okay, maybe I had been doing kind of a lot of crying lately, but those were special circumstances and totally shouldn't count.* "So if it's okay, I'd like to have a different special agent code name . . . like Space Girl."

"Young lady, you are no agent, special or otherwise!"

"Oh." I lowered my head. "Sorry."

"However," she said calmly, "if you can help us figure out a way to close the gate and extract that helmet from enemy hands without tearing a hole in our universe and collapsing all known space, I'll call you any name you like."

"Really?" I pushed closer to the TV. "The aliens told me that the helmet is connected to my bloodline. That I'm the only one who can use it. Is that helpful?"

Commander Cordelia turned away from the camera. There was a long silence. Then she turned back toward us. "You're right about the helmet belonging to your bloodline. Evolarians are on their way to the PUB now, and I can't wait for the One Who Drinks and Dances. Raise your right hand, young lady."

I raised my hand.

"With the powers vested in me by the sacred order of the Knights of Magi, I hereby deputize you interim special agent of the Magi."

"Really?" I started to smile.

Commander Cordelia's eyes pierced mine through the TV. "Closing wormholes is not an exact science, Space Girl," she said. "And a bloodline like the one you're a part of is a powerful and mysterious force. There's no way of telling how this particular helmet will interact with your brain. There are dangers involved. Do you understand me?"

"Yeah." I bit a fingernail.

"You'll do just fine." Father O'Brien patted me on the shoulder. "The One Who Drinks and Dances will be able to use his badge to access the records of what the Magi did in the past to close wormholes, and any intelligence we have on the helmet or the Trondheim, Norway, incident of 1912."

"So then it's happened before?" I asked. "And the Magi figured out how to fix it? That's a good thing, right?" I glanced at Father O'Brien, then back at Commander Cordelia.

"Yes. We did. And we will again tonight," the commander said with restored confidence. "Now brace yourself for the portal from Evolarian command!"

"Huh?"

RRRRrrrrrrr! RRRRrrrrrrr! RRRRrrrrrr! The wail of a siren cut through the air, forcing me to cover my ears. Moving away from the TV and toward the center of the courtyard, I looked up. The sky swirled red and black, and sparks of bright white jetted down at me.

"What's happening?" I yelled. But just as Father O'Brien was about to answer, a beam of bright red light burst down through the hole in the roof, striking the ground between us, and he disappeared. *Whuu!*

"What happened to Father O'Brien?" I shouted at the TV.

"He's gone," Commander Cordelia shouted back. "Only bloodliners have the alien brain center that affords them the privilege to remain in the PUB while Evolarian agents are present. Now hold on, Space Girl!"

"To what?" I glanced back at the TV, but it was all static again. The ground trembled underneath me, and a loud whirling sound came from above, so I hurried over and grabbed on to the picnic table.

The tremors stopped. I looked around. The beam of light was gone, and the sky glowed dark red now, almost black. "Hello again, Courtney."

Ahh! I spun back around. Standing in the middle of the courtyard were my three alien friends, only now they weren't naked and gray. They wore shiny black suits, and their skin was a silvery metallic color.

I stared at the female. She looked so different with clothing on. And her eyes were brilliant explosions of silver and
red.

"You're really pretty," I said, smiling.

She smiled back at me.

The café door banged open, and a man wearing rubber
fishing waders and a white dress shirt and tie burst into the
garden. "Sorry I'm late," he said, striding toward me. The
beer stein in his hand was sloshing liquid all over the place.
"You must be the One Who Cries?"

I nodded reluctantly. "Yes, but actually—"

"I'm the One Who Drinks and Dances," he continued.
"But you can call me Agent de Selby. Or just de Selby. No
relation to the painter."

This guy was a special agent of the Magi? Not just any
agent, but their *best* agent? I glanced at the female alien, and
she nodded reassuringly.

Great!

"Nice to meet you, de Selby," I said, shaking his hand.
"I'm Space Girl now, though. Not the One Who Cries."

He rubbed the stubble on his chin. "Space Girl? That'll
work." He winked at me, then turned toward the aliens.

"How's things, Strings?" He nodded to the tall alien, who
nodded back. "Hot Lips Houlihan, always a pleasure." The
female alien smiled. "Silent Bob. Looks like we got the whole
band back together here, huh? So what's the occasion?"

"What's the *occasion*?" I asked. *Isn't this the guy who's supposed to have all the answers? The one who's supposed to be helping me?* I glared at the TV, but it was total static. *Perfect!*

The tall alien sat down on the picnic table. "We've got a
problem, de Selby," he said. His voice sounded different from
when they visited me in the dumpster—less scratchy. "The
Soldiers of Bilim are trying to use the Solomon-Trondheim
helmet to activate the dormant wormhole underneath the

old Solomon Grace mental hospital. Space Girl's body is in the hospital near the gate, wearing the helmet, as we speak."

"That so?" De Selby pulled out a badge like my grandpa's and shined its blue light against the inside of his wrist. Scrolling symbols and letters projected on his skin like it was a movie screen. "Of course she's wearing the helmet," he said, still reading the symbols. "She's Samuel Dahlen's granddaughter. The helmet's linked to her bloodline. So . . . ah, okay. There's the problem."

"What?" I asked.

"Your presence will trigger the helmet to reactivate the wormhole. And as I'm sure you've been told, once the gate's open, all kinds of bad things can come through the wormhole—and the universes will begin to tear each other apart."

"Listen, I know all this stuff," I said, biting my knuckle. "And apparently no one told *you*, but the gate's already open!"

De Selby's eyes grew wide. "Are you certain?"

"Yeah, I'm certain. I'm the one who opened it!"

"Well, then." De Selby loosened his necktie and glanced over at the tall alien. "I guess we have an open wormhole."

"So transport me back there with your badge!" I said. "I'll shut the gate and sneak the helmet out of the hospital!"

"It's not that simple," the tall alien said. "You're wearing the helmet. It's now locked into communication with parts of your brain you don't even know exist."

"Yeah, okay, but what's the big deal? It's still my brain, right? I can make it do what I want."

"Unfortunately, you can't," the female alien said. "The helmet wants to return home to our universe. Depending on its programming, that could mean it's capable of overriding your human brain and forcing you through the wormhole with it—a journey you won't physically survive."

I gulped. "Won't survive?"

"The wormhole would tear you apart, atom by atom," de Selby said.

"That *would* close the gate and shut down the wormhole, though," the tall alien said.

I gasped loudly, and the female alien shot her tall friend a stern warning.

"Hypothetically, that is," he said hastily. "What I mean is, the wormhole and the helmet are interlinked. Once the helmet passes through and returns home, with or without someone wearing it, the wormhole will cease to exist. But obviously we can't ask Space Girl to jump into the wormhole. It's not an option. She'd die."

"No, obviously not an option!" I blurted out. "But what if I go back there and shut the gate real quickly, then run outside? If I do it fast enough, maybe I can make it out before the helmet overrides my brain or whatever. Will that work?"

"Closing the gate will begin the powering down of the wormhole," the tall alien said. "For a few minutes, anyway. But unless you get the helmet far enough away from the wormhole's energy field to sever their connection, it will simply open the gate and the wormhole back up."

"You would need to remove the helmet far from the hospital grounds," the female alien said, shaking her head. "It won't be easy."

"What if de Selby comes with me?" I asked. "And we run out of the hospital with the helmet, then bring it here to the monastery before the gate can open again?"

"Not a bad plan," de Selby said. "Unfortunately, I'm on assignment seven thousand miles from here, off the coast of Chile. And if I don't get back there soon, my cover will be blown wide open."

"Oh." I bit my thumbnail. "Well, then I'll run out and take the helmet to the diner across the parking lot and hide there until I can get a ride back here somehow."

"That'll work," de Selby said.

I looked at the female alien, but she wouldn't return my gaze.

"Everyone in agreement on this?" de Selby asked, fidgeting with his badge.

"You'd better tell her about the Drazgorns," the tall alien said.

"What's a Drazgorn?" I asked. "Dr. Delmar mentioned them too, but he didn't tell me what they were."

"Drazgorn worms," de Selby said. "Nasty little spidery-legged millipede-looking buggers. Rumor is they're always first out through wormholes. But I've yet to see a live one."

I wrinkled my nose. "I don't like the sound of that."

"Well, they won't like the helmet, and they won't like you," the female alien said sternly. "So you'll have to kill them!"

"You want me to kill bugs now too?" I said, feeling overwhelmed. "Don't I have enough to deal with already?"

"Enough talk," de Selby said. "It's time to send Space Girl back. Agreed?"

"Agreed," the tall alien said. The other two nodded.

De Selby held up his badge and pointed a beam of blue light at my chest. "Ready to beam back?"

"I guess."

"Clear your mind and relax your muscles," he said. "And by all means, when you get there, find your badge! An agent's badge is their lifeline!"

I tried to take a deep breath, but my chest felt too tight to let the air in.

"Safe journey, Space Girl," de Selby said. "I'll be in touch."

Bright white light burst out from his badge, striking me

in the eyes, and my chest went tingly, then warm. The floor beneath me disappeared. *Here we go.*

Just like before, I was falling—*WWOOOOOOSSSHHH*—downward through light like a speeding roller-coaster car. I closed my eyes. Next stop, Ground Zero.

THIRTY-THREE

I **slammed** back into my ghost body with a jarring thud. My knees buckled, but I quickly steadied myself. I was in ground zero, standing next to the electric chair. I touched my head. The helmet felt warm against my fingers.

Right! I had a job to do.

I glanced up at the vent, looking for Haley. She wasn't there—but I jumped as I realized I wasn't alone. The two guards from the old locker room stood ten feet away from me, sweat marks on the armpits of their tight black shirts, their machine guns pointed at my chest.

Not good! How long have they been standing there like that?

"Hi." I said, half waving. They stared at me like they couldn't believe their eyes. Like I was a monster.

The more muscular-looking guard waved the barrel of his gun, and I slowly raised my hands in a gesture of surrender.

Definitely not the time to make any sudden moves! But right behind me was the hole in the wall leading to the brick room! And at the end of the brick room was the gate. Beyond that was the swirling wormhole.

I just needed to climb through the hole and shut the gate. That would close the wormhole and stop the universes from exploding! Then I'd figure out how to sneak the helmet out past the guards.

One little problem: their guns were pointed right at my head now.

Our brilliant escape plan hadn't accounted for this.

"She's making me nervous," the second, scruffier guard barked in an Eastern European accent—like Dr. Delmar's, only thicker. "Knock her down!"

Knock me down?

The muscly guard moved around the side of me, and then, poking me in the neck with the barrel of his gun, he pushed the back of my legs with his foot and I fell down onto my knees. The cement floor dug into my kneecaps.

"Ouch!"

Something moved across the floor behind me; I could hear it scraping across the rough concrete. And hissing, maybe? As I was about to turn to see what it was, I felt a tingle in my head, and I froze. A crackly voice came from somewhere deep down in my brain: *Drazgorns in breach of gate.*

What the hell? The helmet must have activated the alien part of my brain, like the tall alien had said it would, and now it was sending me messages. Not that I knew what they meant or what I was supposed to do about them. I just needed to get through the hole.

I stared ahead at the guard with the scruffy beard, at his finger wrapped tightly around the trigger of his gun. If I was going to turn and bolt without being shot, I needed him to lower his gun.

"Okay. You can put your gun down now," I said. It was worth a try.

Nothing stirred in his eyes, though. He was the serious military type. I tried smiling at him again.

Finally the scruffy guard lowered his gun.

Phew.

But the muscly guard's gun still pointed at my chest.

Grabbing the two-way radio off of his belt, the scruffy guard held it up to his mouth. "Security One to Intelligence."

"Go ahead," someone said on the other end of the radio.

"Freaky alien girl's awake," he said. "And moving. Looking right at us."

Freaky alien girl? That's what they think of me?

"Don't let her out of your sight." The voice on the other end sounded like Dr. Delmar's, but I couldn't be certain. "I'm on my way," whoever it was said.

"Copy that." The scruffy guard clipped his radio back onto his belt and returned his attention to me, and I met his stare.

"So, I'm Courtney," I said. "I'm not a freak or an alien or anything, I swear."

I shifted my gaze to the muscly guard who'd knocked me down. "You can put your gun down too. I'm just lost. I was trying to get back to my hospital room, and I took a bad turn. And somehow I ended up here. So if you just let me go back to my room, everything will be cool."

"No talk!" barked the scruffy guard.

I lowered my head, and started to open my mouth to apologize, when I heard a loud cracking noise behind me. My eyes shot up to meet the scruffy guard's. By the concerned look on his face, he'd heard it too. More crackling noise came from behind, and suddenly I felt a magnetic pull in my head, urging me to turn around and look for whatever was causing the noise. But there was no telling what the scruffy guard might do if I moved.

The floor vibrated, and tiny pieces of cement rained down from the ceiling, littering the floor around my knees. *Oh crap! This can't be good.*

"What are you doing?" the scruffy guard yelled at me. "You're making the walls crack."

"Me? No! I swear." A baseball-sized chunk of concrete plopped down beside my left foot.

"The wall's breaking," the muscly guard said, urgency in his voice.

"Don't shoot or anything," I said. "But I need to look behind me, just for a second. Cool?" Before they could answer, I swung my head around and looked over my shoulder.

The cement wall surrounding the bomb hole was cracking into pieces. Crumbling apart. And the black brick wall behind it was crumbling too, opening up an even bigger, four-by-four-foot window into the brick room!

I sat up on my knees to get a better look through the new window—and the cement wall below it split in half, sending two large chunks of concrete collapsing to the floor. I flinched as bits of cement sprayed my face.

The opening was the size of a doorway now, and I was kneeling five feet from it. I stared through in amazement. The gate was still open—and behind it was the swirling red wormhole! The time to make my move for the gate was now.

I slowly lifted up my right knee, then shifted my weight from my knee to ball of my right foot, like a sprinter at the starting line. *On your marks, get set—*

Shit!

The muscly guard stepped between me and the doorway-size hole in the wall. I froze, one knee up, one knee down. But he wasn't looking at me. He was staring right at the hole. "It's a brick wall, just like they said," he said.

Brick wall? What is he talking about?

"The secret room must be behind it."

What are they talking about? There was no brick wall anymore; it was gone. Were they blind? Unless . . . the tall alien *had* said that normal people couldn't see the gate. Had he meant that not only couldn't they see the gate, but that non-bloodliners couldn't even see into the room where the gate stood? That had to be what was happening. Somehow, even though the brick wall was gone, the guards were still seeing it, like a holographic force-field or something.

Whatever the deal was, I needed to get past the muscly guard and through the wall to the gate. I bit my lip. *Ready. Go!*

I scrambled toward the opening.

"Freeze!" The muscly guard grabbed the back of my hospital gown, and it tightened around my neck like a dog collar.

"Where were you going?" he asked me.

I shook my head, coughed. *Nowhere now.*

He let go of my gown. Then he raised the stock of his gun and tried to ram it through the doorway that only I could see. *Thud!* The gun struck something where the bricks used to be.

"It's a solid wall. She wasn't going anywhere," he said. He looked at me closely. "Maybe she really is crazy."

Oh my God! Not only were they *seeing* a hologram wall that wasn't there—for them, it *was* there, a solid brick wall!

Wait! What if I couldn't get through the hologram wall either?

"Face forward! Now!" the scruffy guard yelled, interrupting my thoughts.

I turned back around to face him, and as I did, the bottom of the muscly guard's boot struck me in the back, sending me sprawling forward. Flat on my stomach now, surrounded by boots, I strained my neck and glanced up. Guns pointed down at me. *Not good.*

"Security One to Intelligence." The scruffy guard held the radio up to his mouth.

"Go ahead," said the man on the other end.

"You need to see this, Dr. Delmar," the scruffy guard said.

I knew it was him! "Oh my God, hey, can I talk to Dr. Delmar?" I asked the guard. "Please! I can explain things."

Ignoring me, he spoke into the radio. "It looks like the alien girl's helmet is talking to whatever is buried down here," the guard said. "The bomb-proof wall is breaking apart!"

"Ha! It's working!" Dr. Delmar yelled through the radio. "Once contact has been made between the helmet and the wormhole's gate, the wormhole's energy field begins to tear down everything between it and the helmet! The bugs can't be far behind. I'm getting on the elevator now. Can you see a brick room? The gate should be at the end of it."

The scruffy guard stared over me. "No room. Just a brick wall."

"It'll happen! I'm coming down now."

Hearing a knocking sound, I looked over my shoulder through the doorway. A giant crack was snaking its way across the black stone ceiling of the brick room, branching out, and twisting toward me. A hunk of the black ceiling fell down to the brick floor, and a streak of bright red light streamed up from the wormhole toward the new hole in the ceiling. *Oh gosh!*

Things were disintegrating, and fast. I needed to shut the gate, quickly, before the whole room collapsed down on us.

A chunk of cement fell from the ceiling above us, bounced off the electrocution chair, and crashed to the ground.

"Are you doing that?" the scruffy guard yelled at me. He shoved me back down to the floor and crushed me with his boot.

"No. I swear, I'm not doing anything!" I twisted my neck, trying to look up at him.

He moved his boot away. I gasped for air.

"Get up on your knees!" he yelled.

Still trying to catch my breath, I sat up on my knees.

"Hands locked behind your head!" he yelled.

I locked my hands together behind my neck like a prisoner of war.

Then I felt something brush against my foot.

Jerking my leg, I looked down and saw a shiny black millipede-like bug with long, spidery legs and twitching antennae clinging to the skin of my ankle. It was so *gross!* *A Drazgorn worm!* It was just how de Selby had described them. The thing was two inches long and as thick as my pinkie finger. But now was not the time to freak out.

I shook my foot, but the bug was latched on.

I snuck a look at the scruffy guard. He wasn't looking at me. I unlatched my fingers and, keeping one hand behind my head, reached down with the other and smacked the little buggy monster. It tucked up into a ball, like the roly-poly bugs I used to find in the woodpile at my grandpa's cottage, and rolled over to the corner. Then it stretched back out and scurried up the wall.

Three Drazgorns in breach of gate, the helmet voice crackled in my head.

I looked around me for the other two spider-legged worms, but I couldn't see any more.

"Check it out." The muscly guard walked over and pointed the barrel of his gun at the Drazgorn clinging to the wall, causing its front legs and antennas to twitch around. I felt the helmet vibrate.

Four Drazgorns in breach of gate. So another must have snuck out through the open gate. Whatever these things were up to, the helmet was totally zoned in on them.

The scruffy guard got back on his radio. "Dr. Delmar. We've got a bug."

"Get it into the cooler!" Dr. Delmar shouted through the radio.

I felt stinging on the back of my right calf. *Ouch!* Two more twitchy-legged monsters had latched onto my leg. I grabbed one and pulled its prickly legs off my skin. Its body was thick, and its oily black skin was ribbed like an armadillo's. It smelled awful, too, like rotten meat. "I could kill you," I told it.

Bending its body backward, it bit me on the finger. *Ouch! Enough!* I threw it as hard as I could against the cement wall. But it just bounced off and rolled across the floor. Then it stopped, stood up on its hind legs, and hissed at me. *Are you kidding me?*

Clenching my teeth, I hissed back at the bug. Then, suddenly embarrassed, I covered my mouth. *What's happening to me?* I wasn't sure. The bug was definitely frightened of my hiss, though, because it scurried up the wall.

Both guards were staring at me now, their mouths gaping open in disbelief. They seemed to have forgotten about their guns.

I quickly grabbed the other bug and threw it as hard as I could toward the brick room. It flew through the doorway, landed on the brick floor, and skidded back under the gate. *Okay.* So whatever was hiding the brick room from normal human view, and had stopped the guard's gun before, had just allowed the bug to sail right through it. This was good! If the bug could pass through, then hopefully I could too.

I glanced at the guards to see if they'd seen the bug go through, but they were still staring at me, jaws dropped, guns lowered. *Right!*

I loosely locked my hands behind my neck again. Then I glanced up at the two bugs. A third one scurried up the wall and joined them. "Are you guys going to catch those things or what?" I asked.

Three Drazgorns in breach of gate, the helmet told me. Which was one less than before. So the worm I'd tossed back through the gate was no longer in breach. Made sense.

The three on the wall were all staring at me now, hissing, like I was the enemy.

Lurching forward, I hissed back at my new enemies, and then I quickly stood up.

"No move!" the muscly guard said, shoving the barrel of his gun between my shoulder blades and stopping me in my tracks.

"I was just trying to help you, I swear," I said.

The scruffy guard picked up one of the organ-transplant coolers and attempted to corral the worms into it with the barrel of his gun, but they scurried out of reach. "These ugly things are tricky," he said, straining to get to them.

"They're Drazgorn worms," Dr. Delmar said, striding into the room through the rusty steel door. "They're only weeks old."

I never thought in a million years I'd be glad to see *him*. But I was.

"Dr. Delmar!" I practically shouted. "This is nothing like you think it is. The two universes are molecularly incompatible. That's what the whole Magi-alien secrecy thing is about. It's nothing against you guys. It's just physics or chemistry or whatever. You're a scientist; you should understand that. Right?"

Dr. Delmar walked over and stared at the two-inch-long bugs on the wall. "Amazing creatures, aren't they?" he asked.

"I don't know about that," I said. "They're definitely ugly, though, and they smell disgusting. But listen, Dr. Delmar. I'm not lying about the wormhole; it's totally unsafe."

"History tells us that Drazgorn worms are always the first species to come through once a wormhole's been activated," Dr. Delmar continued, snubbing my pleas. "They may look like harmless invertebrates now, but in the right conditions they could grow into time-traveling warriors with the intelligence of ten humans. Take a look, people. Locked inside this little creature's DNA is the future of the human race!"

Time-traveling warriors? De Selby definitely failed to mention that little piece of information.

Dr. Delmar lowered his chin and stared over his glasses at me.

"Look at you, Courtney, kneeling there, your helmet lit up like the dashboard of a space shuttle." His eyes were watery, like he was about to cry.

"Give her some space," he told the muscly guard. The gun barrel against my back disappeared, and the muscly guard moved to the side.

Dr. Delmar gazed admiringly at my helmet. "For seven years, some of the world's most brilliant scientific minds have tried to activate that helmet. Without luck. Experiment after experiment—nothing. Four hundred and forty volts of electricity couldn't get it to so much as beep. And then we find you, and the helmet comes to life. What magnificent blood you must have coursing through your young veins, Courtney."

I tried to fake a smile, but it wasn't happening. "Please, Dr. Delmar." I stood up, my hands still locked together behind my head. "You need to listen to me. The wormhole is going to kill us all."

"No! I'm done listening! To you and everyone else. I'm in charge now! No one's going to die. We're rewriting the prophecy! Science is the creator, Courtney. Not God. And the Drazgorn worms are the new prophets. Give me that gun!" He yanked the scruffy guard's gun out of his hands.

Oh great. Not only was he crazy, but now he was pissed off and armed!

Dr. Delmar raised the gun to his shoulder, then pointed it at my leg. "Try anything brave, Courtney, and I'll put a hole through your knee."

Oh please don't shoot me. "I won't try anything, I swear!"

An oily black Drazgorn slithered out from behind me. *Four Drazgorns in breach of gate.*

I hissed quietly under my breath, and it scuttled and squirmed away from me and toward Dr. Delmar's right shoe. It climbed up his ankle and underneath the bottom of his pants leg.

"Owww!" Dr. Delmar jumped backward, and his gun fired six or seven quick rounds up into the ceiling before he dropped it and started shaking his leg. The scruffy guard scrambled over to pick up the gun.

"The little monster is biting me!" Dr. Delmar slapped at his calf. "I'm under attack!" He unbuckled his pants and dropped them to his ankles. This was my chance! I turned and ran through the doorway into the brick room. *It let me through!* Ten feet in front of me was the twisty metal gate, glistening like it was made of hundreds of molten-silver deer antlers. It was beautiful.

"Where did she go?" the scruffy guard yelled.

I glanced back toward the guard's voice. The brick wall they had described was actually made of light and energy. I could see it now, from this side.

"You idiots!" Dr. Delmar squinted his eyes and stared right at me. "The helmet's tricking us. She's made herself invisible. You, block the door! You, find her!"

They can't see me!

Waving his arms, the muscly guard moved toward the doorway. He felt along the brick wall of light, then continued around the perimeter of the room. Dr. Delmar reached his hands out right toward the doorway, but he met the same resistance as the guard. His hand couldn't go through.

Not only could they not see me; they couldn't get to me.

Five Drazgorns in breach of gate.

I turned back toward the gate. Prickly little legs and an oily body slithered over my right foot. *Puke!* I shook my leg, sending a Drazgorn worm tumbling through the air, between the gate's pickets, and right into the spiraling red light of the wormhole.

Whoosh! It disappeared. *Four Drazgorns in breach of gate.*

Nice! I almost pumped my fist.

Eight Drazgorns in breach of gate.

Eight? I looked down to see four more twitchy monsters making their way toward me from the open gate. I bent down and hissed at them like I was a wild animal, and they scurried back toward the gate. They stopped just before it, though, and, standing on their back legs, all four of them screamed back at me with a guttural sound so horrible it made Agatha's torture music sound tame.

I stared at the gate, and a surge of electricity rushed through my head, and I felt myself moving. The helmet wanted to go home. And a part of me wanted to go now too. I was being pulled toward the wormhole, toward my death, and something inside me wanted to let that happen. It was insane.

Get a grip, Courtney! I yelled at myself. I needed to shut the gate. That would close the wormhole. Then I could get the hell out of there.

Crossing the room, I grabbed the gate with both hands and pushed with all my weight. It didn't budge. *Now what?* I wedged my shoulder against it and leaned in, pushing with my legs. Still it wouldn't close. Two more creepy-crawlers slithered out of the wormhole and came toward me.

Ten Drazgorns in breach of gate.

I stomped on one of them, then kicked it back through the gate. But the other one got away.

Nine Drazgorns in breach of gate.

Staring at the swirling wormhole, an idea flashed in my head. I was going about this all wrong.

I grabbed the twisted metal gate again, but instead of

pushing, I pulled, and it swung open wider. *This is crazy. What are you doing?* I slid through the opening and tried to pull the twisted metal toward me; this time it offered no resistance. The massive gate swung closed behind me, and the lock clinked into place.

The gate was shut. And I was on the other side of it.

Now what? I turned. The wormhole was just six feet away from me.

I moved closer.

It was a circular tunnel of light as wide as my sister's trampoline. I peered into it, mesmerized by how it spiraled downward into the ground, like a magical passageway to the center of the earth. I could feel its heat against my skin and its pull against my body.

I was standing still, but the wormhole seemed to be getting closer. I looked down at my feet. They were sliding along the black brick floor. It was pulling me closer! Not only that, but the brick on the floor surrounding the wormhole was crumbling apart: the hole was expanding, growing wider.

Shit! So shutting the gate definitely hadn't shut down the wormhole! *But why?* Maybe it wasn't an instantaneous thing, and it would take some time for the gate to power it down? Or else I'd messed everything up when I brought the helmet inside the gate? *Oh Jesus. Okay!* The female alien had told me that the helmet wanted to go home. So if I just tossed the helmet into the tunneling light, maybe that would fix things and power down the wormhole?

I reached up, grabbed the helmet with both hands, and pulled—but like before, it wouldn't budge. It was magnetically connected to my brain. And worse, it wanted me to jump into the wormhole with it!

No way am I jumping to my death! Back to plan A: get the

helmet far enough away from the wormhole to sever communications between the two.

But how?

Something hard bounced off the top of my shoulder, and I jumped back. It was a chunk of the brick ceiling. I looked up just in time to dodge a second, larger piece. The ceiling above was falling apart. Two more bricks smashed down over by the gate, and I turned to see a chunk of asphalt as big as me crash to the ground.

Asphalt?

I glanced at the gate, at its lock. Then to my left, where its hinges attached to the wall. Carved into the side of the brick wall, halfway toward the ceiling, was a brick step. Then another. I followed them up with my eyes. They led all the way up to the ceiling, and right where they ended I could see red light shining out through a crack as wide as my foot.

Another chunk of asphalt landed next to me, and the crack widened, offering a glimpse of the moon and the night sky outside. This was my way out!

Grabbing one of the twisted antlers on the gate with both hands, I pulled myself up until I could get my foot on top of the hinge. Then I stood up and stretched my other foot over to the first step. There wasn't a lot of room on the steps; they were just bricks sticking out of the wall. But I was running on total adrenaline. Grabbing the bricks with both my hands and my bare feet, I climbed my way upward toward the moon, the light from the wormhole burning against the backs of my legs.

When I reached the top, cool night air brushed against my face. Now I just needed to pull myself up and out without the asphalt breaking away and sending me falling back down to the brick floor—or, worse, into the wormhole.

Wedging my knees tightly against the wall, I reached

a hand up and gave the asphalt above me a gentle tug. It seemed strong. Switching hands, I gave the other side of the crack a tug. The asphalt crumbled apart.

Right.

I reached up to the stable side of the opening with both hands and, bouncing on my tippy-toes—one, two, three—I jumped up and pulled at the same time, stretching my chin toward my hands. Kicking at the wall, I got my elbow out onto the asphalt, then my other arm, and I heaved myself out.

Panting hard, I rolled a few feet away from the crumbling hole in the ground next to me and came to a rest on my back, limbs spread-eagle. I was somewhere in the parking lot. Exhausted, I lay there and gazed up at the moon, smiling. *I'm alive! I shut the gate! I made it out!*

Now it was up to the wormhole to power down and disappear!

And up to me to get the helmet to the monastery.

I just needed two seconds of rest.

THIRTY-FOUR

The asphalt felt warm against the back of my legs and arms. But my two seconds of rest were over. It was time to move! I patted my head to make sure the helmet was there. Still magnetically glued on or whatever. *Thank God!*

I rolled over to get my bearings. I was probably a hundred feet out from the old psych building, but closer to the corner by the service entrance than I was to the dumpster, which was maybe two hundred feet to my left.

Nine Drazgorns in breach of gate, the helmet voice crackled in my head.

"Enough already about the stupid Drazgorn worms!" I yelled at the helmet. But at least the number hadn't gone up since I'd shut the gate.

A loud bang shook the air.

What was that? I managed to get to my hands and knees and crawl toward the service entrance, until I could see around the corner of the building. A big moving truck was parked next to the school bus. Two guys with dollies were wheeling boxes and wooden stools up a metal ramp and into the back of the truck. I recognized the stools from Dr. Delmar's office. *Are they moving him out?* They rolled the dollies, empty now, back down the ramp and disappeared into the building through the service entrance. *Phew.*

I sat up and rubbed the cuts on my feet. It was at least five hundred yards across the parking lot to the street. From there I could flag down a car and hitch a ride to the monastery. Of course, I was covered in dirt and wearing a hospital gown and an alien space helmet, which might make it a little tough for me to get a ride. No, I couldn't risk that. I'd have to run to the Holy Donut and call Agatha.

Wait! Haley's scooter was still parked next to the service door.

I glanced over at the hole in the asphalt I'd escaped out of. It was getting bigger. Haley's scooter was less than a hundred feet away. *Oh wow!* If she'd left the keys in it like she had at our house, I was as good as gone!

Standing up, I started jogging toward the scooter. But the broken pavement cut into my feet, and my run turned into a half-limp, half-jog. When I was halfway there, a pair of headlights turned in to the parking lot from the street and shone toward me. I threw myself flat on the ground, my breathing fast and shallow.

The car grumbled closer, and its headlights lit up Haley's scooter—and then it veered left and drove past me.

It was a refrigeration truck, the kind used to deliver bags of ice to grocery stores, with an air conditioner on top and thick, insulated walls. COSMIC CHARLIE'S ICE CREAM AND DAIRY was painted on the side. WOODSTOCK, VERMONT. *Isn't that where Dr. Straka's other office is?*

The ice cream truck parked next to the moving van, and its headlights went dark.

I sprang to my feet and ran to Haley's scooter. It was the exact same scooter as the one Lauren's brother had. And the key was in the ignition! *Score!* I jumped on the seat, turned the key, and the scooter started up. I twisted the handle grip to D for drive. Then I revved the throttle and took off—toward the road and away from the wormhole.

The scooter tires bounced over a crack in the asphalt,

and a strange buzzing rose up from somewhere. *From the helmet?* Trying to ignore it, I tucked my head down behind the windshield and raced on.

But the farther I got from the old hospital and the wormhole, the louder the buzzing in my head became. I could feel pressure inside my ears, then a sharp pain, like my eardrums might burst.

I stomped on the brakes and put my feet down.

I stood there for a minute, and the buzzing faded a little. *Okay.*

Revving the throttle again, I pulled my feet up and continued toward the road. But the buzzing ramped back up, and then a deafening, inhuman scream shot through my head, squeezing my eyeballs and blinding me. I swerved so far to the right that I was angled back toward the wormhole and the old psych hospital. Immediately the scream went away and my vision came back.

The aliens warned me that this would happen. It suddenly made sense. The helmet was trying to stop me from leaving the wormhole. It wanted to go home. But I had to get it away from there before the wormhole tore the universes apart at their seams! Whatever that actually meant.

Squinting my eyes, I steered the scooter toward the road again. The screaming rose up in my head again, and an image of a scuttling Drazgorn worm forced its way into my mind. *Uck!* It wasn't a memory, exactly; it was more like a movie. I watched the little monster stand up and hiss at me, its legs and antennas twitching violently.

Nine Drazgorns in breach of gate, the helmet told me.

I don't care! I thought back at it angrily. *Why are you telling me this?*

I stopped, grabbed at the helmet, and pulled. In response to my tugs, a sharp pain jetted from the center of my brain to the backs of my eyes. *Owwww!* I rested my head against the handlebars. I couldn't take the helmet off. It wouldn't let me. And it wouldn't let me leave.

Without raising my head, I aimed the scooter back toward the wormhole. Slowly, the pain started to go away. *Okay, one last try!* Sitting up, I revved the throttle and made a sharp turn in the direction of the road again. Crushing pain shot through my eyes into the center of my brain, like my head was in a vise and being squeezed tighter and tighter.

The mission here is not over echoed through my head.

I slammed on the brakes. That was my grandpa's voice!

"Grandpa? What do you mean, the mission here isn't over?" I asked. My grandpa had worn the helmet before. I could feel his presence. But I didn't get an answer.

"Grandpa? Are you there?"

No answer. But I had to trust him, and my instincts. There was more to do here; it made sense, I could feel it. I just needed a minute to figure out what it was. I scanned the parking lot for a safe hiding place. The dumpster was my best bet for now. Hopefully it was close enough to the wormhole for the helmet's liking, and I could figure things out without my eyeballs popping out of my head.

I left the scooter where it was, ran over to the dumpster, and climbed in. Leaning back against the side, I closed my eyes. After a minute, the buzzing and the pain in my skull went away.

"Hello? Grandpa?" I waited.

Nothing.

Maybe the voice I'd heard earlier was some sort of prerecorded message that'd he left in the helmet?

I looked around me in the dumpster. The aliens hadn't explained exactly how long it would take for the wormhole to tear the universes apart, but I imagined I didn't have much longer to go. Time was ticking.

I closed my eyes. "Hello? Evolarian agents? Tall alien guy? I need help!"

I cracked open my eyes and slowly looked around.

No one. Just me.

Then I heard Agatha's laugh.

What the hell? I stood up and looked around, though I knew the laugh had come from inside my head. I was hearing lots of voices inside my head these days; I was almost getting used to it. Then I felt a tingle down the back of my neck.

"Agatha?" I said aloud. I tried to picture her in my head, to connect with her. But I couldn't.

"Agatha? Are you there? Can you hear me?" I whispered to myself.

Suddenly I saw her in my head. She was sitting in her car; the moon was shining in through her windshield, her phone was on her lap, and her horrible music was blaring. "Agatha!" I yelled, but she couldn't hear me. I somehow needed to get into her head and talk to her.

Standing up on the stack of old mattress, I looked over the rim of the dumpster and let the moonlight wash over my face. *AGATHA!!!* I yelled in my head.

I saw her, in my mind, turn down the stereo in her car and look behind her into the back seat, then lean forward and peer up at the night sky.

AGATHA!!! I yelled again. *I NEED YOUR HELP! I'M IN THE DUMPSTER BY THE OLD PSYCH—*

"Courtney?" she said. "Dude, what the hell? Are you in my head? Oh, no way." She rubbed her eyes, then started her car.

Holy crap! I think it worked.

I could see headlights. Not in my head, but flashing at me from across the parking lot, from over by Dr. Straka's office. Then the car's headlights died out.

What the hell? But the car was driving toward me. It was Agatha's car! I could see it in my mind, silhouetted in the glowing blue light, racing across the parking lot.

I jumped down from the dumpster and waved my arms. But bright light struck Haley's scooter from off to my left. *Oh no!* Two figures with flashlights in their hands and guns slung over their shoulders ran toward it. *The guards from ground zero!* I dropped flat on my stomach and rolled against the side of the dumpster to blend in. If they shined their light on me, I'd be done!

I scanned the parking lot for Agatha's car. No sign of it. I squeezed my eyes shut and tried to find her in my head. Still nothing. How could her car have just disappeared like that?

Agatha? Where are you? I whispered in my head. But the connection had been broken. She couldn't hear me, and I couldn't see her.

My cheek pressed against the ground, my arms shaking, I waited to see what the guards would do. Luckily, one of their flashlights sighted the crack in the parking lot that I'd climbed out of, and both guards charged toward it for a closer look.

Then I heard the *thump-thump-scream* of Agatha's death music coming from somewhere around me. Not loud, but just loud enough for me to hear.

Hey, Agatha whispered in my head. *Over here.*

I turned my head to my right, and there was Agatha's car, ten feet from me, glowing in a hazy cloud of bluish light. *Whoa!*

Get in! Agatha whispered.

THIRTY-FIVE

I ran around and jumped in the passenger seat. Throwing my arms around Agatha, I squeezed her as tight as I could. "I'm so glad to see you, you have no idea." Afraid she'd disappear and I'd wake up back in the dumpster if I let go of her, I held on tightly. Tears rolled down my cheek. When I felt certain she wasn't going anywhere, I released her from my grasp and leaned back in the passenger seat. Then I looked at her.

Her eyes were wide, and she looked frightened.

"What's wrong?" I asked. "Agatha? You're scaring me."

Without taking her eyes off me, she yanked her cell phone's cord out of her radio jack and the music stopped. "Dude! You're wearing a sparkling space helmet, and you're covered from head to toe in dirt. And *I'm* scaring *you*?"

"I know," I said excitedly. "The helmet belonged to the first aliens who came to Earth. I stole it from Delmar, but it's connected to my bloodline. You see, there's a wormhole in the tunnels, right under the parking lot, over there." I pointed.

"Hey. Slow down!"

"I don't have time for slow! The helmet's in communication with the wormhole's gate. And it's also totally linked up to the alien part of my brain. It let me shut the gate, which was supposed to close down the wormhole," I continued, unable to slow the rush of words pouring out of me, "but it didn't work, so I need to get the helmet away from here. But it won't let me take it off—"

"Courtney, stop! I know about the helmet. And ground zero and Dr. Delmar and the Bilim, and the wormhole."

"You do?"

"Yes. Father O'Brien's been filling me in. I'm the getaway car. I've been camped out at Dr. Straka's office for the past hour. That's how I got here so quickly when you . . ." She narrowed her eyes. "Don't take this wrong way, dude, but did you, like, beam your thoughts into my head about two minutes ago?"

I smiled. "Pretty cool, huh?"

"Cool? I guess . . . in a paranormal schizophrenic kind of way. Not to mention that I somehow just drove my glowing car right past two guys with machine guns and neither one saw me."

"Oh, wow, yeah, I wondered about that. It's like a force field of light or something."

"Well, whatever it is, it's working for now," she said. "But put your seat belt on. We gotta motor!" She put the car in gear, but I grabbed her wrist and shook my head.

"You weren't listening," I said. "I *can't* leave."

She glared at me, then put the car back in park. "Tell me again why you can't leave?"

"Father O'Brien and the aliens are wrong," I said. "The helmet won't let me get more than a few hundred feet from the wormhole without it crushing my brain because the mission here's not over! My grandpa told me—or, well, his voice did or something. The wormhole's still open, Agatha! We gotta figure out the rest of the mission before the gate opens back up and the wormhole destroys us all."

"Dude, let's just take it easy for a second. You're sounding, you know, a little crazy."

"I don't care! Everyone left all this shit for me to figure

out. Well, I can't figure it out! And yeah, I am crazy—I'm hearing all this stuff in my head, I have an alien helmet magnetically glued to my skull . . . I'm losing it!" My body was shaking from all the adrenaline coursing through it. I rocked back and forth in my seat. "We're all gonna die, and it's totally gonna be my fault. My one job is to get this helmet out of here, and I can't do it!"

"Take a deep breath!" Agatha grabbed me by my shoulders, and I stopped rocking. "It's gonna be okay," she said.

"How do you know it is?" I asked.

She met my stare, and a calmness returned to her eyes that wasn't there a second ago. She looked like the old infallible Agatha again.

"Because I'm here to help you figure this out," she said. "We got this. Trust me, dude."

"I trust you," I said. "I do, Agatha. But *you* have to trust *me* when I say that there's a strong chance it's *not* gonna be okay!"

"Let's cross that bridge when we come to it," Agatha said.

One of the guard's flashlights lit up our windshield, and Agatha ducked down. But the guard just gazed blankly in our direction; then, shining his light over at the dumpster, he walked right by us.

"Did you see what just happened?" Agatha asked, suddenly anxious again. "That guy stared right at us. And he has a machine gun!"

"It's cool. They can't see us because there's a wall of light protecting us," I said. "The same thing happened to me in the tunnels by the wormhole. Not sure how it works, or why it's working on your car, though?"

"Oh, maybe because I have your grandpa's portal machine in my trunk," she said.

"What?" I sat up straight. "You have his machine?"

"Yeah. I went back to his cottage. It's been beeping and glowing all night."

"But how'd you get it out of the ground without the sirens and everything going off?"

"I don't know. It was like it recognized me," she said. "Father O'Brien thinks maybe it's because you activated the badge or something weird like that."

"Yeah. Weird and my grandpa seem to go together," I said. "Wait! Where's the badge?"

Agatha reached back between the seats and came up with my grandpa's briefcase.

I grabbed it and slipped my hand into the secret pocket and pulled out the badge. Holding it up in front of me, I stared into the blue light. My brain tingled. The badge was connecting with my brain!

I rubbed the inside of my left arm against my gown to wipe some of the dirt away. Then I pointed the badge toward my left wrist, trying to mimic what de Selby had done back at the PUB.

"Dude, what are you doing? Shooting alien drugs?" The cocky sarcasm was back in Agatha's voice, thank goodness.

"The badge is like a computer," I said. "If it's anything like the helmet, it feeds off my thoughts. And it's somehow connected to the Magi and alien command. Now, *shh!* I have to concentrate."

I had no idea what I was doing, but de Selby had made it look easy. I scrunched my eyes, and after a few seconds a blue screen lit up my forearm. *Wow!*

Agatha grabbed my leg. "Oh, dude! That's insane!"

Strange numbers and symbols scrolled across my forearm—except they weren't strange at all. Somehow my brain was turning the symbols into thoughts I could understand.

"The badge is connecting with the helmet! They recognize each other—two parts of the same unit," I said, giving Agatha a play-by-play of the info as it came in.

"Look at you," Agatha said with wild admiration. "You're like a special agent ninja or something."

"Shh." Something strange was happening. I could hear de Selby's voice in my head. It was just a mumble-jumble of words and sounds, but I somehow knew that he was sending me a message on my badge and the alien part of my brain was picking it up.

"What's happening?" Agatha asked.

"One of the Magi agents is sending me a message."

"What is it?" She leaned over me to get a better look.

My eyes gobbled up the symbols scrolling across my arm, and the alien part of my brain translated and fed them into my thoughts.

"He says the helmet's programmed to protect both universes," I told Agatha. "That it can read my thoughts. He thinks maybe it won't let me leave because it's registering a threat from something I've seen."

"Tell him you shut the gate but the wormhole's still active," Agatha said.

"Hold on." I wasn't sure how to send a message. But what I needed to know from de Selby was how far I was supposed to go to save the universes. More specifically, if all else failed, should I sacrifice myself and jump into the wormhole with the helmet on? I needed to know if that would still stop the disintegration of the worlds and close the wormhole for good. As horrible as the idea was, maybe that was my mission.

The badge must have read my thoughts and sent them out to de Selby, because his answer popped into my head: *That is your last resort, Space Girl! Last resort!*

"Then what do I do now?" I said out loud.

I've just located an old report on helmets, de Selby transmitted back. *It says there's a peculiarity in the helmet's programming. Even though it knows the gate to the wormhole won't stay closed if the helmet remains within communication distance, the helmet won't allow itself to leave the area if it senses that any alien beings have escaped out through the wormhole. Anything that's escaped has to be captured and sent back into the wormhole.*

A squirming image popped into my head. *The worms. Those little fuckers!*

"What's the message?" Agatha asked, fidgeting.

"He says that the helmet won't leave because it senses that aliens have escaped out into our world through the wormhole."

"What?"

"They're these gross spidery-legged millipede-looking things," I said, shuddering. "We have to find them and force them back through the wormhole. Then we can shut the gate again, and the helmet should be cool with me taking it away from here."

"But I thought the aliens were on the same team as us?" Agatha asked. "Who cares if some of them escaped?"

"Evolarian aliens are our allies," I said, still in awe of my new expertise. "The things coming through the wormhole are a different species—Drazgorn worms."

De Selby was tuned into everything I was saying. *You saw Drazgorn worms? Alive?* he asked.

Yes. The helmet keeps telling me that nine of them breached the gate, I told him.

Then that's it! Get to the wormhole. I'll be in touch! de Selby said.

"Did you just say *Drazgorn*?" Agatha asked.

"Yeah. Why? Do you know about them?"

"Only what your little friend Haley's cousin Jorg told me," Agatha said. "He said they're like the mythical Vikings of the alien universe, except evil. Apparently, they come down on meteorites as tiny worms, and then they grow to twelve feet tall and sprout wings and armor!"

What? Dr. Delmar's description of the Drazgorns as "time-traveling warriors" flashed into my head, and, gulping, I shined the badge at my arm again. Numbers and symbols flashed across my skin; then a sketch of a young Drazgorn worm appeared on my wrist. After a few seconds, it disappeared, and a technical drawing of a full-grown, twelve-foot-tall, winged Drazgorn warrior came into focus on my arm. *Yikes!*

I held my wrist out for Agatha to see.

"Dude!"

"I saw a few when I was trying to shut the gate," I said.

The color drained from her face. "So . . . what's our plan?" she asked.

"Two hundred feet that way," I pointed through the windshield, "is the wormhole. There's a crack in the asphalt and some brick steps that lead down to the gate that protects the wormhole. The Drazgorns should be right around there. We find them, then throw them back to where they came from."

"We're gonna climb down into a hole looking for twelve-foot-tall flying armored bugs? That's your plan?"

"Yeah, kinda. Except the ones we're looking for aren't twelve feet tall." I smirked. "They're more like wormy millipedes, about two inches long, with long, spidery legs and antennae. But they can stand up on their hind legs and hiss and bite. And they smell gross."

"Ew." Agatha wrinkled her nose. "But they're only two inches long?"

"When I saw them, anyway," I said. "For some reason, Delmar and the guards had two live-organ transport coolers they were trying to capture the Drazgorn worms in. It was, like, a big deal to Dr. Delmar. So we need to find the organ coolers too, in case they locked some away in there."

I had forgotten to tell de Selby that part. I shined my badge down at my arm and tried to get it to send my thoughts to de Selby. But I couldn't tell if it was working.

A loud clap of thunder shook the air and crackled across the night sky. Agatha and I locked eyes.

The ground trembled, and suddenly the front of the car dropped down, pitching both of us forward in our seats.

"Ow!" Agatha groaned, rubbing her elbow where she'd smacked it against the steering wheel. "What the hell just happened?"

We both climbed out. I shoved my grandpa's briefcase under the seat and clutched his badge to my chest.

"Uh-oh." A deep crack had opened up in the ground and engulfed the front tires of Agatha's car.

"We're running out of time, Agatha. Agatha? *Agatha!*" I yelled over the rumbling thunder. But she was in a trance or something, staring across the parking lot. She didn't turn around.

Then I felt it: tingling under my skin. I glanced over toward the crack that led to the wormhole. Shards of bright red light were jetting out of the parking lot and shooting up toward the sky!

My stomach wrenched into a knot. "The wormhole's starting to tear away at the universe!" I yelled.

"I know," Agatha said, staring at the light. "It's just like my dreams, Courtney."

I gazed at the bolts of red as they twisted and jumped. "It's the beginning of the end, isn't it?"

"Not if we can help it." She grabbed my elbow. "Come on! We need to find the bugs and shut down the wormhole for good!"

"But what about my grandpa's portal machine?" I leaned into the car to open the trunk.

"Dude! Leave it," Agatha said, tugging on the back of my

hospital gown. I climbed back out and looked where she was pointing.

A white pickup truck with a blue security light on top and the Solomon Grace Hospital crest painted on the door had just pulled up next to Haley's scooter, which was directly between us and the crack leading down to the wormhole. Dr. Delmar was standing there too, talking to the driver of the pickup.

"Great!" I glanced back toward the service entrance, but it was around the side of the building, out of my sightline. "All right. We'll have to sneak in through the service door—it's around that corner. But there might be some people there we'll have to avoid."

"Let's go!" Agatha started jogging across the parking lot.

I was about to follow her, but I couldn't take my eyes off the bolts of red light streaming out through the cracks from the wormhole and stretching up into the sky.

"Dude! Today!" Agatha yelled—and the spell was broken. I pivoted and ran to catch up with her.

She glanced over at me. "Darn, you're really really dirty."

"Whatever." I glanced down at my throbbing feet. "Dirty but cool, right?" I joked.

She laughed. "Dirty but cool, for sure."

I glanced back again; I couldn't help it. The parking lot was alive with streaks of red light. "We should sprint, Agatha."

"Let's do it."

"Go!"

We took off running as fast as we could, past the school bus, to the service door. I creaked it open.

THIRTY-SIX

With no guards or movers in sight, we rushed down the hall to the dilapidated gymnasium. "Oh, that's a good sign," Agatha said, stopping to gape at the *Helter Skelter* graffiti.

"Come on!" I yelled.

We boarded the rickety elevator; then I flipped the lever and pressed B for basement.

"Is this thing safe?" Agatha asked.

"I hope so." The elevator started down, and I stared at Agatha. "Listen, I may have to do something that's a little dangerous. Only as a total last resort. But you have to promise that you won't try to stop me."

She glared her most intimidating glare at me. "What exactly are you talking about, Courtney?"

"Forget it," I said, looking away. "It won't come to that." I fake-smiled, then bit my fingernail.

We stepped off the elevator and ran into the tunnel. Mud squished between my toes, stinging my cuts.

"Ugh. What's that smell?" Agatha covered her nose and mouth with the sleeve of her sexy-witch shirt.

"Wet dirt and decay, I think. Or maybe it's the worms?" It was too dark to see.

We hurried toward the shower room.

"Oh Jesus! It smells even worse in here." Agatha leaned over and heaved.

"Shh! The Bilim's headquarters is just on the other side of the wall," I whispered. "We have to be quiet."

Still leaning over and trying not to throw up, Agatha nodded her head.

I hurried quietly across the tile floor and into the toilet stall, then climbed up on the toilet seat and looked through the peephole into the headquarters. A moving guy was pulling the Soldiers of Bilim photos and maps down off the wall and stacking them in boxes, his gun strapped to his shoulder. The other mover was there too, rushing around the room, throwing books and computers into boxes. No sign of the live-organ coolers with Drazgorn worms in them, though.

Suddenly the tattooed nurse barged into the locker room. My heart leaped in my chest. I ducked instinctively, even though I knew he couldn't see me.

"Let's go!" he yelled at the movers. "Get the computers out to the truck before the roof collapses and the goddamn fire department shows up!"

"We're on it!" one of the movers said.

Tattoo Nurse left.

I crouched back down, and Agatha pushed up next to me in the stall.

"They're packing everything up," I whispered. "But I didn't see the coolers."

"Let me see," she said.

I stepped off the toilet to give her space, but something banged right above us. As we looked up, five ceramic tiles fell off the ceiling and crashed to the floor in the stall next to us. "Oh, dude, that's not good!" Agatha said.

"No, it's not," I whispered.

A large crack snaked down the wall between us and the Bilim headquarters. I grabbed Agatha's hand and yanked her out of the toilet stall. We fled across the shower room— tiles smashing down all around us—and into the closet full of electrical wires at the other end. Water was dripping down from the ceiling.

"Dude!" Agatha looked around. "This is a death trap!"

As if to confirm her statement, the electrical breaker box next to us chose that moment to short out with a loud *POP!* The room went black.

"Yikes."

Agatha pulled out her cell phone, turned on the flashlight, and shined the light around the closet. I grabbed the phone from her hand and pointed the light up at the duct. "That leads to ground zero. I'll help you up."

I set her phone and my grandpa's badge on a dry spot of the floor before locking my fingers together so Agatha could step into my hands. Grunting, I lifted her up, and she wiggled into the duct.

I picked up the badge and put it in my mouth, then I grabbed the phone and shined its light around the closet. Water was running down onto the metal box on the wall I needed to use as a step. I opened the door on the box and pushed the lever down to make sure the power was off. Then I tossed Agatha her phone, stepped up onto the electrical box, grabbed one of the thick wires on the wall, and pulled myself into the duct next to Agatha.

"Follow me!" I crawled past her and toward ground zero.

THIRTY-SEVEN

Reaching the end of the duct, I could feel the heat radiating off the wormhole. I shined my badge at my arm. *Hello? De Selby? We're at ground zero!*

After what felt like a minute, I lowered the badge. "So much for de Selby," I said.

Nine Drazgorns in breach of gate, the helmet told me.

Okay, I hear you. So where are they? I stared into ground zero. The floor was covered in chunks of cement and asphalt.

Agatha pushed up against me and looked into the room. "Dude!" she breathed. "There's the brick room and the gate. It's just like Father O'Brien explained it. And, oh wow, the fucking wormhole. It's like a giant swirl of colors soaring up through the floor! This is unreal!"

"Wait. You can see the brick room? And the gate and the wormhole?"

"Yeah. Why, can't you?" Agatha asked.

"Yeah, I totally can. But normal people . . . So you *are* a bloodliner?"

"I guess so. Lucky me." She grinned facetiously.

I glared at her. It made sense now why I could connect with her mind. "I knew it," I said. "Why didn't you tell me before?"

She shrugged. "I've never been visited by aliens. Not in my dreams or awake. Just my visions of the end of the world and the alien universe. So I wasn't really sure if I had the gene. Now where are these Drazgorn worms?"

"I don't know. The helmet's telling me that nine of them have escaped past the gate." I scanned the room. "There's one of the coolers!" I said. "Next to the electric chair. At least some of the bugs must be in it!"

I spun myself around and started scooting back so I could slide out of the duct and drop down into the room, but just as I was sliding a foot out, I heard the rusty steel door bang open. I hastily pulled my foot back inside the duct, quickly turned around, and shrank back into the shadows next to Agatha.

We watched the muscly guard charge into the room, followed by Nurse Erin. My throat tightened up at the sight of her. Slowly she made her way over to the electric chair.

The guard pointed his gun around the room, then raised his radio to his mouth. "Security Two to Intelligence."

"What is it?" Dr. Delmar yelled through the radio.

"Everything's crumbling apart," the guard said into the radio. "But I still don't see any gate. Or bright red light or anything glowing."

Agatha glanced at me, and I raised my eyebrows.

"Roger that," Dr. Delmar said through his radio. "No lights of the so-called apocalypse up here either. I knew it was Magi propaganda. The parking lot is falling apart, though. So get out before it all collapses."

"Ten-four," the guard said. He clipped his radio back onto his belt.

"We gotta go!" he called out to Nurse Erin.

"You go," Nurse Erin said without turning around.

The guard mumbled something under his breath, then hustled out.

Nurse Erin stepped around the electric chair and gazed toward the brick room.

"What's she doing?" Agatha mouthed to me.

I shook my head. Only bloodliners were supposed to be able to see into the brick room.

Nurse Erin stepped through the doorway and into the brick room.

"No way!" I whispered. "She must be a bloodliner!"

Agatha shrugged.

Nine Drazgorns in breach of gate, the helmet told me.

I looked down at the cooler, and then at Nurse Erin. She was standing right in front of the gate, her back to us. She grabbed onto one of the silvery antler pickets and pulled the gate open.

What the hell?

"I have to get to the cooler and throw the Drazgorns into the wormhole before any more escape," I whispered to Agatha. I started to twist around again, but a loud cracking sound below us froze me where I lay.

"Dude!" Agatha grabbed my arm.

I scooted forward on my stomach and looked down: the cement wall underneath us was totally crumbling apart. As in, there was nothing left below the duct to support it. The only thing holding us up were the screws holding it to the ceiling, and those—

With a loud popping sound, the metal duct tore loose from the ceiling and dropped down, sending us sliding out of the duct and crashing to the floor.

Nurse Erin whipped around and glared at us. "Get out of here!"

"I can't!" I stood up and faced Nurse Erin, my heart thudding against my rib cage. "I have to close the wormhole. The two universes are incompatible. I told Dr. Delmar, but he wouldn't listen."

"I know," she said.

"You do?" I asked. "But—"

"I told Dr. Delmar about the prophecy," she said with

anger in her voice. "He told me it was a Magi lie. He said the Evolarians were too smart to let the worlds destroy each other, and that the wormhole would shut itself down once we left the area."

"But—that's just crazy," I said. "Have you seen what's going on in the parking lot? There's light shooting up everywhere, just like in the prophecy. We're all going to die unless we shut the gate and let it close the wormhole."

"Yeah, you and I know that, don't we, smarty-pants," she said with resentment in her voice. "But Delmar and the others don't. And you already shut the gate once, and the wormhole is still alive. There's no stopping it."

"That's not true," I pleaded. "The gate didn't shut down the wormhole because some Drazgorn worms escaped out of it while it was open. But if I can find them and throw them back through, the gate will shut for good and power down the wormhole. I swear!"

She laughed. "Find your little bugs, then," she said. "I won't stop you."

"Really?" I started slowly toward the organ cooler, still keeping an eye on her. She nodded her head, like it was okay, so I scampered over and lifted up the cooler—uncovering a Drazgorn worm that had been hiding underneath it. The little monster stood up on its hind legs and hissed at me.

"Ew!" Agatha said.

Gritting my teeth, I hissed back at the little monster, and it recoiled in fear. Before it could scurry away, though, the thick wooden heel of Agatha's Viking boot smashed it into the floor, splattering its guts all over the floor and Agatha's boot.

Nine Drazgorns in breach of gate.

"Kick it through the gate!" I yelled. "Dead or alive, they all have to go back into the hole!"

Agatha booted the oozing lump across the floor. Then, kicking it again, she followed it into the brick room. With one last kick, she sent it sliding through the gate and into the wormhole.

Eight Drazgorns in breach of gate.

"One down, eight to go!" I opened up the cooler, but it was empty. "Huh?" I got down on my hands and knees and scampered around the room, hissing, looking for the bugs. But there weren't any. They had to be in the other, missing cooler.

"Where's the other cooler?" I asked Nurse Erin. "I need to find the other eight Drazgorns!"

She just shook her head and gazed at the wormhole.

"You don't understand." I hurried into the brick room. The gate still stood in its center, and behind it was a wormhole spiraling up out of the floor. The ceiling was completely gone now, though. We were standing in a basement room with nothing above it but jetting light, and the moon and the night sky.

"In all my life, I've never seen anything like this before," Nurse Erin said dreamily.

I gazed into the light too, and my insides tingled.

How's it going, Space Girl? de Selby's voice echoed through my head. I quickly looked down at the badge.

I don't know. Not good, I told him. *I'm at the gate, but I can't find the eight missing Drazgorns.*

Well, you better hurry before the wormhole swallows up the bricks holding the gate. Once the gate falls through, there's no closing the wormhole. Period!

Oh no! I said. Glancing at the gate, I realized it was only two feet from the wormhole's edge now.

Yes, exactly. Get to work!

"Listen to me." I grabbed Nurse Erin's arm. "Tell us where the worms are. Please. As soon as that hole catches up to the gate, the gate's gonna fall into it. And then it will be too late to close the wormhole. We'll all die—the whole world. Both worlds. So tell me where the Drazgorn worms are. I saw Dr. Delmar and his guards collecting them earlier. You have to know!"

She jerked her arm away from my grasp, then looked skyward again.

"This world's just not worth saving, girls," she said. "Think about it. If it was, our alien friends would've come down to stop the apocalypse."

"No, it's totally worth saving," I said. "That's why the aliens contacted me. They can't do it themselves, but that's why we're here. Agatha and I are gonna save the worlds."

"It's true," Agatha said, stepping up next to me. "Now tell us: Where are the other bugs?"

Nurse Erin glanced back toward ground zero, at the rusty door leading out to the tunnels. "It's too late," she said.

"No it isn't!" I said. "Please. You walked through the doorway when the others couldn't. You can see the gate and the wormhole."

"So what?" she muttered.

"So you're a bloodliner! This is your chance to help the Magi!"

Jerking her head around, she glared at me.

"If you think the Magi care about me, then you're as crazy as Dr. Delmar," she said. "The bloodline's a curse. The Magi look after their special few, but they do nothing for people like me. I spent half my life thinking I was crazy, being traumatized over and over, losing my mind every time an alien showed up in my bedroom, until Dr. Delmar showed up and explained that everything I was seeing was real."

"Same with my brother," Agatha said.

"We can't fix that right now," I said. "But we have to close this wormhole before we all die."

"I'm ready to die," Nurse Erin said. She pushed past us and walked out of the brick room, back into ground zero.

"Wait!" I called after her. "What about the people who don't want to die? Little kids and their parents, and all the happy people who like being alive? Are you really just going to let them get torn apart? Please"—I was begging now—"just tell us where they took the Drazgorn worms!"

"You really think you're gonna save the world?" she asked, her expression softening ever so slightly.

"Yes, I do. The aliens told me how to shut the gate! They care."

"Oh please." She kicked the dirt floor. "Fine. Dr. Delmar's outside, loading the cooler with the bugs into an ice cream delivery truck," she said. She didn't sound angry anymore. "He's taking them to Vermont, to the genetic research lab run by Dr. Straka's brother; they plan to extract the DNA and use it to create a super gene or something—to take over the world. But I'm betting that there won't be a world five minutes from now."

"We can stop him!" I yelled. "Come on, Agatha!"

I pulled myself up onto the hinges of the gate, and started climbing up the steps toward the parking lot. I didn't have to look to know that Agatha was right behind me.

THIRTY-EIGHT

I stood up on the asphalt, and Agatha climbed out behind me. Bright red light was streaking up out of the cracks in the parking lot, stretching into the sky.

The moving truck was making its way across the parking lot, toward the road. The ice cream truck was a few hundred feet away from the building, but it looked to be standing still.

"There it is!" I yelled. "Come on!"

I had only taken one step forward when something stung me in the back of my leg. *Ouch!* I looked down to see an oily-black Drazgorn worm, spidery legs twitching, digging its teeth into my leg. But wait—what was it doing all the way up here? Glancing down into the brick room we had just climbed out of, I could see the opened gate and the spiraling wormhole. I peeled the Drazgorn off my calf and whipped it down into the wormhole. Then I wiped my fingers onto my gown, trying to get rid of the dead-animal smell. *Uck!*

"Oww!" Agatha swatted at her legs.

I tore a little monster off of her right shin. It bit my finger and jumped free, but Agatha stomped on it and kicked it back into the wormhole. Two more creepy-crawlers scampered up over the ledge onto the asphalt. Crouching down, I hissed at them, and as they reared back, I aimed a swift kick at each one, sending them sailing into the swirling vortex below.

Twenty-two Drazgorns in breach of gate.

"More Drazgorns are breaching the gate!" I said, panicking.

Three more spidery-legged monsters slinked over the edge of the asphalt.

"The ice cream truck's pulling away!" Agatha yelled. I looked over my shoulder; sure enough, it was moving toward the road now.

"Shit!" I said, kicking the three rogue creepy-crawlers back over the edge and watching them tumble down into the spiraling light of the wormhole.

Nineteen Drazgorns in breach of gate.

This is horrible!

Leaning over, I hissed at a mob of bugs making their way up the brick steps. They backed away.

"You stay here and deal with this," Agatha said. "I'll go after the truck. But my car's stuck!"

"Take Haley's scooter! Keys are in it."

I didn't hear a response, so I looked up. Agatha was already sprinting across the parking lot.

"Nice knowing you," I said under my breath, half joking, I hoped. Then clenching my grandpa's badge in my fist, I crawled around on my hands and knees, hissing and spitting, until all the Drazgorns had retreated back down the brick steps.

Nineteen Drazgorns in breach of gate, the helmet told me again.

I KNOW! I grumbled back. I clenched the badge between my teeth, and started climbing down the steps. Gravely inhuman sounds spewed from my mouth, and the bugs scurried down ahead of me, staying just out of my reach. I kept moving down, driving them back toward the wormhole.

Seventeen Drazgorns in breach of gate. It was working! As

long as Agatha could stop Dr. Delmar's truck and steal the cooler back, we might really be able to do this!

I reached the floor of the brick room and stood with a hand clenched around one bar of the twisty gate. The wormhole was even bigger now, not much more than a foot away from the gate. It would only be a matter of minutes before the bricks supporting the gate's posts crumbled away—like de Selby had warned—and the entire gate was swallowed up by the wormhole.

A gang of worms huddled together in a crevice just outside the gate. Maybe ten of them. I slipped through the opening of the gate, ran around and hissed at them, hoping they'd scurry back under the gate, but they didn't move. They just hissed up at me.

Okay. Okay. I reached my fingers into the crevice to the left of the worms and inched it closer to them. One of them bit into my finger. "Ouch!" I yelled through clenched teeth, and I swept my hand into them, hard. I had them trapped! I could feel them squishing around. I grabbed one and pulled it out. Ignoring its squirming and hissing, I threw it through the gate and into the wormhole. Without skipping a beat, I shoved my hand back into the crevice, grabbed another, and threw that one through the gate.

On a hunch, I set the badge down next to me and spat into the crevice; four of the little monsters immediately curled into balls and rolled down to the floor. I kicked them through the gate and spat into the crevice again. Same thing! Three more came out this time. I punted them into the swirling light. Three to go. Crouching down, I got ready to spit again—but two of the worms fled out of the crevice and toward the hinge of the gate.

I stomped one with my bare foot. It didn't squish; it bit back. "Jerk!" I grabbed it with my right hand, and the other one with my left, and threw them both into the wormhole.

Dropping back down, I shoved my hand into the crevice to grab the last worm. I pulled it out by its tail end and let it squirm around for a second, hissing and trying to bite my fingers, before carrying it through the open gate and dropping it straight down into the red vortex.

WHOOOOOSH! It disappeared.

Seven Drazgorns in breach of gate.

I closed my eyes and listened for slithering feet or insect hissing.

They weren't in the brick room. Or anywhere around me. I opened my eyes. They had to all be in the cooler in the ice cream truck.

I picked my badge off the ground and stood with my back to the wormhole. Closing my eyes, I could feel the heat coming off of it, feel its tugging at my helmet. Through the wormhole, on the other side, was the alien universe. The world my ancestors came from. The helmet wanted to go home.

Twenty-nine Drazgorns in breach of gate.

What? I spun around. Slick black creepy-crawlers were parading up the steps again.

"Courtney!"

Oh my God—Mom! She was standing in the parking lot, twenty feet up, staring down at me. My stomach squirmed.

"What are you doing here, Mom?" She was in a dress and high heels.

"One of the nurses called Dr. Anderson and said you'd escaped from the hospital, and that you were running around this old parking lot looking for bugs! Now get up here before this becomes a police matter."

Dr. Anderson stepped to the edge and peered down at me. "A water pipe broke, Courtney, and the parking lot is collapsing," he said.

I glanced at the spiraling wormhole and streaks of red light jetting up through the huge hole in the parking lot.

"Water pipe? Are you serious?" I asked.

"That's right," he said. "You're standing in what used to be a room in the basement of the abandoned hospital. No telling what kind of germs could be down there. It's not safe, so we need you to come up."

I looked at my mom.

"Is that what you think too? That a water pipe broke?" I asked.

"I think you need to quit playing bug collector and get up here, young lady!"

"Look around you, Mom! Can't you see all the—"

"Courtney, please." Mom squatted down and tried to smile reassuringly at me. "Get away from those disgusting bugs. Climb out of there. You're embarrassing yourself."

Oh no! She couldn't see the wormhole—couldn't see any of what was happening. The world was ending, and she was worried about me embarrassing myself!

She turned to Dr. Anderson. "What is that on her head, Roger?"

"It looks like an antique motorcycle helmet," he said.

"Listen, Mom. You gotta get out of here." Rushing to the brick steps, I grabbed the two Drazgorns leading the latest escape wave and threw them back through the gate, then turned and hissed at the rest, scattering the pack.

"Oh, that is disgusting," my mom said. "Courtney Henrietta Hoffman! I am not asking! Forget the revolting bugs and get up here!"

"I know you don't believe me, Mom. About Grandpa and everything else that's happened to me. But I can't leave this spot. And you need to get out of here!"

"Oh goodness, Roger," my mom said. "Look at all the bugs around her. She's standing in a nest or something. I'm gonna be sick."

I looked down. The last few rows of bricks between the

wormhole and the gateposts were beginning to crumble. A crack in the ground had opened. Shiny black Drazgorns were streaming out and scurrying up the walls all around me.

Ninety-seven Drazgorns in breach of gate.

SHIT! Even if Agatha caught up with the ice cream truck and made it back with the organ cooler, how would I get all the bugs back into the hole before the gate collapsed?

"Mom, go, now! Please. I need to think!"

I paced along the front of the gate.

"Courtney, what kind of mother would I be if I left my daughter standing in a hole, hissing at bugs?"

"Mom, you can't see it, but there's a wormhole right here. It leads to an alien universe, and it's open, and I'm the only one who can close it. But the helmet won't let me do it until I get all these alien bugs back into the wormhole. My friend's chasing down an ice cream truck that's carrying some of them right now!"

"Oh my, oh my," Dr. Anderson said, grinning.

Mom looked away for a second. "Oh, look, it's your friend," she said, her tone noticeably brighter.

"What?" I hopped on my toes trying to see. "Where?"

"She's right here, honey. Standing next to me. All your friends are here. They want you to come up."

Oh, nice try. She thinks I'm totally crazy.

I hissed at the bugs scurrying up the wall.

Six hundred fifty-four Drazgorns in breach of gate.

Six hundred? It was getting worse by the second!

"Fine. I'm coming down to get you." My mom kicked off her high heels and, grabbing Dr. Anderson's arm with one hand, she got down on her knees, shimmied backward, and felt around for the step with her foot. "Oww!" She swatted at her leg, then stood back up. "These disgusting bugs are everywhere; I think one of them bit me! Go down and get her, Roger."

"Me?" he said.

She was right. The bugs were everywhere. Gazing at them, I felt dizzy. Everything was falling apart. I wanted to curl up and cry—to kick the ground and bang it with my fists. Or climb up and yell at my mom and tell her I was her goddamn daughter and she needed to believe me!

I rubbed my face. The stench of the Drazgorn worms on my hands made my stomach turn. I bent over and took deep breaths. "This is all on me," I whispered.

I gazed up. The moon was straight above me in the sky. From off to its left, red bolts streaked down at me. I lowered my gaze to the gateposts. One more minute, maybe two, and the gate would tumble into the wormhole and the world would end. I couldn't let that happen.

Dr. Anderson was taking off his suit jacket and handing it to my mom.

Grandpa's badge felt warm in my hand, and I could sense his presence in my head.

"I have to do this, don't I? Send the helmet home?" I asked him. I didn't get an answer, but I knew, it was the only way now. I stepped through the opening in the gate so I was inside again, next to the wormhole. I could feel its heat, but I couldn't turn around and look at it. I clung to the gate and stared up at my mom. She was helping Dr. Anderson lower himself onto the brick steps.

"Mom. There's a priest named Father O'Brien. He was a friend of Grandpa's. I want him to be the speaker or whatever at my funeral. Tell Dad and Kaelyn I love them."

"Courtney! What are you talking about?"

"Nothing." I wiped my eyes. But there was no stopping the tears now.

I turned and faced the wormhole. The swirling light warmed my wet face. "I'm sorry, Mom." I glanced at my grandpa's badge, clenched in my hand, glowing bright blue.

The wormhole's energy pulled at my body as I raised my arms from my sides. "This is my mission."

Eyes closed, I jumped into the light.

THIRTY-NINE

I was standing by the lake with my grandpa when a strange buzzing noise woke me out of my dream. I lifted my head up and banged the back of it into something hard.

"Ouch!" I fell back down, smashing my face against my wrist.

Next to me in the dark, something was flashing: faint strobes of white light.

Gradually, my eyes adjusted, but my thoughts were slow and foggy. I felt like I was in a metal coffin. But that made no sense. Nothing did. I couldn't think straight. Maybe I was still dreaming?

Dreaming or not, whatever I was in, it was so cramped I couldn't straighten out my legs.

Then I remembered jumping into the wormhole. *Am I dead?*

I knew I should be. But I could hear my heartbeat. And I was breathing. I pulled my hand up to my face and saw the blue glow of my grandpa's badge, still clenched in my fingers. *Am I really alive?* I wasn't sure how I could be, but as long as the helmet had made it home and the wormhole had closed, I didn't care. I touched my face. *I'm totally alive!*

But then I felt my head. The helmet was still there.

Oh no! My heart sank. The helmet hadn't made it home after all. *Does that mean the wormhole is still open?*

I angled the badge and shined its blue light around me. My grandpa's transporter machine was right next to me, splashing strobes of white light off the sides of the box I was trapped in. *Weird.* Had I somehow transported to the metal storage box in my grandpa's backyard?

OH GOD! I'm buried underground!

Then slowly another thought came to me: If I'd transported to my grandpa's machine when I jumped into the wormhole, then what had happened to the Drazgorn worms I'd thrown into the wormhole? Were they here too?

I quickly twisted around and shined the light from the badge all over, down at my legs, up around me, looking for bugs. There weren't any. *I may be buried alive, but at least I'm safe from those disgusting bugs for the moment.*

It still didn't make sense that I hadn't died.

Unless . . . maybe the helmet didn't want to go home after all?

Or maybe it did *go home? With me wearing it?*

I turned away from the light of my grandpa's machine and shined the badge around me again. It caught on something shiny: a black leather stiletto boot with a big silver skull on the front. I reached down by my knees and grabbed it. It was one of the same boots Agatha had worn with her red velvety dress when we met in the Mexican restaurant. I was in the trunk of Agatha's car. Of course! It was all coming back to me. She'd told me she had my grandpa's portal machine in her trunk when she showed up in the parking lot!

I started putting the pieces together. My grandpa's machine must have saved me. Actually, it would've been just like him to build something into his machine to protect me. He'd told me once that he was working on a machine that would keep him from accidentally time-traveling, or whatever he called it, into a hostile alien word. I never really knew whether he was joking or not. But he must have succeeded in getting the machine to do what he wanted, because instead of being transported through a wormhole into the alien universe—and being torn atom from atom in the process—I'd just transported to the trunk of a car.

And if I was in Agatha's trunk, and I was still alive, that meant the world hadn't disintegrated!

I banged the inside of the trunk with both palms.

"Help! Anybody. I'M STUCK IN HERE!"

I heard a muffled voice.

"HEY!" I yelled. "SOMEBODY? HELP ME!"

I felt the car wobble. Then something clicked, and the trunk popped open. I kicked it up the rest of the way and sat up. Sure enough, I was in the trunk of Agatha's car, which was still parked in the crumbling lot, right where we'd left it.

"Hey, Courtney." Haley stared at me. The moon hung high over her shoulder; judging by its position—still pretty much right overhead—it must not have been too long since I'd jumped.

I stood up in the trunk and glanced over toward the wormhole. Bright red light was jetting up toward the sky. *WHAT?* The wormhole was still open!

Shit! I stomped my feet, and the car bounced up and down. My plan hadn't worked! I was alive, but the wormhole was still open. The apocalypse was full speed ahead! *What now?*

I jumped out of the trunk and scanned the parking lot for the ice cream truck and Agatha. No sign of either. My mom was still standing by the brick steps leading down to the wormhole, though. I couldn't see Dr. Anderson, but they were two hundred feet away, and even with all the light the wormhole was putting off, it was still too dark to see more than just my mom's silhouette.

I glanced at Haley. For all I knew, the wormhole could

have already swallowed up the gate and we were seconds away from disintegrating into cosmic dust.

Where the hell was Agatha with the missing bugs?

"Oh cool, you still have the helmet," Haley said, interrupting my panic spiral. "The car got stuck in a crack, huh?" She cocked her head. "Wait, how did you get locked in the trunk?"

"Long story," I said. "But the short version is, I tried to jump into the wormhole to save the world, and instead of dying, I came to in Agatha's trunk. Nothing saved."

"Oh, bummer," Haley said. "So, what now? And um . . . do you know where my scooter is?"

"Agatha borrowed it." I glanced up at the sky. There was a crack in the blackness—or a rip, maybe? Whatever it was, a strange bluish light was spilling in through it. A different kind of light than the wormhole's red glow.

Haley twisted her pigtail around her finger. "So there's a giant hole in the parking lot right above ground zero, like twenty feet wide and even longer. That probably means the worlds are starting to tear each other apart, huh?"

I shot her a suspicious glance. For a chick talking about worlds tearing each other apart, she certainly was calm. "Can you see the beams of light shooting up from the wormhole?" I asked.

"Beams? No. I saw the big hole, though. Dr. Delmar told the security from the real hospital that the construction workers ruptured a water line or something. But meanwhile he totally moved all his stuff out of the building. It's like he found whatever he was digging for and took off with it."

"Yeah, makes sense . . ." I bit my fingernail and scoured the parking lot again. *Where are you, Agatha?*

"So, then—ouch!" Haley slapped at her knee and then her ankle. "Gross! Look at these nasty bugs, Courtney!"

"What?" I looked down. The ground to my right seemed

to be moving. Thousands and thousands of two-inch-long Drazgorn worms were slinking their way from the wormhole and slithering toward us. It was like the world's biggest colony of ants had abandoned their home and were on the hunt for a new one. My stomach churned at the sight of the mass of twitching antennae and feet.

"Drazgorn worms!" I said, slapping them away.

Haley climbed into the trunk to get away from the swarming bugs.

Eight thousand, six hundred fifty-seven Drazgorns in breach of gate.

I hissed loudly, and the bugs closest to me scurried back a few feet. I hopped back into the trunk next to Haley, my mind spinning. De Selby had told me that jumping into the wormhole was my last resort to save the universes; now I'd done it, and it hadn't worked. *What are you supposed to do when your last resort doesn't work?*

Leaning down, I started to hiss again, but I stopped short when I felt a message coming through from de Selby. I covered my eyes with my hands in order to concentrate.

"What are you doing?" Haley asked.

"Hold on."

You're still alive? de Selby demanded, his voice running through my head.

"Yes, I'm still alive!" I yelled angrily. "Despite having jumped to my death, and no thanks to you."

"Who are you talking to?" Haley asked.

"Shh!" I waved at her. Then continued my conversation with de Selby in my head. *Now the worms are everywhere! What the hell do I do?* I asked him.

Stay strong, Space Girl, de Selby said. *I've been reading up, and it looks like your grandpa installed a Drazgorn home siren on his portal machine. Activating it should send the bugs running for the wormhole. Then you can close the gate.*

"A Drazgorn home siren?" I said aloud, then glanced down at my grandpa's machine.

You do have access to your grandfather's machine, don't you? de Selby asked.

It's right here, I told him.

Then go! Go! Go! de Selby yelled in my head.

"What's going on, Courtney?" Haley asked.

I hunched down next to my grandpa's machine. "Supposedly there's a bug-go-home siren on this machine. If I can activate it, it'll force the Drazgorn worms back to the wormhole," I said. "Of course, without the worms in the ice cream truck, we're all going to die in a minute or two, siren or no siren."

"Not according to the prophecy," Haley said. "Nobody dies, Courtney."

"Oh yeah? And what prophecy is that?" I asked.

"*The* prophecy. My cousin Jorg says that you and Agatha are going to stop the apocalypse by pushing the gate closed and shutting the wormhole."

I glanced at Haley—her pigtails, her floppy Viking ski hat. Her tattooed wrists. She didn't inspire much confidence.

"Let's hope he's right," I said. I grabbed the big volume dial on the machine and twisted left, then right. Nothing.

Haley hunched down next to me. I flipped two switches, then pressed all the buttons. Still nothing. *Crap!*

"Maybe it's voice activated," Haley said.

"Look at it, Haley. It's from the nineteen-sixties. You really think it has voice activation?"

"You said it teleported you here. So it must be kind of advanced." She smacked a Drazgorn crawler off of her leg. "Hurry! These disgusting things keep trying to bite me."

Nine thousand nine Drazgorns in breach of gate.

"Okay." I leaned my face down next to the machine. "Hello! Machine? Activate Drazgorn home siren, please."

Arrrrreee!!! Arrrrreee!!! Arrrrreee!!! A super high-pitched screech burst from the machine.

"Told you!"

"Wow!" I stood up and covered my ears.

"And look! It's working!" Haley cried.

She was right. The creepy-crawlers were all scurrying, en masse, back toward the wormhole, like a slippery black wave being sucked back out to sea.

"Ahhhh!" Dr. Anderson screamed from over by the hole. I could see him hopping on tiptoes, trying to hide behind my mom.

"My phone's ringing!" Haley yelled over the siren. "It's Agatha!"

I snatched the phone out of her hand. "Agatha?" I yelled.

"Haley?"

I could barely hear her over the siren.

"No. It's me. Courtney!" I yelled. "Where are you?"

"Dude. You're not gonna believe what happened—"

"Agatha! Did you find the ice cream truck or not?"

"Are you with my car?"

"Yeah. I'm with Haley, in the trunk. There's a siren on my grandpa's portal machine that's sending the Drazgorns back into the hole. Wait. How'd you know we—"

"I'm heading your way in the truck now with seven angry bugs!"

I looked up. The ice cream delivery truck was tearing across the parking lot, bouncing and swerving. Its front end was smashed in, and smoke was billowing out from under the hood.

"You're awesome!" I yelled over the siren.

"Dude, it was epic!" she yelled back. I realized that the siren wasn't the only thing making it hard to hear her: the guttural screams of her death metal were also blaring from the truck's radio. "The Drazgorns broke out of the cooler and turned on Delmar," she continued, unfazed by the noise. "He crashed the truck into a telephone pole by the Holy Donut and was totally knocked unconscious. So I stole the truck and synched my phone's music up with its stereo. And the Drazgorns totally love black metal; it calmed them right down."

"Wait," I shouted. "What do you mean, they broke out of the cooler? That thing is solid metal with a huge latch—"

But she'd already hung up.

I climbed up onto the roof of Agatha's car to get a better view. No sign of my mom or Dr. Anderson. Maybe they'd finally freaked out enough to run back to the hospital or go home or something? Standing on my tiptoes, I tried to get a look down into the hole, to see if the gate was still standing or not, but it was too far away; I couldn't tell. I bit my thumbnail. *If we can just get those worms back through in time, this can work!*

Two thousand, six hundred forty-seven Drazgorns in breach of gate, the helmet told me. Which was way fewer than the nine thousand whatever that the helmet had last reported.

"It's working!" I yelled to Haley as I climbed back down to the trunk. The siren was making it hard for me to hear even my own voice. "They're going back into the wormhole by the thousands."

Haley glanced behind us. "I'm guessing that's Agatha in the smoking truck?" she yelled.

Seven hundred thirty-seven Drazgorns in breach of gate.

I swiveled around. There was the ice cream truck— banged up, spewing smoke, and barreling toward us.

FORTY

"**Here** she comes!" Haley yelled over the siren.

The ice cream truck bounced through a pothole and shot past us. I caught a brief glimpse of Agatha as she flew by; she was waving toward the wormhole.

Twenty-two Drazgorns in breach of gate.

"Let's go!" I took off running after the truck.

Suddenly, the truck's brake lights lit up red, and the truck skidded to a stop twenty feet from the edge of the hole. When I caught up to it, I bolted around to the passenger side.

Seven Drazgorns in breach of gate. They were all back through the gate except for the ones in the cooler!

"Courtney?"

I froze in my tracks. My mom was standing mere feet from me, just to the right of the truck.

She glanced toward the hole, then back at me. The siren was still ringing, but we were far enough away from it now that it was no longer earsplittingly loud.

"But you were down there," she said, sounding confused. "And then you disappeared. And all the bugs. We thought—"

Agatha honked the truck's horn. I turned away from my mom and tugged on the truck's passenger-side door handle. It was locked. Agatha shook her head at me through the window.

I peered through the glass—then recoiled when I saw why she wanted to keep the door shut. Crawling up the side of the seat was a shiny black Drazgorn worm. But this one was the size of a loaf of French bread. *Puke!*

Catching sight of me, the worm stood up on its hind legs, sprang forward, and banged its head against the window. It coiled back into itself and hissed.

Whoa! I stepped back.

The window was the tiniest bit cracked open at the top— just enough to let me hear what Agatha was screaming at me. "Get him out of the way!" she yelled. "There's no telling what these things will do when I open the door."

"Him who?" I yelled back.

She leaned on the horn again with both hands and stared straight ahead.

I followed her gaze. Standing fifteen feet in front of the truck, talking on his phone, was Dr. Anderson. Behind him, the ground was falling away into the hole at an unnerving rate.

Dr. Anderson shoved his phone into his pocket. Glaring at Agatha, he crossed his arms over his chest. He was totally blocking the truck.

What the hell?

I ran toward him. "Get out of the way, Dr. Anderson!"

"Hello again, Courtney." Dr. Anderson shaded his eyes against the headlights. "Now tell your friend to exit the truck."

"What? Why?" I glanced back at Agatha and was almost blinded.

Turn off the headlights, I mouthed. She did. I turned back to Dr. Anderson.

"Listen, you seriously gotta get out the way!" I said.

"That's not going to happen," he said. "Tell your friend to get out and leave the keys in the ignition."

"But, no, you don't—"

I broke off at the sight of his arms. The sleeves of his

white dress shirt were rolled up just enough for me see the bottom of his tattoo. The tail of a snake wrapped around a thorny branch. He was a Soldier of Bilim. *That's how I ended up in this hospital!*

I felt sick.

"Mom?" I turned to look for her. She was right behind me, but instead of responding, she walked around me and stood next to Dr. Anderson, putting herself between the ice cream truck and the hole.

"Mom, tell me you don't know what that tattoo on his arm means?" I asked, my voice shaking.

"What it means? Don't be ridiculous. You know I despise tattoos." Her tone was somewhat convincing.

Agatha leaned on the horn.

"Hold on!" I yelled at her. Moving closer to my mom and Dr. Anderson, I gazed past them, down into the wormhole. There was the gate, standing tall. There was still time! All we had to do was open the truck's door, and the siren would drive the Drazgorns down into the wormhole. It was a foolproof plan. *But—*

I stared at Dr. Anderson, at his wolfish grin. If he was one of the Bilim, then he knew aliens were real! And that I wasn't crazy! *This* was my one chance to force my mom to hear the truth from someone she trusted!

"Courtney, listen closely," Dr. Anderson said through his clenched teeth. "I understand there's been a car accident, and that your friend is returning Dr. Delmar's truck. Now I need your friend to get out of the truck so that I can take it where it needs to go. Do you understand me?"

He winked at me.

Gross!

"Oh, I understand you, Dr. Anderson." I ran back to the driver's side of the truck.

"Get out and bring the keys!" I yelled to Agatha.

She shook her head. "No way are you giving him the keys."

Trust me, I got this, Agatha, I mouthed. "Get out here."

Agatha's eyes narrowed.

"Fine!" She killed the truck's engine. Then she pulled the keys out of the ignition and unlocked the door without opening it. "But you better know what the hell you're doing!"

I glared through the window at the Drazgorns. "You'll be home soon," I told them. But if I was going to negotiate with Dr. Anderson and get him to tell the truth, I needed Agatha and the keys out of the truck, and the creepy-crawlers to stay in, for now.

I grabbed the door handle.

"Get ready," I told Agatha. "On three. One, two—" Smashing my face against the window, I hissed loudly, and the two giant Drazgorns I could see scurried over to the passenger seat.

"Dude! Nice!" Agatha jumped out of the truck and slammed the door before any spidery monsters could escape.

I snatched the keys from her hand.

Dr. Anderson rushed toward me. "Give me those keys!" he yelled.

I skirted past him to the edge of the hole. "Stay away or I'll drop them!" I yelled.

"Courtney, quit messing around!" my mom said.

"Listen to me, Mom. The tattoo that you pretend isn't there means that your stupid boyfriend is a Soldier of Bilim. He wants the ice cream truck because he's after the Drazgorn worms. They're an alien species from another universe. Dr. Anderson and his buddies want to extract DNA from these bugs so they can take over the world or something."

"No bugs are going hurt us, sweetie," she said. "Now just give Roger the keys."

I shook my head. "You talk to me like I'm crazy, but I'm not. Dr. Anderson lied to you, Mom. He told you I was crazy, but he knows there's nothing wrong with me. He had me locked up in the hospital with Dr. Delmar because the Bilim needed me to put on this helmet and open up the wormhole so the Drazgorns could come out."

"Actually, Dr. Delmar paid him a lot of money to bring you to Solomon Grace," Haley said. "I heard them talking—"

"You're out of your mind, Haley!" Dr. Anderson yelled. For once, he seemed to be losing his cool.

"Roger?" My mom's eyes narrowed into attorney cross-examination mode. "What is she talking about?"

Ignoring her question, Dr. Anderson rolled down his shirtsleeve to cover his tattoo. "Your mind is not well, Courtney," he said. "And now you are negatively influencing your friends. You need psychiatric care. That is the reason I brought you here. To help you."

"Oh, you're gonna help me. Right now!" I said. I held up the truck keys for him to see.

"You want these keys, then tell my mom the truth about the Soldiers of Bilim. And the aliens. And my grandpa, and what I am."

Buttoning his shirt cuff, Dr. Anderson shook his head in disappointment. "This is much, much bigger than you, Courtney."

"That's not what you told Nurse Erin the other day, Dr. Anderson," Haley said, walking up beside me. "You told her that Courtney was the only one in the world who could open up the wormhole, and that she was going to make you all very rich."

"All right! Enough bullshit." My mom stomped over so she was face-to-face with Dr. Anderson. "Time for the truth! Roger! I'm talking to you!"

"Shut up, all of you!" Dr. Anderson snapped. "I don't like

bugs. It's no secret! But with Dr. Delmar incapacitated, this entire operation suddenly falls on my shoulders. And you girls are not going to stop me!"

"Did you just tell me to shut up?" my mom yelled. "Nobody tells me to shut up!"

"Mom, stop! Just listen." I yelled. "Tell her the truth, Dr. Anderson. Now! Or I'm throwing the keys into the wormhole!"

My mom glared at Dr. Anderson, then shook her head and turned toward us.

"I've heard enough for one day, girls," she said. She sounded apologetic, almost ashamed. "Give Dr. Anderson the keys, Courtney, and I'll take you girls home. I'm sure Father O'Brien and your other Magi friends at the monastery will forgive you if Roger sneaks away to his clubhouse with a few stupid bugs to show his friends."

What? I never told her about the monastery!

"Mom? Are you saying that you know that the Knights of Magi are real?" I asked.

"Oh, no way!" Haley quickly covered her mouth for interrupting me, but her eyes were wide with shock.

"If I say yes, will you get in Dr. Anderson's car with me before the police get here?" my mom asked. "We're leaving him here."

"Dude!" Agatha yelled, pushing past my mom and Dr. Anderson to get to me. "We've got a wormhole to close!"

"I know!" I yelled.

I locked eyes with my mom. "You know about the Knights of Magi?" I sneered.

"Oh, don't look at me like that," she said. "I had to put up with all this for eighteen years with your grandfather. Of course I know about the Magi. I know all about men and their silly secret clubs and tattoos."

I felt the blood drain from my face.

Agatha grabbed my arm.

"Not now," I told her. Impending apocalypse or not, I wasn't finished with my mom yet.

"You knew that Grandpa was part of the Magi?" I scowled. "You knew about my tattoo, what it meant? And you didn't tell me?"

"Settle down, Courtney," my mom said. "I didn't tell you because I didn't want you to end up like your grandpa."

"But Grandpa wasn't crazy."

"Crazy or not, he was dangerous. And whatever notions he put in your head about being special or made of alien DNA or whatever it was, I needed you to forget! And if it took locking you up in a hospital to accomplish that, then so be it!"

Agatha slunk her way back to the truck while I stared at my mom in disbelief. "You put me in the hospital so I wouldn't find out about Grandpa? It was so important to you that you locked me up in a goddamn mental hospital—*twice*?"

"Oh, get over it," my mom said. "You're not the first person in the world to inherit some weird brain anomaly or creepy ability to see things that may or may not be there. Just because you're different doesn't mean you have to run around shouting about it. We're all different. But smart people figure out how to act normal."

This was getting worse by the second.

"Courtney?" Haley said. "We gotta get the bugs into the hole."

My eyes were locked on my mom's. "So all this time, you knew I really was seeing the aliens in my bedroom?" I asked. "You made me think I was crazy, that I was losing my mind. But you knew about my brain, that I was different. You knew grandpa wasn't crazy! That the aliens were real!"

"Don't tell me what I knew!" my mom yelled. "All I knew was that your grandpa believed in aliens. That he thought he was chosen and special, and better than the rest of us. I knew that he loved the Knights of Magi more than he loved me or my mother. He abandoned us—his family—for aliens, imaginary or not. So I will not have a daughter who follows in his footsteps!"

I shook my head in disgust. "So you lied to me about Grandpa and my tattoo? About what happened at the cottage? You made me believe that Grandpa was crazy . . . that he almost *killed* me."

"So what if I did?"

"So what? *UGH!*" I kicked the ground. "Do you have any idea what that did to me? How confused and scared I was? How guilty I felt for not being the normal daughter you always wanted?"

"It was for your own good," she said. "People who are different don't become heroes in this world, Courtney. They're locked up for being crazy, or they live in their parents' basements and spend the rest of their lives watching public television and eating microwave dinners without a friend left to talk to."

I glared at my mom, speechless. I couldn't even breathe.

"Dude!" Agatha interrupted. "Let's do this."

"You're right. Let's." I looked away from my mother, disgusted, and flipped the keys high up in the air.

"Oh totally!" Haley said.

The keys did two loops, then started falling.

Dr. Anderson scurried to the edge of the hole and stuck his hand out to catch the keys, but he couldn't reach quite far enough. Together, we all watched them plummet straight down into the hole and disappear.

"You little bitch!" Dr. Anderson yelled.

My mom's mouth dropped open. But before she could

yell at Dr. Anderson, Agatha yanked on the door to the truck, and two Drazgorn worms the size of possums scurried out onto the asphalt.

My mom's face turned white.

"Shut the door!" Dr. Anderson screamed, spit flying from his mouth. "You'll ruin everything!"

He charged toward Agatha, but the two Drazgorns stood up on their hind legs and hissed at him.

"Ahh!" He ran behind my mom.

She turned and socked him in the gut. "Get away from me, Roger!" She socked him again. "And don't ever speak to my daughter that way again."

The Drazgorns scurried past them and down into the hole.

Five Drazgorns in breach of gate.

I walked over and kicked the side of the truck. Five more giant Drazgorns scuttled out, their spidery legs and antennae twitching wildly.

"No! Back in the truck!" Dr. Anderson yelled. He waved frantically at the Drazgorns. "Shoo! Shoo! Go! Back!"

"Yeah, nice try," I said. Hunching over, I rushed at the bugs, hissing as loud as I could. They dashed past Dr. Anderson and my mom and straight down into the wormhole.

Dr. Anderson dropped to his knees and held his head like a kid who'd just missed a wide-open soccer net in the final seconds of the game.

Zero Drazgorns in breach of gate.

"Is that like all of them?" Haley asked.

Sitting down on the edge of the hole, I nodded my head and allowed myself to smile.

"What are you doing?" Agatha yelled, snapping me out of my peaceful moment. "Get down there and shut the gate!"

"Shit. Okay!" Securing my badge in my mouth, I flipped over onto my stomach, gripped a crack in the asphalt, and lowered myself onto the top brick step. Then I scrambled down to the last step, but I was still at least eight feet up. With one hand and one foot clinging to brick steps, I swung myself over to the edge of the gate. Then I carefully shimmied down and across the antlers, to the middle of the gate. Taking a deep breath, I jumped down to the ground.

Standing on the safe side of the gate, I grabbed it with both hands and pushed with all my weight until I heard the lock click.

"It's shut," I called up to Agatha and Haley.

"So, apocalypse fixed?" Haley asked, peering down at me.

"I think so!" I yelled up. But then suddenly Haley wasn't where I could see her anymore, and she didn't answer.

I stared through the closed gate at the wormhole and took a deep breath. I was crying and smiling at the same time. "We did it!" I couldn't believe it was over. I felt a rush of something strange—happiness!

"Something's wrong!" Agatha yelled down. "I can still see the wormhole!"

She was right! "But I shut the gate like I was supposed to," I said, confused.

"I see that. But there's still red light shooting up into the sky. The apocalypse isn't over!"

I looked up. Agatha was standing at the edge of the hole. Alone. "Where's Haley?" I asked. "And my mom and Dr. Anderson?"

"I don't know," Agatha said, looking around. "They disappeared."

What?

Agatha's phone rang, startling us both. Finally, she answered it.

"It's for you, Courtney," she said.

"Huh?"

She dropped the phone down, and I caught it. Then I put it up to my ear.

"Nicely done, Space Girl," said the voice on the phone.

"Commander Cordelia?" I asked, knowing it could only be her.

"Yes," she said briskly. "You've done good work. Now you must throw the helmet into the wormhole."

"Throw the helmet?" I repeated slowly. The helmet was part of me now, part of my thinking. Why should I have to give it up for good? "Are you sure?"

"Send the helmet through! Now, Space Girl!" Commander Cordelia ordered.

"Okay, okay." I reached up and tugged—and the helmet slid off of my head with no resistance. It felt tingly in my hand. I stared at it for a moment, taking in the twisted metal and glowing black stones. Then I stepped back from the gate and heaved the helmet up and over.

Whoosh! It disappeared.

"Now the badge," Commander Cordelia said, as if she'd seen me throw the helmet.

"But, no. I can't. Please!" I protested. "It's my proof, and my link to the Magi!"

"Quickly, Space Girl. Now! It's life or death!"

I stared down at my grandpa's badge. Tears streamed down my face. "Okay." I wiped my eyes. Then I tossed the badge through the antler pickets. And it was gone.

The wormhole disappeared.

The hole in the brick floor, where the wormhole had been, filled back in with bricks.

The gate was gone.

I was standing in a brick room with no ceiling.

It was like the wormhole had never been there.

"Dude! You did it! It's over!" Agatha grinned down at me.

I nodded to her. Then I raised the phone to my ear again.

"Now go home, Space Girl," Commander Cordelia said.

"Home?" I whispered into the phone. "But I can't stand my mom, and my dad travels during the winter, and my mom—"

"A wormhole between the universes was opened, then closed." Commander Cordelia spoke matter-of-factly. "Energies and powers have shifted, the universes altered. You need to go home. It's where you're safe!"

Safe? "No, wait! You don't understand, Commander. My mom's boyfriend is a Soldier of Bilim. He was after the Drazgorns, and he saw me close the gate. He hates me, and he sleeps over at our house. How can that be safe for me?"

"When you closed the gate, the helmet projected an energy wave that altered the memory of non-bloodliners, erasing parts of their memory and moving their minds backward in time," Commander Cordelia said.

"Seriously?" I asked. I glanced up at Agatha, then to where Haley had been standing, and over to where my mom and Dr. Anderson used to be. "Like how far back?"

"Just far enough," Commander Cordelia said.

I glanced down at my bare feet. This was too much.

"Wow, Courtney." The voice came from above me. I looked up to see Haley standing next to Agatha again.

"What the hell?" I mouthed to Agatha.

She shrugged her shoulders.

"What are you doing?" Haley shook her head. "Wait. My cousin just called me and said you were locked in a trunk. But . . ."

Haley didn't remember rescuing me from the trunk, or helping me with my grandpa's portal machine, or apparently anything else after that.

What's wrong with her? Agatha mouthed to me.

"I guess the helmet did it," I said. "Memory."

Suddenly my mom and Dr. Anderson pushed past Haley to the edge of the hole. Butterflies rushed into my stomach.

"Dr. Delmar called and said you'd escaped from the hospital," my mom said. "And that you were running around this old parking lot looking for bugs! Now get up here before this becomes a police matter."

Oh wow! She didn't remember any of the conversations we'd had in the past hour. *Wait! Oh no!*

I turned away from my mom and whispered into the phone, "My mom doesn't remember anything about the wormhole, or the Drazgorns, or Dr. Anderson yelling at us?"

"No," Commander Cordelia said. "Secrets need to be kept."

"Then she doesn't remember admitting to me that my grandpa was part of the Magi? And that she knew all along that I was like him, that I wasn't crazy, that the aliens in my bedroom were more than imaginary?" I whispered angrily. "And she doesn't know Dr. Anderson is evil?"

"It doesn't matter what she remembers, Courtney. It's what you know that matters," Commander Cordelia said. "It always has been. We're proud of you, Space Girl. Now go home."

"But I don't want—"

She hung up.

Shit!

"How did this ice cream truck get here?" Dr. Anderson asked with confusion in his voice. "What's going on? Where's Dr. Delmar?"

"The truck broke down, Dr. Anderson," Agatha said. "You're supposed to drive your car over to the Holy Donut and meet Dr. Delmar. Something about a mission." She shot me a quick wink. Then stared at Dr. Anderson. "Don't you remember?"

"What? Yes. Of course I remember." He stomped away from the edge.

Brady G. Stefani

"Roger, where are you going?" my mom asked.

"For a drive," he said. "Where's my car?"

"It's over there, by the school bus," Agatha said.

"Ah." He stormed off.

My mom took off after him. "But what about Courtney?"

"Come on, dude! Get up here," Agatha whispered loudly.

I put the phone in my mouth and gazed up at the brick steps. Now that there was no gate to help me climb up to them, I wasn't sure how to do it. Standing on my tiptoes, I tried to grab the bottom step, but it was too far up.

"Why the frown?" someone called out in a Scandinavian accent.

I looked up. A tall guy with long dyed-black hair and bright blue eyes glanced down at me. It was Jorg. He didn't have any corpse makeup on now, but the tiny skulls hanging around his neck were a dead giveaway.

"What are you doing here, Jorg?" Agatha sneered. "We've got this handled!"

"I was just in the area, hoping the world wouldn't explode," he said. He grinned as if Agatha weren't shooting him the world's dirtiest look. "And it didn't. So I thought I'd pick up a souvenir from the near-apocalypse to take back home. Aren't you ladies going to introduce me to your friend?" he added, smiling down at me.

"So wait..." Haley glanced around, confused.

"Courtney, this is Haley's cousin, Jorg," Agatha said. "Jorg, Courtney."

"I know who you are," I said, staring up.

"Do you now?" he asked.

"Yeah." I was about to tell him how I saw him with Agatha in the church in Norway, but I bit my lip instead. "Um... We found a Magi letter with your great-grandfather's name in it," I said, stumbling to recover. "Joakim Skoglund. He was a chief high priest or something back in Norway."

298

His stare grew more intense. "A hundred years ago, the Knights of Magi tricked my great-grandfather into letting the Magi come to Scandinavia and dig up our churches and the pagan temples they were built over."

"Oh. Right." I glanced up at Agatha. "There was something about that in the letter."

"Well, I bet your letter didn't explain how the Magi stole our transport helmet and the rest of the artifacts of our Evolarian ancestry, completely destroying our portals of communication with the alien universe?"

"No, not really," I said. "Haley mentioned something about that, though."

Jorg turned to Haley and started speaking in what I assumed must be Norwegian, or maybe Swedish?

Haley spoke back to him in the same language, shaking her head.

"Apparently she doesn't remember rescuing you from the trunk of the car, or seeing your grandfather's portal machine," Jorg said to me. "The gate must have manipulated her memory."

Haley took her Viking hat off and rubbed her head. Then she sat down on the ground. "I don't feel good."

"Take Haley and get out of here, Jorg!" Agatha commanded. "Before Delmar or his goons show up."

"What about me?" I asked, staring up at the twenty-foot brick wall.

Jorg dropped to his knees, then he scaled down the brick steps using only his hands, like he was on a rope ladder. When he reached the bottom step he let go, and landed on his feet just a few feet away from me. I backed away from him, but he moved closer.

My heart jumped in my chest. I looked around, for some place to run, an escape route, in case he attacked me or something. Then my eyes caught Jorg's, and I froze.

Something in the way he was looking at me told me I could trust him.

Closing the gap between us, he leaned his head down so his mouth was level with my ear. "You frightened me when you jumped into the wormhole," he whispered.

"What? You saw that?" I whispered back.

"From the roof of the old hospital," he said. "When the wormhole didn't disappear, I figured that your grandfather's machine must have been programmed to save you. That's when I called Haley and told her you were in Agatha's trunk."

"But . . . How . . . ?" This didn't make sense.

Jorg reached into his leather jacket and pulled something out. A badge like my grandpa's—but different.

"You've got a badge! Are you with the Magi?" I asked.

"No." He shoved the badge back into his jacket, and his eyes burned into mine. "Like I told you, the Magi destroyed our Point Utterly Between."

"Oh wow, sorry," I said.

"Yes, 'oh wow,'" he said. Then he cracked a smile. "But you just stopped the apocalypse. So I'm going to help you again." Before I could react, he grabbed me by my waist and lifted me onto his shoulders, then boosted me up to the steps.

I climbed my way up the steps, toward Agatha and Haley.

"Jorg! There's some chick standing on my car," Agatha yelled down. "And by the looks of her, she's a friend of yours."

"That's the One Who Screams," Jorg said. Jumping up, he grabbed the bottom step, then climbed up behind me.

The One Who Screams? I crawled onto the asphalt and glanced over at Agatha's car. A black Jeep was parked next it. And sure enough, a lady with long red hair, wearing a tight black dress with a flowing skirt, was standing on Agatha's hood, staring over at us.

I couldn't see her eyes—she was too far away—but just the sight of her staring in my direction sent a chill through me.

Agatha grabbed my arm and twisted me around. "Don't even look at her," she said.

"You know her?" I asked.

Without answering, she narrowed her eyes.

I glanced at The One Who Screams again, and I could feel her stare cutting into mine.

"We helped you out of the trunk," Jorg said. "So now we're borrowing your grandfather's portal machine and taking it back to Norway with us as payment."

"What?" I broke off my stare, and gazed at Jorg. "No way! That's my grandpa's. It's all I have left. You can't take it!"

Agatha shot me a nervous look. "He just wants to borrow it," she said. "Right, Jorg? She'll get it back?"

Jorg put his arm around my shoulder. "You shut the wormhole. You stopped the apocalypse, Space Girl," he whispered in my ear.

"Wait. How do you know that name?" I asked.

"I have sources. And we're all grateful. But we need your grandfather's machine to open up a Point Utterly Between back in Trondheim. To make things right."

I shot Agatha a pleading glance, but she quickly shook her head. "Let it go."

I pulled at my hair. "All right, I guess," I said. "But you have to give it back when you're done. Swear on your life!"

"I swear on my life." Jorg laughed. Then he squeezed my shoulder in a sort of hug. "Rest up. We'll be in touch." He let go of me and started walking toward Agatha's car.

I turned toward Agatha, and shook my head in anger. "What am I going to tell Father O'Brien and Commander

Cordelia?" I hissed at her. "That I gave Joakim Skoglund's great-grandson my grandpa's portal machine?"

Agatha shrugged her shoulders. "Could be worse." She scraped at the dirt with her Viking boot. Then she smirked. "Right?"

I felt my lips part. "Yeah, way worse, for sure." I was smiling too. "We stopped the apocalypse, didn't we?" I asked.

"That we did, Space Girl," Agatha said, nodding her head and smiling.

"Hell yeah, we did," I said, wiping tears of happiness from my eye. "And that's *Ms.* Space Girl to you."

"Wait." Haley raised her head from the pavement where she was resting. "Where's my scooter again?"

FORTY-ONE

Rolling onto my side, I adjusted my pillow and stared out through the gap in my ugly yellow curtains to the sky: sunny and cloudless.

I heard the front door slam shut, then the *click-clack* of my sister's soccer cleats running up the stairs. "Courtney!"

Ugh. I covered my head with my pillow. I couldn't figure out what was worse about being grounded, phone and all: Not being able to leave the house, not being able to call Agatha, or having to constantly answer Kaelyn's questions about the hospital and why I was barefoot and covered in dirt when I got home Thursday night. Today was Sunday. Tomorrow I'd have to show up at school, and face the rumors about why I wasn't in school last week. Right now, though, I just needed sleep.

"You got something in the mail," Kaelyn said, standing next to my bed now. "You want me to open it?"

"No!" I whipped off my pillow and flipped over to face her.

In her hands was what looked like a shoe box wrapped in thick brown paper.

"Where did you get that?" I sat up.

"Someone dropped it off on the porch," she said.

I grabbed it from her. "Someone like a mailman?" I asked.

"No. Just some guy," she said. "Aren't you gonna open it?"

Courtney Hoffman was handwritten in black marker

across the front. No address, just my name. *Weird.* Good or bad, I had no idea. But definitely weird.

"Oh. I remember: it's just my shoes and stuff from the hospital," I said, lying. "Yeah, one of the nurses said he'd drop it off."

I wrapped my arm around the package and crawled under my comforter. "Thanks. Now shut my door."

"Oh jeez." Kaelyn clomped back down the stairs.

When I was sure she was gone, I sprang up, tore open the brown paper, and pulled the top off the white box inside. It was filled with crumpled newspaper. I pulled it out to reveal—*oh my God*—an oval badge made of twisted metal.

It was different from my grandpa's badge: it was smooth and had a large red stone embedded in the metal, whereas his had had lots of tiny blue ones and a rough feel to it. But there was no mistaking what it was.

The red stone in the center glowed up at me, and I felt a smile stretch across my face.

I rested my forearm against the crumpled-up newspaper on my bed and shined the badge on it. That's when I saw that the newspaper wasn't written in English. Norwegian, maybe?

Oh God! I quickly lowered the badge. What if it was from Jorg? What if he and the One Who Screams were trying to recruit me to their side?

I smoothed out a piece of the newspaper and studied the print. It was written in Spanish. *Okay. Phew!*

That could make more sense. De Selby had said he was on assignment in Chile. And who knows where Commander Cordelia was physically located? Or where the badges came from?

I picked up the badge again, angled it in my hand. I could see the Magi crest etched into the center of the stone.

Smiling, I shined it at my eyes, and my brain started tingling.

A message came through from Commander Cordelia: *Space Girl, your presence is required at the PUB. Acclimate yourself to your badge, then transport in. We will be waiting.*

"Holy shit!"

I couldn't stop smiling, even as I composed my response.

Message received, Commander. Give me two minutes to figure this thing out, ten seconds to fix my hair, and I'll totally be there. Space Girl out!

Acknowledgments

Thanks to my mom and dad, Marilyn and Mike Stefani, for their endless support of my writing. To my late grandmother, Regina Stefani, from whom I inherited my writing spirit. To my brother Jeff Stefani—thanks for teaching me mindfulness.

Above all, thanks to my beautiful wife, Heather, for putting up with me, being the world's best mother to Beckett and Blaze, and repeatedly pointing out to me that I was writing a book about two things I knew nothing about: teenage girls and extraterrestrial beings. Hopefully she'll read the book and realize I do know one thing: what it's like to feel crazy.

Extra special thanks to Brooke Warner for helping me craft my writing into a polished story. Without her, there would be no book—literally! Along those lines, thanks to everyone else at She Writes Press and SparkPress who helped turn my story into a book (in no particular order: Krissa Lagos, Megan Connor, Taylor Vargecko, Lauren Wise, Kristin Bustamante, Karen Sherman, Janay Lampkin, Hannah Sichting, Julie Metz, and Crystal Patriarche. To anyone I'm missing here: I apologize, and thank you).

A warm shout-out to the talented photographer Michaela Frunek for making Jade look like Courtney. Pretty cool cover photo.

Cheers to Jimmy B Almost—the best backroom idea

man east of the Mississippi—who taught me to never ever underestimate the paranormal.

Lastly, thanks to Dr. Melvin Bornstein for helping me understand how the human mind works, and what can happen when someone believes that theirs doesn't.

About The Author

©Stela Zaharieva

Brady G. Stefani has a bachelor's degree in creative writing, and a graduate degree in law. During law school, he spent time as an involuntary commitment caseworker for the Massachusetts Department of Mental Health, where he interacted with patients suffering from severe thought disorders, including numerous patients presenting with subjectively real memories of being visited and abducted by alien beings (commonly referred to as *alien abduction phenomenon*). It was through his study of these patients, along with his own struggles with anxiety and cognition, that Stefani became aware of just how deceiving, mysterious, and powerfully resilient the human mind can be. After law school, Stefani wrote and directed a feature film, *The Wind Cried Larry*, which received Honorable Mention at the East Lansing Film Festival. In addition to working on a second YA novel that continues the storyline from *The Alienation of*

Brady G. Stefani

Courtney Hoffman, Stefani continues to write YA fiction for his website, exploring issues of mental health in the context of our boundary-less imaginations.

SELECTED TITLES FROM SPARKPRESS

SparkPress is an independent boutique publisher delivering high-quality, entertaining, and engaging content that enhances readers' lives. Visit us at www.gosparkpress.com

Within Reach, by Jessica Stevens
$17, 978-1-940716-69-5
Seventeen-year-old Xander has found himself trapped in a realm of darkness with thirty days to convince his soul mate, Lila, he's not actually dead. With her anorexic tendencies stronger than ever, Lila must decide which is the lesser of two evils: letting go, or holding on to the unreasonable, yet overpowering, feeling that Xan is trying to tell her something.

The Revealed, by Jessica Hickam
$15, 978-1-94071-600-8
Lily Atwood lives in what used to be Washington, D.C. Her father is one of the most powerful men in the world, having been a vital part of rebuilding and reuniting humanity after the war that killed over five billion people. Now he's running to be one of its leaders.

Serenade, by Emily Kiebel
$15, 978-1-94071-604-6
After moving to Cape Cod after her father's death, Lorelei discovers her great-aunt and nieces are sirens, terrifying mythical creatures responsible for singing doomed sailors to their deaths. When she rescues a handsome sailor who was supposed to die at sea, the sirens vow that she must finish the job or face grave consequences.

Blonde Eskimo, by Kristen Hunt
$17, 978-1-940716-62-6
In Spirit, Alaska on the night of her seventeenth birthday, the Eskimos' rite of passage, Neiva is thrown into another world full of mystical creatures, old traditions, and a masked stranger. When Eskimo traditions and legends become real as two worlds merge together, she must fight a force so ancient and evil it could destroy not only Spirit, but the rest of humanity.

ABOUT SPARKPRESS

SparkPress is an independent, hybrid imprint focused on merging the best of the traditional publishing model with new and innovative strategies. We deliver high-quality, entertaining, and engaging content that enhances readers' lives. We are proud to bring to market a list of New York Times bestselling, award-winning, and debut authors who represent a wide array of genres, as well as our established, industry-wide reputation for innovative, creative, results-driven success in working with authors. SparkPress, a BookSparks imprint, is a division of SparkPoint Studio, LLC.

Learn more at GoSparkPress.com